[Insert Self-Discovery Here]

To the organizers of National Novel Writing Month, without whom this book would never have been written.

And to my wife, Arden, who will always be my safe place.

First paperback edition August 2019
Second paperback edition July 2020

Book Design and Illustrations by Arden Rachel
www.ardenrachel.com

ISBN 978-0-578-56080-9 (paperback)

[Insert Self-Discovery Here]

A Novel

Belinda Roddie

JUNE

It's nine o'clock on a very hot suburban night. On a desk in a dimly lit bedroom, there are three empty containers that used to contain Chinese chicken chow mein and moo shu pork. Next to the remains of the coping mechanism is yet another one, a half-empty bottle of Zinfandel warming up by the window. And next to that, an opened laptop, replaying songs organized in a playlist titled, "Sadness," with several pictures of Emily Anderson lighting up the screen.

I've kept track of the days since she said goodbye. It's turned into three weeks, and I've shown no signs of recovering from the blow.

But can you blame me? Emily Anderson had been my girlfriend for four years. She had been my high school sweetheart. She had taken me to prom, even making me wear a red tuxedo to match her dress. She had pushed for me to go to the same university she did so we could stay together. She had encouraged me to become a teacher. In short, she sort of molded me into everything I am today.

Imagine devoting four years to a woman you were lucky to see every day after class, constantly reminding her of how much you loved her, how willing you were to make it work, how once school was over, you'd be able to move in with her and finally start a whole new life with her since she persisted that she wouldn't be ready to share a place until she was out of college. All in all, a shitty pay-off for a fairly large and dramatic build-up.

Needless to say, it's been a messy after-college existence for me so far. I really do mean it when I say that most of what I did, I did for Emily. I got both a bachelor's degree in history and a teaching credential in the same subject in four years. I worked my ass off for them — no joke. I got on the chancellor's list every semester, too; I wasn't going to graduate without honors. It was all so I could rip off my robe and pull on a blazer and get right to work as a nerdy high school history teacher with a nasal drip and a penchant for being overly pedantic. Then I could get Emily and me a nice apartment and start from there.

Yeah, that worked out nicely, didn't it?

I pick up the bottle of Zinfandel and retch after taking a swig straight from its neck. The wine hasn't been corked for a while, and it's probably half-vinegar by now. I've already choked down enough potential salmonella from the Chinese take-out; I don't need to go into toxic shock while in mourning. I've planned out my night thoroughly, and I'd hate to see it go to waste. I switch from my "Sadness" playlist to my "Guilt" playlist, ready to re-evaluate where it had all gone wrong.

And where had it? Emily had given me plenty of excuses.

She had told me that she was looking for someone to fulfill her passions, someone who could be successful, someone who wasn't entirely automated, someone who could *improvise.* That last one kills me. I've never been an improviser, and truth be told, Emily hadn't asked me to be one. I had created a whole life plan because I figured that I loved her so much that I wanted to cater to her every whim. I guess I just failed at making her happy. There's no one I can blame but myself.

The guilt trip starts again, which is super appropriate, given the playlist I've selected to listen to. I drink more of the spoiled wine, recline back on my swivel chair, and let my brain sift out thoughts like thick, dense flour. I can feel my eyes slipping toward the back of my head, the tension building just above my eyebrows. The tears will come eventually; they do every night. All I hope is that my mom doesn't walk in two hours later to find me comatose on the rug with some whiny emo's voice singing about betrayal on my laptop as the battery drains away.

[…]

I go downstairs the next morning around 11:30 because I find no reason for getting up any earlier. My mom is home because it's summer, and the schools are all closed until August. She calls herself a "traveling music teacher" and always says that I must have been inspired to become a teacher because of her. She's way too proud of that pseudo-accomplishment, but I don't bother correcting her.

My daily routine since the break-up starts without a hitch. I eat a bowl of generic cereal shaped like o's and return to my room to log onto my computer and stare at an array of collages and photos of Emily and me that I've arranged throughout the years. I've got my photo albums when the Internet's down, but venturing through the various posted pictures on all of my social networking sites is my preferred method of masochism during my lingering depression. Plus, I get to visit her profiles and cry a bit about every status and snapshot she puts up. Good old public viewing option.

It hurts me to look at her, but I still do. I focus way too much on her long, artificially red hair, her big brown eyes, the way she puckers her lips in most pictures, especially in the ones of her and me. There's a photo of her clinging to my T-shirt as she kisses me near Disneyland. And there we are at Disney World, too. And in front of the Golden Gate Bridge. And at the diner we went to with my college friends. All the way to the last picture of us in our graduation robes, hugging and smiling for my father's point-and-shoot camera. It wounds me every time.

I know if I keep looking at the pictures, it'll hurt me more. But I know if I don't, it'll hurt me more. See the psychological catch-22 I've stupidly created for myself?

My mom knocks on the door to check on me, and I tell her to go away. She informs me that she was thinking of going out to watch a movie, and I feel bad, but I let her know that I'm not interested. She asks to come in, and I remind her that I don't want her to see me like this. I'm ready to cry again, but I try my best to stifle it because I don't want my mom to freak out and go into over-the-top-comforting mode. Finally, she says that she can order me a pizza. That offer I do take.

My mom's been taking it easy on me since Emily ended it all. She liked her a lot, as did my dad, and four years together is nothing to sneeze at. In the first week after everything fell apart, my mom regaled me more than once with the saga of how she fell madly in love with a handsome sculptor from Oslo, Norway, only to have her heart broken when he flew to Venice without her and stayed with an Italian woman who made good espressos. I'm actually not sure if the Venice part happened; come to think of it, I might have just made that up. Regardless, after a while, my mom figured out that empathy and story time weren't exactly helping me coping-wise, so now she's following the next best strategy: Leaving me, most of the time, alone.

Around three o'clock in the afternoon, I realize that I've lost track of time, and I lie back on my bed, my headphones snapped around my ears as a sad country song twangs from my laptop. I don't even like country — then again, everybody says that, and they always listen to it in secret — but the way the lyrics cater to my personal melancholy is absolutely spot on. I inhale and exhale with each beat and drawling syllable of the morose vocalist and think that if I focus really hard, the tears won't fall for once. I think about calling Emily. I don't, of course, because I know what the response will be:

"Jamie, stop. Just stop."

I wish I could, but I can't. I haven't been able to. My chest tightens like I'm about to have an asthma attack, and I don't even suffer from asthma. From what I can tell, based on my limited knowledge of romantic comedies and tragedies, either the person who's been dumped never gets over it, or they get over it in approximately three to six months. I guess there's still hope for me; it hasn't even been a month yet. Hang in there, old sport!

There's a knock on the door again. Mom says my pizza's here.

It's no Chinese food substitute, and eating it doesn't make me feel much better. It's a wonder that I haven't been gaining weight like crazy since the break-up. I blame the young adult metabolism that'll self-destruct by the time I'm thirty-five.

My father comes home, and we exchange quick hellos. He's a man who works until six every day for a six-figure income to feed two other people. I never thought how helpful having a sibling could be until now, but my parents had decided that after me, they were good. In the end, I'm not comfortable about spilling my emotions to my parents. To a sibling, maybe. A brother more than a sister, sadly enough. If I had had a sister, she probably would have turned into a prep or a cheerleader type and labeled me a crazy dyke. She wouldn't have been wrong, though.

By the time the sun starts dipping behind the hills and casting me in darkness, I'm back to the "Sadness" playlist, and I'm craving chow mein despite my stomach being loaded with overcooked pepperoni and congealed lumps of fake cheese. I'm remarkably lethargic by this point at night, what with the heat and the slow tempo of my song selections and the raspy voice of the plaintive singer sharing in my misery. Without Emily, it's safe to say that I don't have anyone else to turn to. She was always able to make me laugh with little sappy bits of advice and corny jokes. She knew the best places to take me for consolation dinners if I ever got anything lower than an A on a paper or an exam. She even wrote silly poems for me whenever I had an especially bad day; neither of us were good at poetry, but we had fun. My college friends, I'm starting to realize, were the bystanders to the beautiful show that was Emily. Without a main character to pivot around, they don't really have a purpose in my life.

So I don't call them. They're too far away from my hometown, anyway. They wouldn't make a move to visit me; they're just not that kind of people. Most of them have summer jobs to slave away at, cursing the day they were born while standing behind a cash register, wearing a heavy green apron, and taking seventeen orders for lattes in under two minutes. In retrospect, my five or so buddies from my university were never equipped to deal with sad stuff. Usually, they just tried to douse me in beer and take me to sports games and get me to act like a complete dude like they did. Not really my style, and definitely not a way to help me.

"All By Myself" starts playing on my "Lonely" playlist. A classic. That comes after the "Guilt" playlist. I lie on my stomach on the floor with my laptop pressed against my exposed elbows. My eyes feel itchy in the summer air, and I bite my tongue to keep from cussing out the world. Not that the world itself did anything to me, but hey, Emily's living in it.

Downstairs, my parents are doing crosswords and watching the latest *Jeopardy!* episode. They're good, quiet parents that way. I nestle my head on the rough carpet because clearly, my bed isn't kind enough to me. It's now been three weeks and one day.

June's felt really long. I'm expecting an even longer July.

JULY

On my twenty-second birthday, I receive an unexpected call from, of all people, Devin Abrega.

I have not spoken to Devin Abrega in well over three years. The last time I had seen him, he was at a bar in my college town, just about to travel to Colorado to explore the great outdoors. I remember his cheeky grin and his oily long dark hair. He's half-Portuguese, half-Irish, and it shows up in his skin, which can't seem to decide if it wants to be ruddy or olive in tone.

His voice on the other end confuses me at first, as I pull away from the table where a cupcake with a single candle has been laid out in front of me because neither of my parents can bake, and I never exactly asked for a birthday cake. For one thing, I wasn't even aware he still had a cellphone. Knowing his mentality, I'm surprised he didn't try to contact me by passenger pigeon; then I remember they've been extinct for years. Still, why is he calling me?

"Devin, why are you calling me?"

He sounds out of breath on the other line, like he's been out camping and just got chased out of his tent by a pissed off puma. I wouldn't put it past him.

"What's up?" he asks. "Am I interrupting something?"

Clearly, Devin doesn't remember that it's my birthday. I don't remind him. He can hardly remember what he ate for breakfast each morning — at least, that was the way he was in high school.

"It's fine," I say, then repeat myself. "Why are you calling me?"

"Dude. Meet me at the Lair tomorrow, two o'clock. I'll be in town by then and we can talk."

I know that if I push him about what he wants to talk about, he'll get cryptic. "Where are you now?"

"Kyle's," Devin replies. "He let me crash at his place. You know who Kyle is?"

"No. I don't." I don't think I've ever had an acquaintance named Kyle, let alone a friend.

"Good buddy of mine. We met when I was playing mountaineer. Dude, what's the deal? You sound awful."

I do sound awful. I feel awful. Birthdays suck after you've spent the last four of them either underage drinking with your girlfriend or eating junk food. Or both.

"Don't bother asking," is what I say instead of conveying my honest feelings about the matter. "Look, Lair at two. I'll be there."

"Promise?"

"I legitimately have nothing better to do."

"For real?"

"I'll be there, okay?"

I'm fairly certain that Devin is choreographing a victory dance on his side of the call.

"Awesome. See you there. What I have to say is going to blow your mind. Like, through the roof."

Then he hangs up. I sit back down at the table, where my parents have been practicing how to have the patience of a saint, and blow out the candle on my cupcake. I wish for nothing else but sanity. Mongolian beef and selfies of Emily await me upstairs.

[...]

Little back story on Devin: The guy never got his high school diploma. It's not necessarily a bad thing, but he was never built for school. By the time he turned eighteen the January of our senior year, he just bailed. From what he tells me, his parents didn't care, as long as he didn't stay at their house after August of that same year.

Devin's a self-identified nomad and has been known to excessively travel by everything besides personal car or commercial plane. He's hitchhiked, bussed, biked, even helicoptered all around the United States; luckily, he's never been the pilot of said helicopter. He's crashed at houses and shacks in every state on the east coast, from Virginia to Rhode Island to Florida. He's camped out in RVs and trailers, told stories on trains like a millennial hobo, carved his initials into every tree he likes, and attempted to maintain a blog about all the hole in the wall restaurants he's frequented (the last entry was eleven months ago). You'd think he would've been declared a public nuisance in some of the states he's been to by now, but no matter how opinionated or "free-spirited" he is, no one's seemed to hate him. I know this because of the slew of photos I find online every time I look at his social media pages, which I'm surprised he updates. It should be weird to see him smiling next to a redneck with an AR-15 or giving a thumbs-up with a senile busker in New York City, but that's Devin. It doesn't surprise me anymore.

I can't tell if I should be proud of or sad for the guy, but from what I can tell, he's loved life without anything chaining him down. He's never stuck with one goal for over a year. He's always journeyed alone, and he's never attempted to get me to tag along. Still, we were pretty close in high school. I mean, we hung out all the time, being anti-jocks: The hippie and the butch lesbian, like we could produce our own unconventional buddy film. But no matter how good of friends we were, Devin's always considered me one of "them," as in someone willing to give their life and money away to the "broken education system." And seeing how cozy I got in the structure of college, he probably wasn't willing to bother me with his incessant desires to be the next wise man on a mountaintop before he got bored of that, too.

Anyway, the Lair he's talking about is a small, remote diner on the edge of my hometown where he and I used to eat after school. It's not actually called the Lair: It's called Marty's, but it's always been dimly lit in these red and silver lights that give it the aura of an adolescent hideaway. The broken jukeboxes, prog rock playing from a tiny stereo kept in the kitchen, and tired-looking waiters in crimson shirts add to the ambience, though the place still has the kitschy looking menus with big neon-colored pictures and standard "All-American" fare — oh, yeah, and the clichéd, "signed" picture of Elvis on the wall, too. We used to call it the Den, but Devin claimed it made him sound too much like a suburban dad.

According to him, nicknaming it the Lair sounded creepier and, "more legit."

And we loved it. Before a standard visit to the Lair, we would go to the home football games and baseball tournaments at our high school as an act of irony because the jocks couldn't stand Devin, and they really hated me. Most of the ire came from the quarterback because I went out with his crush for about three weeks in sophomore year before she decided she wasn't into girls after all. It was a thrill to see him seethe when he stomped into the diner with his teammates and caught my scrawny, derelict-looking buddy and me scarfing down Melty Clubs with big grins on our faces.

So at two o'clock, I've already gotten a glass of water, and I'm squirming around in my booth because it's been a while since I've been exposed to sunlight, let alone been outside my house. It feels kind of funny to be moving around so much, and I feel like I've lost a part of myself, like an insect shedding an exoskeleton. Some piece of me is lying out in the July sun, decaying, as I try to act like an actual person again by entertaining myself with the prospect of a burger. And then I see Devin come in.

He's shockingly a lot thinner than I remember, but his hair's just as long, if not longer. I guess he hasn't updated his profile picture in a while because he's now sporting a pretty thick, dark goatee that I don't recall him ever being capable of growing back in high school. He's all sweaty around his forehead, and his hands are buried in the pockets of his patched brown corduroy pants. Despite his vagrant-esque physique and wardrobe, he's grinning from ear to ear, and he looks more than happy to see me. It's unnerving to witness someone besides my parents smile at me again, especially when it's a, "So great to see you," smile rather than a, "I'm sorry for your heartbreaking but at the same time kind of creepy loss," smile.

"Devin," I utter simply, rising from the booth to give him a conventional high-five. Instead, I feel my bones compress as he swoops me into a bear hug. I smell the ocean, tobacco, and Kentucky bourbon on his torn leather jacket. I don't remember him ever liking whisky.

"Jay-may!" he roars. "My little buh-day! How've you been?"

"Little?" I scowl. "I resent that."

He releases his monster grip on me and scowls right back, a little cartoonishly. "Well, compared to me, dude, you've always been tiny."

If he means my height and not my weight, then sure, I'll buy that. He reassembles himself into the seat across from me and doesn't even scan the menu.

"Fuck, how long has it been since we've been here, man?" he asks. "I've missed this place!"

I'm not interested in nostalgic conversation, and I'm really not amused by how much he stares at me for an answer to his question. He's probably perusing every bit of me. I'm suddenly very self-conscious about my mussy, shaggy hair poking out of my beanie, and I suddenly regret my choice of the wrinkled black tee I threw on to look somewhat presentable. And don't even get me started on the bags under my eyes that are large enough to store all the sand on Lincoln Beach. Not much I can do about those, though; I've been sleeping a lot, but I always feel tired.

I call a waiter over and try to order. "Chocolate milkshake for me, and..."

"Two Melty Clubs!" Devin bellows before I can finish. "And a big ass root beer! All on me!"

"Devin, for Christ's sake..." But the waiter's written it all down before I can protest. He asks if we want anything else, and I don't even bother changing the order.

"Yeah, sure, it's fine."

I hate being such a killjoy, especially when everything around us seems to make Devin the giddiest guy I've ever seen. He dances a bit to the Rush song wafting from the kitchen speakers, and he keeps rubbing his hands together and licking his lips, like the sandwiches we're going to get are going to be gifts from heaven or nirvana or whatever dogma he believes in now, if he does believe in one. I get even more disjointed when he abruptly reaches across the table and seizes my shoulder, as if trying to pull me toward him.

"So. I'll ask again. How've you been?"

I shrug the best I can, given how hard Devin's hand is pressing down on my scapula. "Worst two months ever. Yourself?"

"Oh, me? I'm the best, dude. Man, I wish I could send some good vibes to you. Should I ask history questions and make you feel all smart and shit?"

"Devin."

"No, seriously, I'll quiz you. Who was the seventh president of the United States?"

"I don't remember."

"Okay, fine. Then describe the effects of totalitarianism on Eastern Europe in the 1940's."

"Fuck off."

I'm not kidding on the not remembering part, either. Just

because I did well in social studies when I was at school, doesn't mean that I recall any of it. Kind of sad, the reality I live in: I'm a history student who can't even remember history two months out of college.

Devin gives up on the impromptu trivia round. "Well, anyway. You're probably wondering why I called you."

"No shit, Sherlock," I grumble. "It's been years since you've graced me with your presence."

"Hey, man, after you decided to keep going to school…"

"Yeah, yeah. Part of the system. No hope. No soul."

"I wasn't going to say that," gripes Devin. "It's just that I figured you have your own things to care about."

"Had."

"Aw." He makes a sad face. It annoys me. "I know. Little Emily broke your heart."

So he does check his friends' profiles at least occasionally. That annoys me even more.

"Look," I demand, "is this really about meeting up with an old friend? Or do you have some sort of stupid agenda for me?"

"Ooh. You've got good intuition. I like it."

"Stop patronizing me!"

I'm close to crying because I'm short-fused and I can't help it, and Devin has probably noticed because he goes stiff for a moment, like he's worried I'm going to have a nervous breakdown right in the middle of the Lair. The whole space makes me feel uncomfortable for some reason, like I'm some hermit who can't stand being around others. It bothers me to be here, but it bothers me even more that it bothers me to be here. It's almost as if I can't function on a normal human level anymore, which just makes me want to stop trying to function on a normal human level altogether.

Then, by the grace of God, the Melty Clubs finally come, and Devin stops talking and starts tearing into the spongy white bread and heavy-duty layers of gooey American cheese and dripping, greasy pastrami. I get myself to eat because it's a way for me to feel better, if only temporarily. My sandwich is pretty good, though. Hard on my stomach, but easy on my tongue.

"Okay," Devin chews out, spraying bits of shredded meat at me. Shoot, I was enjoying not having to contribute to a conversation. "Enough beating around the bush. I have a job offer for you."

That stops me in my tracks. I manage to soften up the wad of bread in my mouth enough to respond. "Since when have you cared about jobs?"

"No, no, just hear me out. Picture this: Complete serenity in the wilderness. Trees. Fresh air. A creek trickling in the morning. A safe haven far away from civilization. Sounds like a dream come true?"

I finally gulp down the chunk of processed dairy that's been lingering against my tongue. "Sounds like an advertisement for a retirement home."

"Jamie, I'm talking living in and taking care of a cabin. Complete and total tranquility. Getting away from the constant drama of the modern world."

Okay, now it sounds like a horror story, being in a cabin in the woods. But I let him keep talking because, honestly, why not at this point.

"You remember my uncle Aaron?" Devin asks me. I'm guessing it's relevant, even though he hasn't entirely gotten to the point yet.

"Yeah. From that reunion party you convinced me to go to. He said we looked cute together."

"Yeah, har, har. Funny joke. Anyway, he owns this big, awesome property up in this little place called Pensalado. It's got three cabins, and he needs some folks to take care of them. Now, mostly he does it all himself, even invites people to stay so he can get some extra cash. But get this: He's got the traveling fever in him, too, and he's going to Portugal to rediscover his heritage. Which leaves me with the keys to his place."

There's a lot to digest here, literally and figuratively. I'm halfway through my Melty Club, but I've forgotten about eating the rest of it because this whole thing Devin's thrown at me is just completely unexpected. "Go on."

"So," continues Devin. "I'm going to be the head caretaker. You know, try to stay in one spot for longer than a month. Crazy, right? And guess what? I can take three people with me. I've already decided on Kyle. Poor dude wants out of his parents' house for... well, religious reasons. Plus, he's totally into the outdoors. I asked my cousin earlier, so that's two down. Which leaves..."

He doesn't even have to finish his sentence. I already have an answer. "No."

"C'mon."

"You're ridiculous."

The chocolate milkshake next to me has turned into chocolate milk. I'm shaking my head.

"Why not?"

"Because," I protest, "I wouldn't be a good fit."

"Aw, dude, snap out of it!" groans Devin. "Look at you! Look at your clothes. Look at your face!"

"What, are you a fashion consultant now?"

"No, I'm a guy who sees how fucking miserable you are. I mean, seriously, have you looked at yourself in a mirror lately? You are so wrapped up in your own self-pity, kiddo, that I can barely see the old Jamie. Look, I get that Emily was hot, but was she really worth this much?"

"You don't get it."

He shrugs. "Maybe I don't. Maybe it's a gay thing."

"Come *on*, dude."

"But," persists Devin, slipping into an obnoxious tone of sincerity, "I get how liberating it is to drop everything and get out, explore, try something new. Jamie, I never thought I'd want to be some groundskeeper for my uncle. Now you have a chance to escape from this bullshit, too. And if you take me up on this, it'll be an officially paid job. Not just some favor."

The waiter asks how everything is, and we dismissively give the okay signal. I'm not paying attention to anything else around me. I'm just zeroing in on Devin's face, his eyebrows never lifting from their furrowed position, the determination never dissolving from his eyes. And now, he's just tapped into a gold vein in the deep mine that he's dragged me into.

"Paid?"

"Yep."

"Like, actual money?"

Devin gives me a look. "No," he replies sarcastically. "The fake money you get when you play Monopoly. Yes, real money, you fucking dingus."

I lean forward against the table.

"What would I have to do?"

He smiles slyly. "Oh, now the little fishy wants to hear about the bait," he teases. "All right, dude, here's what's up. For nine months – well, give or take — you get a bedroom all to yourself in one of the cabins, and you're set to clean, paint, chop, plant, weed, and rearrange. Uncle Aaron's shown me the place, and it needs a good look-over. Dead trees need to be ripped up, stuff needs to be fixed, everything needs a good old-fashioned sprucing. And you and me and everybody else would be in charge of making the place presentable. That, and we'd have people renting out the guest cabin every month, so we need to play host, too."

"Okay. So like a bed-and-breakfast sort of deal."

Devin chuckles. "More lumberjack, less cute little old lady offering her guests scones."

"Whatever. Proceed?"

"So. Uncle Aaron will give you seven hundred bucks a month for living expenses, and he's totally willing to give you a reference for future jobs if you ever need to write up a résumé. I mean, think about it. Seven hundred bucks for a little housework and gardening. Put that money together with three other people, that's twenty-eight hundred dollars a month, and we don't even have to pay for rent or repairs or supplies. My good old unc' will take care of that. So what do you say, Jamie? A little adventure into the wild never seemed so bad, huh?"

I have to admit, he has me there. I mean, what other choice do I have? For the past two months, I've been lounging around my house, eating and sleeping and listening to bad music and doing very little else. I can't do that forever. I'm just another one of those punks who can't seem to move on after some stupid break-up. Which, of course, doesn't feel stupid to me, but I don't like my present state as much as I pretend to.

The waiter brings over the check, and Devin slaps down a fifty, telling the pubescent boy in a red shirt to keep the change. It's probably some cash he's saved up and kept in a box all these years because, surprise, surprise, he hates the big banks. I fiddle with the straw that came with my milkshake, and I honestly can't believe I'm considering his offer, but I am. And I'm taking it seriously.

I give him the most suspicious look I can muster.

"When would we leave?"

[...]

At the end of August, I am going to Pensalado. That means I have three or so more weeks to huddle in my room, listening to downer music and eating cheap Chinese food.

My parents are pretty chill with the whole set-up. They've always liked Devin, since he never enticed me to run away from college, and at this point, they know I can break down if they say no to any of my demands. My dad thinks that my being away from home and in the middle of nature instead will be healthy, and if I'm getting paid for taking care of this property, well, then why not? Nothing like his kid learning a little bit of responsibility. So, yeah, I have their blessing.

I guess it can't be that bad. I'd be staying at a new place. I'd have some sense of independence. I'd be getting away from my parents, obviously. And who knows, maybe it won't be so weird to stay with Devin. I have to admit, reuniting with him like that in the diner, no matter how disgruntled I might have been, was kind of refreshing. It did bring me back to the good old high school days when we had started hanging out by the soccer field, eating microwave burritos that we had snuck out of the cafeteria and talking about God knows what as the girls walked by and looked at us with a sort of beautiful skepticism. We acted like we gave a shit at the football games when all we wanted was to piss off the players and flirt with the cheerleaders. We were assholes back then, now that I think about it. Emily seemed to find it sexy. She treated me like I was some sort of rebel when I had always been a goodie-two-shoes who kept a high GPA and stuck to history textbooks.

Of course, I won't be shedding away my remorse and regret so easily. My little laptop will be coming with me, and my cellphone, and my photo albums. I'll do the dirty work expected of me for this job, but I will make damn sure I have the time and self-loathing to keep up with every stage of grief as best as possible. Can't let myself down in letting myself down, right?

As I finish off a midnight pity snack of cashew chicken with extra fortune cookies, all containing messages that I read way too much into, I find that I'm not crying as excessively anymore. Sure, I feel like shit, but I feel like shit with a purpose. And soon, I'll be somewhere entirely different, even if I'm pretty sure I'm not even close to getting over Emily.

You know what, who am I kidding. I am so not ready to get over her.

AUGUST

I feel a car horn go off outside my window around six o'clock in the morning. And I mean feel, not just hear. It sends vibrations up and down my bed, and as I push myself upright and wonder if we're being attacked by bomber planes and World War III has finally started, I spot a flashy red car waiting for me in the driveway. A car that obviously can't be Devin's.

Sure enough, however, he's standing by the passenger's side, waving frantically at me. Leave it to him to show up early; he's probably way too hyped up for this whole trip. In the driver's seat must be Kyle, who I can't see very well but appears to be built like a dark, muscular mammoth. He honks the horn again — well, more like punches it, as if it insulted his mother or something — and nearly splits my eardrums.

"All right!" I bark through the open window. "I'm coming, I'm coming, I'm coming!"

Luckily, I packed everything the night before — everything

except my computer, that is. I needed my sick, forlorn Emily fix somehow. I stuff it into my backpack and grab a decently sized suitcase with the essentials before heading downstairs. Big shocker, I slept in my clothes, and all I have to do is pop into my sneakers, throw on a jacket, and get this show on the road.

My dad's awake and says goodbye to me, giving me an appropriate papa-loves-his-daughter hug and telling me how much he'll miss me and that I should call every week. I tell him to say goodbye to Mom for me, as she's out on one of her very early morning jogs, and I disappear into the mist that cools down the morning only a little bit before the summer heat attacks my senses.

I wordlessly toss my suitcase into the trunk, and then I sidle into the back seat like a sleepy sloth. It's clear that despite his enthusiasm, Devin's tired enough to hold back on the chit-chat at least for a while. Kyle, however, seems much more awake — adventurous, even — and flashes me a toothy grin as I pull on my seatbelt.

"Jamie, right?"

I nod. He holds out a hand that's big enough to crush my head.

"I'm Kyle. Devin's told me all about you. Glad we could finally meet."

I shake his hand and get a vibe from him that's not entirely unexpected of a man who pretty much looks like a lumberjack. The perfect buzz cut, the big black beard, the denim jacket, and the carpenter jeans should look simple enough to any heteronormative passerby. But he's got this spunk in him that people like me can detect from a distance; his rich, silky baritone voice can't hide it. Any other time in my life, I would have started to like him, but I can't take too much bubbliness right now, especially not before seven AM.

"Okay!" There's Devin, launching his wiry frame into the passenger's seat. "We good? We packed? We've gotten to know each other? Awesome. Now we drive for three hours 'til Pensalado, et voilá! Home, sweet home."

"On it, Devin boy," sneers Kyle, revving up the engine a few times before lurching out of the driveway.

The car looks nice and runs just as nicely, and I wonder if Kyle's parents bought it for him. He looks to be about Devin's and my age, maybe a year or so older, and he's a remarkably safe driver. I would have predicted that, like the average douchebag with an expensive car, he'd be speeding and cutting people off and refusing to use his turning signal the whole way, but it's like he glides onto the freeway, and the ride is marvelously smooth. Of course, I realize rather quickly that Kyle probably drives like this so asshole cops don't flag him down; I mean, he does happen to be a black guy driving a nice automobile. Sorry to be a killjoy, but racism ain't dead yet.

I feel ready to nod off again and stop my wandering mind. That's wishful thinking on my part, as Devin drops the drowsy persona and starts talking.

"So! Kyle. You're probably stoked for this gig, huh?"

"Are you kidding me?" scoffs Kyle. "I love it. Pensalado's a cute little place. And it's right next to...you know where, Jamie?"

"No."

"Hearnsville!" Kyle cries out triumphantly, as if he were announcing a verse from a sacred gospel. "The place that the homos victoriously brought back to stability and fabulousness after years of shit. And I intend to indulge in said fabulousness."

Okay. I was right about the vibe I got. He's gayer than a watermelon jolly rancher.

"Surely, Kyle, your queerness would sail a thousand ships," declares Devin, before he casts a simpering look my way. "You know what that's like, right, Jamie?"

"Fuck you."

He laughs and waves me off.

The buildings and shops on both sides of the freeway have disappeared, leaving nothing but browning hills and scorched ranch land, where the cows lumber mindlessly all around us. The drive during this part of the trip is almost entirely uneventful, save for one asshole who decides to slow down to forty-five miles per hour in the left lane for no reason. We don't plan to make any stops; there are groceries packed up in the fairly spacious trunk, and Devin informs Kyle and me that there are many more dried, canned, and packaged goods awaiting us on the property. Apparently, Hearnsville has a big enough store for us to browse whenever we need more food, and that's a relief to me. At least I won't be too far away from civilization.

Halfway through the trip, the trees begin to appear, and the road becomes more winding. Kyle finally gets us off the freeway, and we're propelled into complete nature land. Kyle is fairly focused on his driving, but Devin and I chat a bit. Devin fills me in on his latest adventure to Arizona, where he visited the Grand Canyon and was half-tempted to jump off the edge, "just because." I inform him that the decision not to die was a good one, and he agrees. We go on about high school for only a couple of minutes, because after a while, I start thinking about Emily. All I want to do is look at my computer. The backpack it's stowed in is awkwardly

pressed against my thigh, so there's a physical, as well as emotional, reminder.

"That's one thing I need to do when we get up to Pensalado,"
I sigh. "Check my stuff. I've got profiles to update, pages to read.
Need my little den all planned out."

Devin gives me an awkward look from the passenger's seat.
Uh-oh. Not a good sign.

"Jamie," he murmurs, "there's no Internet access on the
property."

I blink. I don't exactly understand in my still lethargic state.
"Why not? Not allowed or something?"

"No, I mean there's no wi-fi." Devin pauses, perhaps waiting
for my inevitable rage. "Well, except for the café close to the
Pensalado general store, but it's only open Thursday to Sunday,
and it's five bucks an hour."

I stare at him like he's grown horns out of his head. "Are you
serious?"

"Yep. Oh, and you can't use your cellphone, either. No
reception."

"You're killing me, Devin!" I groan.

"But hey, MP3 players still work. You brought one, right?"

I start banging my head against the window nearest to me.
Kyle is not pleased.

"Hey, hey, watch it!" he scolds me. "No smudging the glass!"

"Devin," I complain after rubbing my aching forehead, "couldn't
you have clarified that when you said out in the wilderness, you
really meant out in the actual wilderness?"

"It's not like we're camping or Amish or something!" Devin
argues. "I mean, we've got electricity, heaters, running water, a

refrigerator, a stove, a microwave..."

"Three French hens, two turtle doves..." Kyle adds teasingly, his eyes still glued to the road ahead.

"But my computer!" I whine.

"Too attached to technology, I see."

"Not true and not fair!"

Devin throws up his hands. "Oh, really? Then why is it such a big deal?"

I give up the fight then and there, sinking back against the plush cushioning and shutting my eyes in defeat. Just my luck. I blindly decide to stay in a cabin in the woods for nine months and didn't think for one second that maybe, just maybe, I'd be more than somewhat disconnected from the outside world. No Internet, no cellphone, no MP3 player. So no sad playlists to tide me over, and I'm fairly certain, now that I think about it, that there are no Chinese take-out places around, either.

Thank God I have my photo albums; I need to feed my sorrow somewhat. It's like a habit for me now — I can't help it, and it's like Devin just waltzed in and tried to pull the metaphorical needle out of my arm.

"Hey." Kyle stops effortlessly at a stop sign and tries to give me a comforting smile through the rearview mirror. "Don't worry about it. This is going to be good for you. Devin told me all about your — "

"No-no-no-no-no-no-no."

I clap my hands over my ears like a five-year-old. Devin elbows Kyle. "Don't push it."

After the stop sign must be Hearnsville, and it looks as fabulous as Kyle made it out to be. From the rainbow flags, to the neon signs, to the little local theater, to the flashy bars, it really is a nice, quaint town. Any other time, were I still in a healthy relationship, I would have liked hanging out here because it seems cool, and I guess it has a lot of history. But seeing as I'm not in a healthy relationship, and I feel lousier than lousy, and I couldn't give a fuck about any city's origin right now, Hearnsville is just another spot to look at as we breeze across the intersections back into the wilderness.

This is when the roads start to get narrower, and Kyle becomes a slower and more paranoid driver. We slither through dips and up hills and down inclines, and every time we make a sharp turn, Kyle blares his horn. Not just squeaks, I mean outright roars, as if some truck is going to come barreling out of nowhere and smack us to the side, causing us to careen into the jagged rocks below because there's no railing protecting us.

"You never know what might happen," Kyle mutters, as if he's reading my thoughts. "Some asshole comes around, and boom, we're falling into a ravine or something. Devin, you're a little bitch for making me drive these roads."

"What, would you rather have us die sooner? I'm shit when it comes to driving."

"Jamie, you want a go at this?" Kyle asks me.

"Fuck, no!"

We ascend another hill, and sure enough, I can see the bare bones of what must be Pensalado. And Christ, Devin wasn't kidding when he said, "little place," though I'd disagree with Kyle about it being cute. For one thing, it's very gray. Like, all of it. The church, the general store, the hardware store, even the fire department building. The café is the only colorful addition — bright blue — and it flashes right by in a blur. Then in another minute, Pensalado's gone, and we're still driving.

"The property's still a little ways away," explains Devin. "But you get to see the creek."

Yeah. Half dried up and not very exciting. I see various cabins and houses popping up along the thick foliage. We've gone from all gray to green and brown. It should be vibrant, but everything looks kind of dull to me. I get bored of it easily, but the car keeps pushing forward.

I feel fidgety all of a sudden. I pull my knitted beanie further down on my head. It's a present from Emily — she gave it to me for our second anniversary. Some things I don't let go of if they look good on me, no matter who gifted it.

We're still bobbing along the edge of the road. Still no railing. Still barely enough room to fit two cars. Kyle keeps hitting the horn even when we're not turning.

"Little bit more now," Devin insists, before I can even ask.

It feels like forever, but then I see the gate. It's like the entrance to a hillbilly prison: strict iron and wood and chains. Devin tells Kyle to stop so he can get out and unlock the rickety thing. I watch him fumble with a fistful of keys, all different sizes and shapes and colors. In the distance, through the trees, I can see at least one of the cabins. Bright red.

"The other cabins are green and blue," Kyle says, once again appearing to be psychic, as Devin pushes the gate open with a loud, uncomfortable shriek. "The green one is the guest house."

"C'mon, gang!" calls Devin. "Move it!"

We start coasting onto the property, and Devin runs beside the car like a lunatic. What's left of the creek can be seen to the side, and while there are branches strewn about, crooked half-dead trees, and unkempt grass and weeds, the acreage is still decent-looking. A rope swing lies abandoned by a large patch of poison oak, so that's a little weird, but the cabins look sound enough, even though they're a bit faded paint-wise.

We roll onto the rocky driveway, and I go into sensory overload from all the green around me. Moss droops from the trees surrounding us. Green tufts of grass blossom like random hairs from the gravel. Green grows from abandoned tree stumps. Green even lingers on the walls of the tool shed nearby. There is so much goddamn green that I feel like a leprechaun who's finally made her way home.

I pull myself out of the car and shakily find my footing. The dry leaves and twigs crunch loudly beneath my shoes, and I try to pop the bones in my back and neck back into place. Then I feel a hand smack my shoulder, and I turn to see Devin staring at me as if he's expecting me to erupt with glee at my new circumstances.

"Well?" He stretches out his arms. Straight out of a clichéd movie scene. "What do you think?"

[...]

I'm going to go crazy here.

Devin wasn't kidding when he mentioned the lack of twenty-first century technology. I know that I should turn off my cell phone right away because it's already freaking out about the lack of reception. There's no television, no radio, not even a CD player. All I have for music is a shelf of vinyl records by artists who aren't depressing enough in my current state.

Oh, hey, but we have a landline phone! So we're not totally shut off. I make a mental note to call my parents after I unpack.

I'm told that I will be staying in the main cabin (the red one), while Kyle and Devin will stay in the other not-guest cabin (the blue one). I guess both cabins have two bedrooms and one bathroom each, so it works if there are four of us.

"Where's the last person, by the way?" I blurt to Devin after surveying my bedroom, which is normal for a bedroom. Bed, dresser, closet. Boom. Done.

"Last person?"

"You know, your cousin. They're the fourth person, right?"

"Oh!" Devin snaps his fingers. "Right. Yeah, they won't be here until October."

"Why? Busy with something?"

"In Washington. They're visiting a friend."

Oh. Lucky.

"Anyway, Uncle Aaron is sending all four of us money for September, so don't worry about that."

Devin gives me an exaggerated wink before going to fetch the groceries from the trunk of Kyle's car. It's like everything is an exciting show for him, and he's just a part of the script. I am not amused by it, but then again, I'm not amused by much these days.

I take the time to explore the main cabin. Sure enough, the cupboards in the kitchen are packed, and it does look like we have everything we need. Kyle and Devin eventually walk back in, weighed down with stuff like milk and meat and cheese and bread, and in a few minutes, the refrigerator's crammed. I just watch the two boys work because they're certainly not asking for my help, and I step outside to see if I can get some fresh air.

Turns out that here, it's super cold, even in August. I don't take off my jacket. I wonder what time it is, and when I check my cell phone before I turn it off, I can hardly fathom that it's not even nine. All I want to do is sleep, so I do. I barely take another look at the property or acknowledge it for its so-called splendor; instead, I just march into my room and fall onto the bed.

As I drift off, I think about the photo albums that I've laid out on the dresser beside me. There are plenty of Emily pictures for me to look at and mope about while I'm here. I know I'm a masochist, but I can't stop thinking about her. I tell myself that despite all sense and logic, I still love her, but the thought is unbearable because I know nothing will come of it. I don't dare dream about a day in which Emily comes running back to me, so it makes the whole experience even harder.

I sleep in erratic bursts, and Devin and Kyle don't bother me. They probably will let me off today but get tough on me tomorrow. After all, I'm getting paid to be here, no matter how odd it seems. I am, pretty much, a groundskeeper. A caretaker.

I don't know if I like that idea.

SEPTEMBER

I'm going to kill Devin for this.

I was willing to give this job a chance. I got over the fact that
he had destroyed my cyber cocoon and forced me to begrudgingly
metamorphose into a cynical moth, and I did plan on making
good use of my time. And by making good use of my time, I mean
isolating myself and staying away from the rest of the world for
most of the day. Who knew that I'd be relying on an old record
player for that purpose?

I'm not ready to heal and be all sunshine and butterflies, but
God damn, if Devin and Kyle aren't trying to shove their adven-
turer optimism down my craw. Every morning, they wake me
up around six or seven o'clock by abusing one of my five senses.
Devin occasionally decides that it's fun to fling open my shutters
and blind me with the impending sunlight. Other times, Kyle strolls
into my room, boisterously singing that, "Good Morning," song,
and I don't remember where it's from, but I have to stop myself

from tying up the guy with my bedsheets and locking him in the closet as a form of irony.

If my sight or hearing aren't molested, then it's my sense of smell. I wish I could say it's always a good smell because Kyle's a great cook, and sometimes he makes these amazing waffles that become the next ultimate comfort food for me, even though they're not steamed rice or sweet and sour pork. But Devin will try to give his buddy a break, and he'll serve up this disgusting mosaic of what used to be ham and eggs but now looks more like a fourth grader's art project. I don't like starting off my day with the taste of burnt sulfur in my mouth.

I wouldn't mind the whole, "C'mon, be happy," vibe so much if it weren't for the fact that Devin seems so freakishly energetic about this whole set-up. It's like a vacation for him. He blabs on and on about how he gets to tend to this or manage that, fix this or build that, and suddenly, I hardly know him. He never used to be the person who enjoyed working, in any form. Hell, he would even complain about the homework we got for what I thought were our easiest classes. Maybe wandering around the country for so long made him question whether or not he wants to be a homebody now. But whatever the reason, he's painfully chipper about his newfound daily life, though I often wonder if in the thick of night, he sneaks out of the cabin to go hiking or stargazing or bear wrestling or something.

And then there's the work. It's not difficult or challenging; that's actually the reason why I don't like it. Recently, Kyle and Devin have been getting up early to work on the guest cabin. They're mending the roof in preparation for the rainy season, which here, from what Kyle has told me, is almost all year round.

When they're not hammering away on new shingles, they're tightening window panes, re-hinging doors, and shuffling around furniture. I honestly would not mind this sort of work. I appreciate doing some manual labor, and while I've never considered myself strong enough to do it as an actual career, I think I'd feel pretty empowered with a hammer or a screwdriver in my hand.

But, no. I get to be the painter, cleaner, and secretary for these two assholes. I have to add a new coat of paint to the main cabin, so in the first week, two of my good shirts are splotched with red because I didn't have half a brain to bring up older clothes to work in. Devin insists that I vacuum the cabins, I shit you not, every other day. I run the laundry, wash the dishes, water the potted plants (why do we even have potted plants here? Mother Nature's done wonders for us already!), and rigorously scrub down the bathrooms when all I really want to do is wield a saw. The only things that are missing are the frilly apron and a frying pan so I can cook dinner every night, offering a fresh salad with every meal.

"Just so you know," Devin says to me one night, as I dust the fireplace for what feels like the forty-second goddamn time that day, "we're not making you do this because you're the only girl around. It's just that Kyle's a really good carpenter, and I want to learn from him."

"Yeah, sure," I mumble. "Just let me know when I can fetch you your beers, and you can slap my ass as I'm sashaying away."

Devin cringes. "Ew, bro."

"No hetero, obviously."

Don't get me wrong: I don't actually think that Devin is misogynistic when it comes making me do the housework. I just think he's seriously undermining my gay cred when it comes to being a handyman. No pun intended.

The main cabin is the most spacious of the lodges here, but it also means that I have the least privacy. Obviously, we have meals there because that's where the kitchen and the dining room are. Also, because we don't have Internet, which is the worst thing for modern business ever, I have to use a wall calendar to confirm and re-confirm and re-re-confirm stays at the guest cabin. Even after I get off the phone, which has the shape and weight of a conch that you pick up on the beach so you can pretend that you're listening to the ocean, Devin waltzes in and tells me to double check everything. He fusses like this even though the only guests in September are his immediate family, whom I'm not keen on entertaining when I have nothing substantial to offer when it comes to my presence.

And that's the thing that burns me up the most, more so than being a maid or being woken up by a science experiment for breakfast: The fact that I feel completely and totally worthless all the time. The boys do try to cheer me up, though; whenever I hole myself up in my room with the record player after stealing it from the living room, listening to the saddest song I can find on the Genesis vinyl, in comes Devin or Kyle, checking up on me and encouraging me to break away from my hermitage. But once I'm with them, having dinner or playing cards or screaming about some stupid board game, I feel more like a burden than a friend. I can't tell stories. I can't draw fun pictures. I don't like taking walks anymore. I don't find the books up here worthwhile. I'm horrible at that generic trivia game we have in the cabin (which, to be fair, is so old that it still classifies Russia as the USSR), especially the history questions because I keep mixing up names and almost getting the right year but never hitting the mark. I'm even worse at basic conversation, primarily because I have literally nothing interesting to say.

I am essentially a hired hand who should make little to no verbal or physical contact with any other people while I'm here. Let me just stick to dusting the chairs while everyone else has fun. I'll stay in my corner and get tired of seeing the same glossy photos of Emily in my photo albums when really, all I want to do is see if she's getting antsy yet and wants me back after all.

[...]

By the time Devin's family shows up for their stay at the guest cabin, the rain starts coming down. It's cold, harsh rain that creates percussion on the tinny roof and makes it difficult to sleep. The weather forces me to stop painting the cabins for the time being, which I don't mind holding off on, and I think maybe I can finally get some extra time to sulk and subject myself to purposeful solitary confinement. But this is Devin's family we're talking about, not mine; they don't understand boundaries.

The week starts with Devin's parents and two younger sisters crowding around the doorframe of the main cabin, dripping wet, eager to have a family gathering. Devin lights a fire, and I collapse onto the gaudy black and white couch in the living room as the family pulls up chairs and begins working on a jigsaw puzzle they found in our clumsy tower of boxed games. They talk the whole time, Devin of course talking about his many adventures; I've heard the tale about how he helped birth a piglet on a Mississippi farm about four times since we came up to Pensalado. Just a typical conversation at dinner, you know.

Devin's father is bigger than I remember him being, with more gray hair, but he seems to recall everything about me after our two or so meetings back in high school. "If I didn't know any better," he says to me, as Donna and Danielle — yes, all D names for the kids — turn on the Beatles' White Album and start awkwardly dancing to it, "I'd say you've gotten a little taller."

"I haven't," I mutter. "I think I stopped growing when I was sixteen."

"Oh, must have been mistaken," Devin's father replies. "But you look taller, anyway. Look a little green around the gills, though. You eating right?"

I've tried. Inexplicably, I've been losing weight since I got here. I had always been kind of chubby in high school and college. Not so much anymore.

Devin abruptly strides into the room with two bottles of champagne, and the family toasts and drinks before Kyle's even put dinner on the table. The rain doesn't bother anyone except me. My fingers are numb all the way from the knuckles to the tips, and my skin and hair feel damp even though I've hardly been outside today. I want to snatch the record player from Devin's sisters and run with it back to my room, where I can bury myself in quilts and try to drift into awkward musical dreamland. But I can't do that. I'm now a host, and I'm meant to entertain. I could hardly entertain my own dog when I was little. He would always get bored with my antics and go off to chase his own tail or something. That reeks of failure.

Devin's parents and sisters are pretty much as "free-spirited" as Devin is. His father is a fisherman who would let the poor things go if he didn't have to make money off them. His mother runs an independent knitting store, where she sells bundles of yarn and needles while encouraging new and "innovative" designs. Given the way our hometown is, the shop is a never-ending cash cow. Donna and Danielle, being twins, tried to be as different as possible from each other but ultimately are both writers, and at the dinner table, I am undesirably exposed to their artistic sides.

"It's like a muse controls me whenever I'm sitting at my desk," Donna informs us, as I pick at the pork chop that Kyle's thoroughly cooked and seasoned. "Like an out-of-body experience. I just give myself up to the energy surrounding me, and the writing just flows."

"Wouldn't it be more liberating to write with a quill instead of a pencil?" Danielle pipes up with a mouthful of brown rice. "Having a cute little inkpot, needing to use your resources wisely. Letting the writing itself become art so the words are powerful inside and out. I totally should try out calligraphy."

Kill me, kill me, kill me, kill me, *kill me...*

"So!" It takes me a moment to pull out of my fatalistic state and realize that Devin's mother is talking to me. "I heard you decided not to become a history teacher after all. Going to take more risks in life?"

I wouldn't consider getting seven hundred dollars a month as a semi-functioning landlord to be much of a risk, but I humor her with a nod. "Sure. May as well try something new."

"Honestly, I didn't think Devin would last four days up here," Devin's dad chuckles, slapping his son on his bony back. "After he spent only a week in a tent by the Hudson River, I figured he'd never stop moving!"

"What can I say?" jokes Devin. "I'm like the Energizer bunny. I just keep going and going and going…"

"Well, I won't drag you down with too many bad memories, Jamie," Devin's mother suddenly and audaciously states, "but I think it's super that you're dealing with all your troubles with such determination and perseverance. I'm very proud of you for that."

What, now she's my mom, too? I give the evil eye to Devin, determined to use my fork to fling a chunk of pork right at his forehead. Then, in order to tamp down on my violent and wasteful urges, I loudly excuse myself to use the bathroom when I just want to leave the table. Sure enough, in comes the gangly peace-maker himself, grabbing me by the arm.

"Would it kill you to try socializing a little more?" he demands.

"Are you kidding me?" I growl. I'm livid now. "You're the one who decided that everyone had a right to know my sob story. Seriously? You had to tell your mom that I was dumped?"

"All I'm trying to do is surround you with people who care for you," Devin snaps. "Make you a little more, I dunno, in love with life?"

"I don't need your pity party! I can take care of myself!"

A roar of rain above our heads seems to accentuate my words of vitriol. Devin is frozen, his nostrils flaring, his greasy hair framing his locked jaw. Outside the small hallway, back in the dining area, there's laughter. I guess our little tiff doesn't seem to be disturbing anyone else except us.

Of course, leave it to me to start crying. I try to wipe the offending water away from my eyelids, but the hyperventilating makes up for it. Devin's face falls, and in my blurred vision, I see him reaching toward me. Then my wet nose scratches against his jacket as he pulls me to his chest. I don't care how ridiculous we both look. I'm too upset and overwhelmed to care.

"I miss her," I whimper into the fabric.

"I know."

"I fucking miss her."

"I know, Jamie."

He rubs my shaking back with one hand while clinging to my sweatshirt with the other. I try to calm down, but all that's repeating in my head is a reel of Emily's face and smile, her laughter and the way she pursed her lips just before she kissed me. Even when everything seems so colorless around me in real life, she's so vivid in my memory and my imagination, all the way down to the purple tank tops and the black skirts and the blue wedges she always liked to wear, no matter what the occasion was. She's like a dragon that flew into my castle, cooked me with fire breath, consumed me, and then spat the bones out. I've got no meat to offer now. I've been picked clean as if by vultures.

Devin keeps hugging me and waiting for me to stop crying until Kyle checks on us. His lips are drawn into a concerned pout, and he lets us know that dinner's been cleared away, and we're welcome to have caramel toffee bars and sparkling cider or wine whenever we're ready. Of course, my stomach says yes, and I pull away to partake in the baked goods that my new mate has provided.

Danielle and Donna are reciting poetry now — original pieces, which is clearly evident by the writing itself. They're not bad at their craft, but in their attempts to be open-minded, they come across as snooty. Danielle shares a sonnet with us that's meant to be about life and finding freedom by living in a car and shrugging off material needs, and it's just so hackneyed and over-the-top that I think even Jack Kerouac would roll his eyes. Still, I can't fault her for trying; despite being related to people who claim to be hippies, her life is very run-of-the-mill and suburban. And that makes being even slightly original all the more difficult.

As for me, I occupy myself with the toffee bars, which are like gifts from God, and let the sparkling cider tickle my raw throat before cooling me down. No matter how chilly it is inside, and no matter how much it rains outside, I now feel warm and stifled in the space. I prop my feet up on an available chair, try to listen to Donna's ode to revolution in a small rural town, and end up spacing out.

[...]

The rest of the week carries on with no other incident — or at least, no emotional breakdown from me — and the rain lets up for the last two days of the Abregas' trip. I'm treated over and over again to Devin's family's creative whims, receiving a notebook filled with haiku from Danielle and a knitted scarf from Devin's mother (which, to be fair, could come in handy in this weather). The faint rays of sun allow me to re-paint two walls of the main cabin, while our guests enjoy their nature walks and their blackberry expeditions, and I only socialize with them once Kyle has taken the berries and turned them into a phenomenal cobbler.

No matter how disillusioned or disenchanted I seem to be or act, Devin's family adores me. Maybe it's because of the demeanor

I've had in the past, which, to be fair, was rather enthusiastic, if not a little sardonic. Maybe they find me clever, or they think I'm secretly a suffering Poe-like figure, even though I certainly didn't lose Emily to tuberculosis, and she sure as hell wasn't my thirteen-year-old first cousin. Either way, they shower me with goodbye hugs and kisses, promising to visit again if they ever find the time or money for the stay.

Devin is glowing from the success of housing our first lodgers, regardless of the fact that they're related to him. The stay is fifty dollars per night, which also covers the meals we cook for them, so we've made three hundred and fifty dollars from them. We put the check in a box, and Devin and Kyle travel down to Hearnsville to deposit it at the bank for safekeeping until Aaron comes back.

That's another thing: The boys go down to Hearnsville at least once a week. Sometimes they swim. Sometimes they fish. Most of the time, they drink, and I'm sure that Devin tries to hook Kyle up with some mountain man whenever he can. And every time, they've tried to get me to go with them. I've always refused. I might set a new monthly record for how many times I've declined invitations to do allegedly fun stuff, but I doubt that's something you can find in the Guinness Book of World Records. Devin and Kyle try to lure me with anything: Food, drinks, dancing, hot girls, you name it. They even tempt me with bribery, as in paying for everything I could ever want. But I still say no. I'm not in the mood to leave the property. Even with the offer of hourly wi-fi for four days a week, I don't even visit the café in downtown Pensalado — or what little could be classified as downtown, anyway.

So once Devin and Kyle have given up all hope of me coming with them and decide to leave me alone, I wander around the main cabin for a little bit before disappearing into my room. I get what they're trying to do: They're probably terrified that I'm going to go crazy and do something drastic, like smash all the windows or burn down everything in sight. But I'm not the manic kind of sad; I'm just the sad kind of sad. The harmless kind, where you should just shrug your shoulders and say, "Poor Jamie. We'll see what happens. Leave her be." It's not like I've become a lazy slug; I do my share of the work without complaining vocally, even if mentally, I'm frustrated and exhausted. But I think they're getting tired of dealing with my baggage. I mean, they could've found someone else who would make the most of this experience, but hey, Devin had high hopes, didn't he?

At the end of the month, I call my parents. Nothing's changed on their end, but they're surprisingly eager to hear what I've been up to. I leave out the emotional drama and tell them about what tasks I've been working on, and they seem to take it as a sign of healing. They remind me of how much they love me and how they'll tell everyone I say hi, even though there isn't anyone I'd say hello to at all. I hang up the phone feeling just as dazed as I've felt for the past few months, and I return to my somewhat updated routine.

Right now, I'm the only one who stays in the main cabin. The space belongs to me and me alone. Then again, it's almost October.

OCTOBER

The rain has not stopped since the new month began. It's intolerable. I can't get any outside work done on my end, and I feel like if I step out of the cabin, I'll drown while standing up. Kyle and Devin are more than welcome to act like troopers in the torrential downpour, attempting to remove dead chunks of trees so we don't have the monstrosities toppling down on us and killing us on impact. I'll just stick to the housewife role for now. It's safer, at least.

Because the weather isn't getting any better, we've received cancellations throughout all of October. It's pretty bad, and obviously, Devin's the least happy about it. He's tried to convince guests to reconsider and just enjoy the outdoors for what they are, but we've got open slots all over the calendar that no one is touching. They're not interested in coming up here, especially not on these roads. It's like all of Pensalado becomes a hazard zone in the storm season.

Oh, yeah, I'm not kidding about the storms. They started at the end of September, and I'm becoming accustomed to lightning and thunder. I'm waiting for God or Zeus or Thor to grow tired of me and just hurl a bolt right through my window, frying me like a flabby chicken thigh. The wind is bad, too, and it keeps me up all night. If you think my mood's lousy even after ten hours of sleep, imagine how off-kilter I am without being able to doze off at all.

"Maybe think about changing the record now, Jamie?" Kyle pleads with me one day as the rain continues to come down in sheets. He's making sandwiches for lunch, even though I'm not hungry. I've played the same side of Pink Floyd's *Wish You Were Here* for the past two days. The vinyl's a bit warped, so the pitch of the music shifts once in a while when the needle hits the curve.

"Don't touch the record player."

"Jamie, come on."

"Don't touch it!"

He waits for me to use the bathroom before hiding the record and putting on some jazz. I'm ready to go Medea on his ass when Devin whirls into the room, tracking in puddles and looking more than perturbed.

"So," he wheezes. "Just heard on my radio that the storm's going to get worse before it gets any better. So methinks we gotta go into town and grab some things."

"Radio?" I gape at him. "You have a radio?"

Devin gawks back at me. "Yeah. A portable. I've been listening to it while cleaning up the guest cabin."

"Devin! You have a *portable fucking radio?!*"

"Yeah! I just said that!"

I lash out at the little black device that I now see clipped onto his jeans. "Give me that!"

"Whoa, whoa, easy!" Kyle takes only two steps from the kitchen to block me from outright assaulting his friend. "You've hogged the record player all week. You don't get to claim Devin's radio, too. We use that for emergencies and weather reports."

I point a finger accusingly at Devin. "But he just said he — "

"Jamie." Kyle's voice is now the lowest and coldest I've ever heard it. He's not screwing around right now. He's gone from baritone to bass. "Leave it be."

A growl of thunder is the orchestra that accompanies his words. I back down, but I'm still pissed off. All this time, I had no radio to listen to and no way of knowing what was going on outside my little bubble, and Devin's had one the entire time? What did he expect me to do, hire a town crier?

"So are you going to go out or not?" I ask.

"Kyle and I will go," says Devin. "Kyle's a crusader — he can drive in this rain. We'll get some fire starters and some flashlight batteries in case we lose power for a bit."

"Lose power?" I stutter. "Who would be around to bring it back up?"

"Dude, don't worry about that. We're going to be fine. You can stay here and look after the place."

"Christ, the bitch job again?"

"You've never wanted to go into town, anyway," retorts Devin. "Why are you suddenly caring now?"

He's got me there, but in my sleep-deprived state, it's a little different now. For the first time in a while, I don't want to be left alone. Still, Devin and Kyle are pulling on dirty raincoats and bracing themselves for Mother Nature's wrath. I only hear a few more words from them before the sliding glass door closes and the winds swallow them up.

"I'm a crusader? Seriously? Fuck you for making me drive."

"Oh, c'mon, it could be worse."

Could it be? I think that to myself as I collapse onto the same ugly black and white couch, the noise outside disorienting me. I try to close my eyes and settle down, but the weather won't let me. I know what will happen if I can't sleep. I can already feel my mind going on high alert, overly vigilant while still lost in fragmented thoughts.

It's been a while since I've suffered an anxiety attack. I used to have them pretty frequently, even while I was still dating Emily. I've been known to have a frenzied and overanalytical mind, but my ex was good at calming me down. She had a way with rubbing my back at just the right angle, whispering to me that everything was okay and I could stop thinking so hard about everything. Her lips were like soothing aloe for my emotional sunburn. I didn't think I could ever manage the crazy chemical soup that is my brain without her.

However, now that I'm single and by myself in a cabin on a property in the middle of the wilderness, with the rain streaming down like a river from the sky, I find myself reverting to my old habits. There's no one to comfort me now, no one to tell me not to go into panic mode. So I start mentally wandering. Worrying about the future, dwelling on the present, and reminiscing too much about the past.

It's October, but I'm thinking about last May. It's storming, but I'm thinking about a heat wave in Southern California. Graduation. I fold my arms and press them against my chest, attempting to keep calm. I feel like I'm slipping through time like the water slipping across the cabin's eaves and gutters. Everything is fluid and inconsistent. I'm not paying attention to clocks, but I'm going back through the years, anyway.

May. October. Five months. Five months since four years came to an end. Four years since she asked me to prom. Told me she liked me. I liked her, too. Sure, let's try this out. Fuck the haters. We're so fabulous that it makes our faces hurt. Four years.

There's a dirge playing in my head. Everything is now chrono-logical. All structured. Going down the line. Four years. Prom. High school graduation. "I can't believe we're going to the same college! Isn't that amazing?" "You know, you'd make a great teacher."

No, I wouldn't make a great anything. I don't even make a great history buff. It was different before. Back in college, I was able to absorb dates and names and rattle them off during dinner or hang-outs. I passed out fun facts and informational tidbits from Greek mythology and the medieval times and the Industrial Revolution like business cards. You want to hear the story about how much Nikola Tesla loved pigeons? I was your girl. Interested in knowing more about the Soviet Union's space program? Dude, Yuri Gagarin studied tractors before becoming Russia's space hero (why do I remember that?). Thinking about the Civil War, but not sure why it started? Slavery. The answer is always slavery.

But I hardly remember anything I learned now, besides the random nonsense I just cerebrally spouted. It's like a giant blank with only a few illegible scribbles. Like the last four years meant nothing.

History was my life. My existence. And the thing about history is that it ends. It becomes a stamp, a "from here to there" status.

The fall of empires. The collapse of politicians and kings and dicta-tors. Birth and death. Beginning and end. I'm not a history teacher. I'm a history book. And the Jamie-Emily dynasty has concluded.

I can't take this. I can't take this. I know I'm being dramatic, but I am history. There is nothing left.

I find a pillow to cover my ears with, as if muffling out the thunder will help me. But I'm stiff and tense all over my body. My heart is practically in my mouth. Everything feels so cold around me. Anxiety is here, and it has accepted me as its bitch, baby.

And then the power goes out.

[...]

I find a flashlight after gathering my breath and pulling myself out of my panic attack, the silver beam barely illuminating the space. I shine the light on the battery-powered analog clock on the wall, and it's eight o'clock at night. When did Devin and Kyle leave? How long has it been?

I want to call someone, but the phone line is, of course, dead. Without the hum of the refrigerator, the rattling of the heater, or the buzzing of the lights, everything feels catatonic. Even with the thunder rumbling occasionally and the rain pummeling the roof, it's eerily quiet. The occasional lightning only serves to startle me in its momentary offering of natural electricity. I push myself into a chair in the dining room and don't move.

This power outage could mean anything. It could mean a fallen telephone pole, a wrecked wire, maybe a tree taking out towers. Who the hell is around to fix that stuff? Do we even have a backup generator? In short, I come to the conclusion, in my nearly hysterical state, that I am adequately fucked.

I stay in the dining room for what feels like eons, clinging to my flashlight, hoping it doesn't putter out. My feet grow icy, even though they're pulsing in my socks, and I have to clench my jaw to stop my teeth from chattering. I half-expect to see my own breath wafting in front of my face. It really is like a scene straight out of a horror film: Alone in a cabin on a stormy night, and the power goes out. I should have known what would happen after Devin left me here to fend for myself; he must have decided that I would be the first to die in a nightmare scenario, cut down by some serial killer, or chainsaw enthusiast, or just a traumatized dude with a unique facial scar. Now all I need is for that person to knock on the door.

Oh my God, someone's knocking on the door!

I jump up and stifle a shriek, whipping the flashlight at the main entrance. The main cabin has two ways to get inside: The sliding glass door, which currently is locked and concealed by blinds, and the front door. Devin, Kyle, and I hardly use the latter, and even our guests usually go in through the side door for meals. Because of this, we consistently keep the front door locked, since we figured no one really uses it to go in or out. And now, someone is knocking on it.

I try to react quickly without making too much noise. One misstep, and I could be flat on my back on the hard tile floor, vulnerable to a vicious attack from a psychopathic monster. I sidle against the brick that engulfs the fireplace, the flashlight twitch-ing in my hand, and grope for something, anything, to serve as a weapon. My fingers rub against the sooty handle of a poker.

The thunder crashes with beautiful timing. There's another

knock. Then I hear someone jimmying the knob. Shit — he's trying to break in! The fucker's impatient, so he's just going for it! I yank the poker out of its little iron bucket and brandish it in front of my face. The rain is like a war drum as I near the entryway.

Everything seems to get louder the closer I get to the perceived threat. The storm, the creaking knob, even my own breathing. I try to press my feet into the floor like I'm a rooted tree. I hold the poker straight out. I hear jingling, rustling, coughing. Then, the door swings open just as lightning conveniently flashes.

Bellowing, I jab the poker forward and hit nothing but air, watching as the intruder tumbles into the house, shoes audibly slipping on the floor. There is a loud thud and clatter behind me — the perpetrator has fallen, taking something down with him. A large weapon? I ignore the rain trickling into the cabin from outside, the wind picking up around my ankles. I raise my poker like a sword and swing my flashlight so I can see the bastard's face.

"Holy shit, man! What the fuck?"

I jolt. Lying before me, hands splayed out and mouth half-open, is a girl who can't be much older than I am. Her dark, curly hair lies in wet tangles against her coat, its collar clinging to the soaked skin on her neck. I slowly realize, caught in the faint glow of the flashlight, that the heavy object that is lying beside her is a decently sized suitcase.

It can't be. Is this the cousin I've heard about? I don't let down my guard. Not in my frazzled state. I wave around the poker in a sad attempt to look threatening.

"Who are you?" I try to interrogate her. "What do you want?"

She looks at me like I have two heads, and they're both speaking in gibberish. She struggles to her feet, pushing her suitcase aside. I see now that she has a key in her hand, which explains the jingling; she must have knocked on the door initially to see if anyone was home first. I imagine, in fact, that she did so in order to avoid spooking anyone.

I quietly and shakily lower the poker.

Well. This is weird and embarrassing.

Right as the newcomer attempts to stand up after my attempted assault, two things happen. The first is that Devin and Kyle's silhouettes crowd the open doorway, the former looking especially pale in the dim light. The second, oh so conveniently, is that the power suddenly comes back on, the rush of brightness disorienting me and forcing me to shut my eyes like I've been confronted by hundreds of camera flashbulbs.

"So." Devin sounds more amused than puzzled. "I see you two have already met."

I can't believe it. Not only is this my cabin mate, but I also just tried to go samurai on her ass.

Devin and Kyle carry in one grocery bag each, their hair wet from the rain. Devin hands his bag over to Kyle, pulls his cousin to her feet, and offers her a hug. As she reciprocates, she keeps sending dirty looks my way. I don't blame her; I did just try to stick a poker through her because I thought she was a burglar, or a madwoman. Her hazel eyes sear into me, one dark eyebrow arched.

"Devin," she says, pulling away from her cousin's arms, "please don't tell me this is my cabin mate."

I suddenly feel very small and set my sights on the fireplace. I then scurry over to put the poker back in its rightful spot, turning off the flashlight and tossing it onto the nearest piece of furniture, all while trying to act as cool and collected as possible. Devin looks me up and down, clicking his tongue, as if he's a veterinarian examining a sick dog.

"That is indeed your cabin mate, my dear cousin," he replies with a small smile. "Jamie, may I introduce to you the lovely Rachel. The daughter of my dear Uncle Aaron."

Rachel, for what it's worth, looks nothing like Devin. In fact, I'm shocked that they're even related. Where Devin is tall and gangly and seemingly harmless, Rachel looks like the kind of girl who can take down guys in a fight. She's not overtly buff, but she's definitely well-toned under that coat, her jawline very prominent and her cheeks almost looking like they're built out of brown marble. It's all the more intimidating that she looks ready to tear out my jugular with her bare hands.

I reluctantly extend my hand as both a greeting and an apologetic gesture. "Nice to meet you, Rachel."

She laughs and shakes her head instead of shaking my hand. "'Nice to meet you,'" she repeats. "She tries to stab me with a poker as soon as I walk through the door, and now she's saying, 'Nice to meet you.'"

"Oh, give it a rest, will you, Rachel?" coaxes Devin. "She didn't mean it. She probably just thought the worst."

"Eh, well, don't we all." Rachel stoops down for her suitcase and flashes a smirk at her cousin. "Do me a favor. Be a gentleman, and get my guitar and CD player out of my truck. It's unlocked, and I figured you don't have to live like old men up here with your phonograph."

A CD player. I would be more enthusiastic for a more advanced form of technology, were it not for the fact that I don't have any

CDs to play, and the record player is starting to grow on me. But Devin seems more than eager to help out. Guess it comes with the family dynamic.

I very quickly head for the kitchen to get away from Rachel, finding Kyle there opening up some beers. He looks surprisingly chill after driving through one hell of a storm. He even smiles at me as I approach.

"You okay?" he asks me.

I tentatively reach for a bottle. "Kind of, I guess."

He nods. "Go ahead and take one." He grabs a bottle for himself and downs a good quarter of the contents in just a couple of swallows. "I guess the power grid sort of glitched around here. Too many people using their heaters, I guess? Everything went dark in town when we were leaving, but it looks like it's all cool now."

"You think this rain will ever let up?" I ask.

Kyle shrugs. "Has to at some point, right?" He picks up two more beers in his enormous fist and calls over his shoulder. "Rach, you want a welcome drink?"

I guess they already know each other. Once again, Devin has a way of getting everyone connected except me. Maybe he's doing them a favor.

I decline the offer to stay in the living room and head back to my own space. I'm too light-headed and humiliated to interact with anyone. First, I come to this place with no other desire but to brood, and now, I'm proven to be a complete dumbass to the person I'm supposed to be living in the same cabin with for another seven months. Who, I remind myself, is another chick.

Oh, well. I sit on the corner of my bed, drinking my beer. I'm so out of it that I don't even cater to my Emily habit for the night. I have to shake off the smell of failure first. But hey, maybe no hard feelings between me and Rachel, right? Everything's going to be cool by tomorrow, and we'll all be fine and dandy the rest of the time we're up here, right?

Christ, who am I kidding? This isn't going to end well.

NOVEMBER

I never thought I was going to be doing this during our epic stay in no man's land, but I'm trying to regularly maintain good hygiene now. The day after Rachel showed up, I walked into the kitchen so I could devour Kyle's delicious Belgian waffles, and all I got instead were her judgmental eyes piercing into me. I think I've gone through more deodorant and shampoo in one week than I have in the past three months. By this point, I wouldn't be surprised if I smelled like a goddamn meadow full of lilacs and daisies by the time I got out of the bathroom every morning.

The whole dynamic has shifted in the cabin since Rachel moved in. As in, I can't live in a messy hobo-like environment anymore. Not only do I share a place with Rachel, but I also share a bathroom with her, meaning I'm still getting used to all her toiletries cluttering up an already tiny sink. I'm actually hanging up my towel and cleaning out the tub after I shower— all the hair that I pull out of the drain reminds me that I'm way overdue for a trim. Rachel rearranged all my stuff and put a lot of my things into the medicine cabinet as soon as she settled in, which threw me off-kilter just when I was about to go into my Fortress of Solitude with a Chicago record and a bottle of cheap beer.

Since Rachel seems completely unwilling to maintain normal human contact with me, Devin fills me in a little on her back story. Apparently, since she was eighteen, she'd been living in a little town called Lunanoche — because in this state, we like our cities to be named after two Spanish words, thank you very much. She didn't give a damn about college, making me the only person on the property who most likely wasted four years and thousands of my parents' dollars on a worthless degree. Yeah, Kyle's a college drop-out, though he probably could have gotten a Bachelor of Fine Arts in oxymorons, given his macho flamboyance.

Anyway, Rachel worked in retail, mostly, switching from store to store and position to position, selling everything from electronics to groceries to poorly designed T-shirts that normally got pulled from stock due to We Knew It Was Offensive, But We Didn't Know It Was *That* Offensive Syndrome (or WKIWOBWD-KIWTOS. Sorry, I'm no good with acronyms). Most recently, while she was slaving away at one of those classic paper and office supply stores, one of her assistant managers decided he could use an extra spoonful of paranoia in his life and convinced the boss to fire her. According to Devin, his conspiracy theory was that Rachel was going to oust him from his blue polo throne just by selling enough cheap appliance warranties and rewards cards to earn herself a one hundred dollar gift certificate to a frozen yogurt parlor. After that, no one was really biting for an extra cashier or guest services grunt, and she couldn't afford her rent, especially after her roommate decided to move to Ecuador on a whim. Just another leaf on the wind, I guess. Hence why she's here.

I am surrounded by so-called free spirits. I've got Devin, the former drifter; Kyle, the gay Brawny Paper Towels man look-a-like; and Rachel, the token female hard-ass from all the action films I've watched. I feel totally separated from them, especially job-wise. At first, I expected Rachel to take on more administrative and clerical tasks so I could become less of a wuss, but, no! She's out there splitting wood for the nightly fire and toiling away at the cabins' infrastructure like a boss. I can tell she revels in it, too; she dresses the part by wearing scraped up jeans and T-shirts and a baseball cap from some team I don't care about. She even got a denim jacket from Kyle that's way too big for her, but she still keeps it on while she works.

Obviously, Rachel is perfectly capable of what several people would nastily call, "men's work," but here I am, stuck with a vacuum cleaner and a toilet brush, looking like a loser. How is it that she's pulling off the stereotype better than I am? Is she gay, too?

"Bisexual, I think," Devin tells me privately when I manage to ask him. "Or pan. I don't keep track of that shit, man."

I have never cared this much about what my friends think of me. At least, I like to consider them friends, but it's probably more of a "trio with extra baggage" scenario than a healthy, sitcom-worthy quartet. Oh, but hey, I got somewhat of an upgrade on the job front. Now I'm weeding and mowing the lawn before winter starts. My fingers need to be thawed out every shift after being scratched up by tall green nuisances, and the lawn mower leaves me smelling like diesel as soon as I walk into the house. I feel so much better now. Sarcasm free of charge.

I want the boys to just give me an axe so I can stop feeling so emasculated every single day of my life. Can I even feel emasculated, given my gender? I'll leave that question for enlightened college students to debate at a women's studies seminar.

With the rain finally dissipating for the rest of October, we start getting more calls from prospective guests. Of course, as soon as a rich couple shows up at the start of November with two teenage girls who use all their air to complain about no cellphone reception (I mean, how do they think *I* feel?), what should decide to become a magician and disappear but our hot water. I'm keeping to myself in the living room the night it happens, reading a sports and entertainment magazine that Devin snatched for free from the Pensalado general store. Sportsball team number one is losing hardcore against sportsball team number two. It is a dark day in the middle of nowhere.

Rachel is in the kitchen, popping open a bottle of white wine that's probably way too sweet for my liking. Last week, it was Riesling, and this week, well, I'm pretty sure it's still Riesling. She pours herself a glass, exhales as if she's found paradise, sidles past me without even saying, "Excuse me," and sits down on the nearest couch with her back facing me.

Yeah, it hasn't exactly been chill between the two of us. I mean, we obviously don't hate each other, but I don't think we necessarily like each other, either. Keep in mind, I'm not the cheeriest person to hang around with at the moment, making me unnervingly sensitive to any shred of negative tone. Rachel happens to be very loud, brassy, and snarky — qualities that Devin and Kyle, of course, adore — and they're all like bros. But as soon as she sets her eyes on me, the smile that's lit up on her face, whether it's after a game of cards or a spontaneous dance session to a Beatles record, just falls off like dead skin. It's like I kill her happiness just by existing. I don't know if I could feel any guiltier than I already do about my situation, but she's certainly not making me feel any better, especially after the whole, "Yeah, sorry for almost stabbing you with a dusty poker," incident.

In short, we don't talk to each other. That's the easiest way to skirt around any potential issues that will probably re-surface at some point and bite us both in the ass. But hey, we're young adults, and who needs to develop communication skills when someone's got Riesling to drink?

The silence in the living room, as Rachel savors her wine, is punctuated by a banshee-like scream from the guest cabin. I jump up immediately, thinking that someone's being strangled, the magazine scrunching up like a flimsy accordion between my hands. Rachel almost spills her drink, which I'm sure, to her, would be a mortal sin that she could never atone for. The screech of the sliding glass door signifies Devin's entrance, and he scampers in, looking rather agitated. His long hair hangs in awkward ringlets over his eyes, and the sleeves of his sweatshirt hide his blatantly shaking hands.

"Bad news, guys," he gasps. "One of the daughters just got a blast of freezing cold water in the shower. I think our heater's blown."

"Oh, no," I whisper, immediately thinking doomsday — or at least, doomsday in first world terms. Rachel's reaction, however, is entirely different from mine.

"Where's the heater?"

We tramp out into the cold night with shoes clinging to our

bare feet, foregoing the socks in this type of emergency. The water heater sits sadly between the main cabin and the tool shed, not even a sad groan emitting from it. I take one look at the metallic behemoth and suddenly feel the urge to prove myself as a useful human being. Maybe if I can get this thing to buck up and start working again, I could be somehow validated as an individual in the eyes of my friends and colleagues. Because random feats of competence always do the trick!

But before I can even say a word, Rachel is kneeling beside the heater, using a flashlight as her visual guide. "So is this a newer propane unit, or what?"

"I guess," Devin stammers, and Rachel gives him a dirty look.

"You guess? I don't want to do anything to screw us over even further if we don't know for sure."

"Okay, then, it's a newer heater. Just say it's a newer heater."

I'm wondering if Devin's reconsidering this whole caretaker thing and planning to run away to Indiana to live on a fifty-acre ranch and learn how to milk a cow. No, wait, he's already done that.

"No, don't just say it's a newer heater," growls Rachel. "Find out if it's a newer heater so I can know what I should fuck with."

"What's going on, guys?" Kyle has finally joined the party, wearing an old flannel shirt and holding a glass of cheap butter-scotch-flavored whisky because that's how he rolls.

"Oh, hey, Kyle," says Devin, seemingly eager to break away from Rachel's demanding expression. "Yeah, we're just, uh, trying to fix, uh..."

"Oh, for God's sake."

Rachel appears to believe that it is, indeed, an updated propane water heater after some inspection, which really gets to me. When did she become an expert on this shit? I mean, chopping firewood, I'll tolerate. Doing manual labor, okay, I won't get all uppity about that. But now knowing things about heaters? That's beyond absurd. Next thing I know, she'll be building elaborate treehouses with balconies and constructing a toaster out of scrap metal because it's, "more energy efficient."

I reach for what I think is the heater's control valve, only to feel a blunt pain rattle through my fingers. Rachel has decided to slam the flashlight down on my hand like a teacher hitting a kid with a yardstick.

"Ow! What the hell?"

"Don't fuck with the heater, dude!"

I grab my throbbing fingers in my unscathed hand and take a sharp, angry breath. "You could have broken something, you crazy person!"

Rachel laughs mockingly, which really grates on my nerves. "Aw, poor widdle Jamie. Did I hurt you?"

"Fuck you!" I spit viciously. Interestingly enough, despite all the ire we're trading off right now, this is the longest verbal exchange we've had so far since Rachel made it up here. However, Devin's more than willing to put a stop to it, given his frantic mood.

"Girls! I'd love to watch your catfight, but I've got a pissed off family demanding a refund if we don't fix this thing! Rach, can you handle this, or do I have to get a repairman down from Fort Lawrence?"

"All right, all right, all right. Don't get fussy on me. I'll take care of it."

Rachel finds a way to ignore me and my aching hand and

focuses on the very thing that I was going to twiddle with myself. Only it's not the control valve I was about to touch; it's the thermocouple, and she makes it well known to me, making me feel like a full-fledged idiot.

"Maybe," she mutters, "if I can just re-tighten the thing...God damn it, my fingers are numb. Hold this, will you, widdle Jamie?"

"Would you knock it off?" I snap as I swipe the flashlight away from her.

"Yeah, Rach, cool it," Devin cuts in, and I'm amazed that he might be defending me. "Take it easy on her. She's still healing."

"Right." Rachel spits a wad of mucus out the side of her mouth and shakes her head. "'Healing.' Whatever. Just give me a minute on this, okay?"

We wait for a moment before realizing that, "give me a minute," translates to, "leave me alone, now, before I re-tighten *your* personal pair of thermocouples." Devin and Kyle take me back to the kitchen before I have a chance to throw a temper tantrum in front of the guesthouse. It's not just that Rachel is, well, being kind of a bitch to me: It's that she's being bitchy while still proving to be justified in said bitchiness. I *am* whiny. I *am* a bummer. Rachel didn't even hit me that hard with the flashlight; I'm just a wimp when it comes to any level of pain. I get it, but no one reminds me more of that than myself. This girl doesn't have to march into my life and refresh my memory on all of my character flaws. The thought of Emily being gone is enough.

Kyle treats me to some sugar cookies he's just made using his lumberjack love, because of course he was making cookies and drinking whisky by the time the water heater died on us. I've eaten six of the damn things like a gluttonously sad puppy when Rachel trudges back into the cabin, her face flushed from the late autumn air but still holding an aura of triumph. She steps into the kitchen to wash her hands, which are noticeably grimy from all the moss and rust that's gathered on the metal she's been tinkering with. Then she pulls her baseball cap off her head and tosses it onto the counter as if throwing down a prized enemy flag.

"Give the family two hours," she announces. And sure enough, the water's warm again by eleven o'clock.

I retire to my room to bang my head repeatedly against the wall in self-harming exasperation, collapsing onto my bed and refusing to leave despite Kyle's demands to eat more of his cookies. But no amount of sugar will appease me now; I'm ready to crack like a damn egg. Rachel comes into my life, reorganizes the bathroom, only speaks to me when she wants to cut me down, slightly taps my hand with a flashlight, and now has the audacity to be productive and fix a water heater so we won't lose revenue from our angered guests. The nerve of her!

Realizing that if my thoughts were amplified, I'd sound like a bona fide brat, I calm down and decide that it would be a good use of my time to gaze mindlessly at the ceiling. The door opens, and I don't look to see who's there, but the voice obviously gives it away. Rachel barely gets my name out when I roll over on my side and melodramatically exhale like a tragic literary character.

"If you're here to ridicule me further," I say, "I'm not interested."

"I was going to say sorry for being an asshole, but sure, if you want to leave it like that."

"You don't have to say sorry. I deserve it."

I don't have to look at Rachel to know that she's rolling her eyes. "God, are you always like this? You're like Debbie Downer over here."

"Travel back in time before May," I retort. "Maybe you would've actually liked me."

"Devin told me you had a bad break-up. But I mean, was it really *that* bad?"

Now I lift myself up and look at her. Her eyes don't waver as she brushes a strand of black hair away from her forehead. Once again, I'm reminded of the good old cinema.

"You ever seen the movies in which the guy or girl has a nervous breakdown after they get cut off from a long and committed relationship, only to wind up in a hospital and reevaluate their life choices?" I ask.

"Yeah?"

I shrug. "I'm halfway there."

Well. Maybe I've made her uncomfortable enough to leave me alone. But for the first time since I met her, that tough exterior seems to fade for just a second. She even looks a little upset about what I just said. But then she lets a groan rush out from between her clenched teeth as she slams the door behind her on her way out of my room. I have to admit, she's not someone who lets herself get dragged down into other people's shit. I've always wondered if that's a good thing.

"Thanks for fixing the water heater," I manage to holler at the wall, hoping that Rachel hears me. I don't ask her how she's learned to fix heaters or where that sudden burst of repairman spirit came from. I just don't bother.

My thank you is the closest to a truce that we get for a few more weeks.

Thanksgiving rolls around, and none of us at the property plan to be home for the holiday. My parents don't put up much of a fuss about it; as long as I promise that I'll be home for Christmas, they'll be fine. To be fair, most likely they don't want to have to cook nearly as much food for their little feast if I'm not around. Once again, I have an appetite that could launch a thousand ships. Only instead of being laden with gold and treasures, these ships' hulls are packed with delicious treats.

In the meantime, we have guests to tend to for the week, and they happen to be an older couple seemingly scooped straight out of the Bohemian side of the coastline. I'm first introduced to them when they slip out of their environmentally friendly coupe in brightly colored shirts and shawls, their hands wrapped together like lace as they coo about the beautiful landscape and kiss each other's wrinkling cheeks. They introduce themselves as Sally and Cindy Wainwright, together for thirty-seven years – yes, exactly thirty-seven. They're keen on reminding us of that number. I'm happy for them, but my memory's not so shot that I need such a fact repeated ad nauseum.

The next thing I know, Sally and Cindy are camping out in the living room, playing a banjo and a fiddle respectively. Rachel seems so unbelievably stoked about their musical abilities. At first, she just sits and listens, her eyes wide and her mouth slightly open in a lazy smile, as Sally twangs away and Cindy's bow glides across the violin strings like she's afraid of breaking them. The two of them balance each other out perfectly, one wearing red and the other green, sitting cross-legged on the fraying carpet and following a perfect melody, while I can't stay on key to save my life. It's pretty adorable, though it does make me think about relationship goals that I can no longer aspire to.

I assume that Rachel just likes folk music, or hippies, or hippies playing folk music. I guess I also should have suspected that my new housemate is a musician herself. And a good one, too.

The second day of their stay, our guests entertain us with both seemingly original tunes as well as the classics, from Cat Stevens' drawling stories to Bob Dylan's ramblings to even Heart's rousing duets. Somehow, they make it all work with just two instruments and their rough, raspy voices scraping the air like blunt knives. Halfway through the session, Rachel excuses herself and disappears into her room for a minute before, sure enough, out comes the guitar. It's obviously a bit beaten up from so many years of being played, but the sound it makes is, for lack of a better word, stunning. Rachel tunes it quickly, begins strumming a Beatles song, and proceeds to prove to me once again that I should not underestimate her raw talent.

I wind up enjoying the music, especially Rachel's singing, which is raw and Joni Mitchell-esque and really relaxing to listen to. Her callused fingers nearly meld with the strings when she plays, and more often than not, she communicates with the older couple through notes and chords rather than with words. It's almost as if Rachel feels safe and at home when she's cradling her instrument in her arms and making it speak, so that's why I don't hold too much of an envious grudge toward her when it comes to acknowledging her skill.

Because Devin has essentially forced me out of the bedroom and ordered me to socialize, I'm happily exposed to this new little

band performing for us. Bit by bit, however, I start to head into
the living room of my own volition, taking a seat in the corner
easy chair with a glass of beer and a book that I don't plan to read.
Being by myself while things are happening outside my room
these days feels claustrophobic, almost as if I've been walled off
from the real world. And for the first time, I'd rather tear those
walls down than stay behind them. Thanks for the trite imagery to
convey my point, Pink Floyd.

I never thought I'd say this, but I like Sally and Cindy. They're
not exactly conventional — and in many ways, I think that's inten-
tional — but they're a real kick, and it's the good kind of kick. The
kind that knocks you out of bed in the morning and boots you
to where you need to be. Obviously, I'm not one hundred percent
made better by their presence, but their being in or around the
main cabin does help, even if I still can't get myself to smile all
that much. In order to remedy that, I try to show that I'm content
or pleased with something or someone by moving my eyebrows,
usually raising them if I'm impressed with some random musical
ability or belted high note. During one particular jam session,
Rachel notices my little facial dance and decides to create an
eyebrow language between us.

"What's with you?" she seems to ask, using arches and
creases.

I furrow my brow as a sign of, "Meh." It's my go-to body
syntax. She buys it.

After a couple of days with our Thanksgiving guests, I find
that I'm observing a lot more and not burying my head in the
metaphorical sand as much. For one thing, Sally's hair is silver, and
I do mean silver, not gray. She pulls it back in a neat bun so it looks

like a falcon is roosting atop a rainbow jacket – a jacket, mind you, that she adores walking around in every day. She wears all these bright colors, hues that I would normally find vomit-inducing but now see as just brightening up the space. I also notice that Cindy's nose is extremely pointy. It's kind of cool, actually; she could perch a pair of glasses on the bridge of that nose, and they'd probably stay straight. The pointiness accentuates her smile, which she flashes to me whenever she seems to sense that my admittedly sour mood is becoming tarter.

"Have you ever considered becoming a songwriter, dear?" Cindy asks Rachel the day before Thanksgiving, after Rachel has gone through several covers of Creedence Clearwater Revival's repertoire. She's just finished, "Bad Moon Rising," and her voice is hoarse from the rambunctious chorus.

"Oh, no. See, I can sing. I can't write." She sends me a sly look as if informing me that she's not a perfect individual – talented, yes, but not perfect. I never thought she was, but the reminder doesn't bother me.

"But you should still perform, dear. Maybe someone can write for you," suggests Sally.

"Yeah. Maybe."

Don't look at me. I can't write worth shit.

Thanksgiving is a day I find myself looking forward to, if only because of all the amazing food. Cooked by Kyle, no less — well, save for the mashed potatoes, which are my job, and really, you can't screw up obliterating spuds and serving their flattened and mangled carcasses with melted butter on top. I even add some garlic just to pretend it's super special. Devin contributes to the celebration by decorating, even arranging place mats and name tags scrawled out on white cardboard tabs in sloppy Sharpie. This is a first, since I'm normally the one who does the cute little jobs around the property, which include setting the table and even cutting up wildflowers to show off in a mason jar because we don't have a lot of vases. Soon, a table is set up outside because the weather, even if cold, is pretty nice. There's also no wind, and we can eat without too many disturbances.

I mean, we could get eaten by a wild coyote that can smell the turkey from a mile away. But hey, we all gotta live a little, right?

I sit down between Devin and Kyle at the table once the feast is served. Barbecued turkey sizzles on the foil, accompanied by hot stuffing and a silver boat of gravy with the residue dripping from its tarnished lip. All we need now is the pie, which, thank God, Kyle got to bake. Maybe he's fulfilling an entirely different stereotype than his exterior presents, but he's a fabulous culinary artist. For the first time, I try to take in my surroundings, and suddenly, everything seems very vivid and very loud. I can hear the rush of the creek nearby, bloated with the year's rain so far, and I've never even bothered to walk alongside it. I look at the intimidating oaks looming over me, their leafy heads drooping in the sparse sunlight, and I've never bothered to roost under them. I have been so adjusted to staying inside and being isolated that just experiencing the late afternoon air makes my body feel lighter and my skin not so dry and abused.

I graciously offer to serve Rachel some turkey before I dig in, like a gentleman would. She sits next to Sally and Cindy, who are already enjoying the food, I can tell. To both my surprise and relief, they are eating the mashed potatoes I've made with determination and relish.

"I must say, you young people are fine hosts," Cindy compliments us after dumping some more lumpy starch on her plate. "I have never had such a lovely Thanksgiving."

"You don't have family to visit?" Kyle asks a little tactlessly. His mouth's brimming with shredded turkey, too.

"Oh, we sure do," Sally replies. "But after thirty-seven years of the same old politics at the table, we just wanted to escape and have our own little trip. And the mediocre food. Oh! I am so glad you all can cook!"

"Except me," Rachel interjects, and again, she smirks at me as if to say, yet again, how not perfect she is.

"And me," Devin admits. "But I am good with scrubbing a few pots."

"I thought that was my job," I interject.

"Oh, are you offering?"

"No," I reply quickly, digging my fork into my mosaic of deliciousness.

We share a small laugh after that exchange, and then Sally and Cindy become interviewers. They're so grateful to celebrate Thanksgiving with us even though they barely know us, but maybe we remind them of themselves somehow or, like Sally said, we're part of their escape. To them, we represent something new, something exciting — something *young* and *fresh* and *open-minded*. I guess after thirty-seven years, that kind of starts making sense.

"Jamie." It takes me a bit to realize that all eyes are now on me. Cindy is talking. She points her fork at me, the tines gleaming with grease. "It is Jamie, isn't it?"

I slowly swallow a glob of gravy, my lips growing sticky. "Yes, ma'am."

"Now, I know all about Devin and Kyle. I could write a book about them, come to think of it. Devin seems to be a real traveler. Lots of stories to tell us about his exploits."

I can't help sneering at her comments about my high school buddy. "Did he tell you about the time he stood on top of a living and breathing alligator thinking it was a rock while visiting Florida? 'Cause I've heard that story before. A lot."

"Then maybe come up with stories of your own, Miss Sassypants," teases Devin, scratching at his goatee. It's starting to grow back after he shaved it last month, but at least he and Kyle can pull off the scruffy facial hair without looking like creeps.

"Anyway," Cindy continues, as if our little tiff has only served as extra entertainment for her wife and her, "we also know that Kyle here is quite a kindred spirit. Big handsome activist. Used to work with children, if I remember correctly."

See, I didn't know that, but Kyle adds a little detail before sipping some red wine. "I worked with kids who had been kicked out of their homes 'cause of reasons," he explains to me, and I am already very aware of what one of those reasons could be. "Could've been drug issues, could've been abuse, could've been anything. Lot of queer kids, though, who just needed someone to talk to them and let them know it was okay. Course, you can't pay rent with that kind of part-time or volunteer work, so..."

"So he decided to be a pioneer like the rest of us," Devin finishes for him, clapping his big buddy on the back. "I met him while hiking in Nevada. He was with his oh-so-accepting family, pardon my sarcasm."

"But you," Cindy finishes, waving a now full fork at me. "You,

I'm not so sure of. You don't talk much. But there's bound to be a bit of back story with you, dear. Always is. So tell me, Jamie. What would you consider yourself to be?"

"What would I consider myself...?" My voice trails off. I'm admittedly confused by this sudden interrogation.

"You know," Cindy presses, eyeing me cautiously as if worried I'm going to bolt from the table like a scared rabbit. "Your friends here have all these dreams and goals and stories. So how do you fit into this crazy narrative we call life?"

I'm not quite sure I understand the question, as I chew on a strip of dark turkey meat. "This crazy narrative we call life?" Is this supposed to be some kind of story we're writing? I mean, are we all being assigned roles? Is Devin the hippie and Kyle the gay black dude and Rachel the tough girl with a heart of gold? Leave it to me to be the lesbian emo of the bunch, the depressed girl who just needs someone to love her. I must be taking way too long to reply, so Rachel jumps into the psychological fray.

"Jamie." She gesticulates at me. "She wants to know what your passions and interests are."

"Oh." I let out a light but sharp laugh. "Those. I didn't think I was expected to have any. Do I get a selection to choose from?"

Okay, apparently, that's not funny. Well, not funny for most of them. Devin lets out a chuckle that falls somewhere in between genuine and apologetic. Kyle doesn't react at all, occupying himself with the contents of his plate. Cindy just waits expectantly, while her wife runs two fingers through her very silver hair before sipping loudly from her glass of wine. Rachel, of course, rolls her eyes. She communicates with me via eyebrow-ese again, letting one rise higher than the other as if to ask, "Take this seriously just

for once, please?" And while normally, I'd scoff at such a suggestion, I get a sense that this time, she's earnest about getting me to
open up.

I sigh and put down my fork. I'm still hungry, but I can't let
food get in the way of my oncoming monologue. Above me, the
sky is turning a pretty cool shade of orange, so I let my eyes focus
on that as I talk so I don't get weird or panicky.

"Let's see," I begin. "For a long time, I thought I was going to
be a teacher. Not because I was dying to be one, mind you. I mean,
it's just that I got caught on that old saying. You know, 'Those that
can't do, teach.'" I laugh to diffuse any possible tension; I don't
know if it worked, as no one's facial expressions have changed.
"Don't worry, I don't believe that. But I mean, I was a good student.
Doesn't mean I could be in a play or rock out in a band or kick ass
in a sport. Devin can vouch for me that I was just someone you'd
hang out with playing video games or goofing off at a diner or
trying to act cool with a high GPA."

"Amen to that, brother," Devin exclaims, thumping the table
with the palm of his hand.

"Thanks, dude," I snort. "Anyway, I thought to myself, 'Jamie,
you're kind of weird and uncool. You're not quite sure what you
want to do when you grow up. Being undeclared in college is a
disaster waiting to happen. How can you make the most of your
future?' And, well, that's when I started kind of looking into a
history degree."

Kyle finds that to be wildly funny — which is fine, given that
the joke I was trying to make was that my future lay in learning
about the past. Sally and Cindy are enthralled. Rachel, of course, is
skeptical.

"History?" she repeats. "What, you know about all the great European wars or some shit like that?"

"You know what?" I answer, almost too proudly for my own good. "No. I don't. And if I did, I don't remember anything now."

Now everyone is intrigued. All forks are down, and not even alcohol is being consumed at the moment. This shit just got real, so I press forward.

"See, I went into college to essentially bullshit," I explain. "I don't really remember anything I was taught — I just held onto it as long as I could until I had to turn in an essay or pass a test. I mean, am I supposed to care that much about the different Chinese dynasties and their legal systems? Or about the Code of Hammurabi or the logistics of trench warfare or how much Kennedy almost screwed up the Cuban Missile Crisis? Nope, but I still glued myself to the textbooks and got A's for that shit. Why? 'Cause I wanted to get the stupid degree, and I'm not exactly special at anything else besides absorbing information."

At this point, I'm leaning back in my folding chair, my legs stretched out in front of me as the smell of the surrounding foliage and dirt suddenly punches me in the nose. I can't help but grin like a goofball as I continue to speak, perhaps against my better judgment.

"Basically," I declare, "I learned about the past because...well, it seemed more interesting than my future would ever be."

There. That wasn't a bad zinger to end my little rant. I wave my hand for the salt, and Devin passes it over quietly. Nothing like a little extra sodium on my potatoes to make me feel better about my mediocre oration skills.

"So," I hear Rachel say even when my eyes are still on my food,

"you can't just rattle off the names of the kings of Scotland or
something?"

"Nope!" I cry out, startling myself with my own outburst.
"Fuck, no. I can't even remember most of the presidents of the
United States. I got my teaching credential just to spew everything
back to kids and hope they cared more about it than I did. Want to
give a rat's ass about the effects of Marxist government on American youth? Fine, go for it. Doesn't mean that at the end of the day,
it's going to be the thing that keeps me wired."

"But don't you think what you learned has a purpose?" opines
Cindy, as if she wants to give me some perspective. "One of the
most interesting classes I ever took was about the effects of
imperialism on African tribes and micronations. Sally has family
and friends who participated in the Civil Rights Movement and the
Stonewall riots. You care about those things, don't you?"

"Of course I do!" I exclaim, then try not to get too defensive.
"I just...don't think I'm the right person to teach those things. Not
because I don't find history interesting or important, but because...I
don't know. I don't have the passion or the willpower or even the
brain capacity to be a history *teacher*. I mean, you realize how little
those people get paid, right? You really have to *love* teaching to do
it, because God knows, you don't get much else out of it besides
that."

That should do it for spewing out my soul for now. At least, I
hope it does; I'm feeling kind of tired and wrung out, and I don't
want to argue about my sorry state any further. I already feel
bad about seeming indifferent to obviously significant historical
moments, and I just want to eat the rest of my dinner before it
gets cold.

Cindy and Sally could not seem any more fascinated than they already look. They nod and hum even after I'm done talking, as if they've been thoroughly and properly entertained. I wipe the dried excess stuffing that rims the corners of my mouth, and I notice that Rachel, interestingly enough, doesn't seem annoyed or taken aback or even disoriented by what I've said. She just looks thoughtful about it.

"So," she muses, "if you don't want to teach history, then why did you spend four years and all that money to get your degree and credential?"

Eesh. Here we go. I guess I have to mention the very thing that's been bothering me this whole time. The thing that would serve as an elephant in the room if more people were concerned about it. I exhale, tell myself that if I cry, I will never forgive myself, and try to give Rachel a simultaneously humorous and honest answer.

"Because," I explain, "my ex-girlfriend thought it'd be really hot to marry a nerd."

Cindy and Sally laugh, Sally nearly choking on her Cabernet. Devin starts clearing plates as if he's ready for me to explode like a wet bomb of sorrow; I'm not going to, but his worries are still justified. Kyle just focuses on the rest of his meal and doesn't offer pie until he's one hundred percent done with the food on his plate. Thankfully — which is appropriate, given it's Thanksgiving — I don't have to expose anything else about my life, and I get to look forward to pumpkin dessert and the sound of a fiddle, guitar, and banjo in the living room.

I have to say, though, opening up like that about myself and Emily after so long doesn't hurt as much as I thought it would. It's kind of liberating, like I can finally mention her without breaking down into wild episodes of tears and self-flagellating guilt. At the same time, she keeps lingering in my mind, and the more I think about it, the more I realize how much she dominated my life for all those four years. Tonight, I'm not sure what to deduce from it, but I'm sure that I'll be analyzing it long after the festivities.

Rachel sings well and plays well, as usual, but she keeps giving me looks, and they're far from judgmental. They're kind of sympathetic, like she understands something that maybe I can't even scrape the surface of yet. I'm sure Devin's told her some things about Emily, but probably not much. He obviously doesn't know every crucial fact, let alone have all the nitty gritty details. But the more Rachel keeps glancing at me, the more I wonder how much she's thinking about it.

Oh, well. Overall, it's a nice Thanksgiving, even if it's far away from my family. Cindy and Sally are good company, and Devin and Kyle seem more willing now to have me around them for games and music time. I find myself enjoying the trivia adventures that I used to hate, of course not doing so hot in history, but seriously pulling it off in the science and nature categories. Mostly because I get all the weird questions, like what a polyorchid has three of. I jokingly guess that the answer is testicles, and Devin laughs so hard that he starts choking on his own spit because I'm absolutely right, and I get a green wedge for it from a giggling Rachel.

At the end of the night, I chill outside for a bit because at this point, I may as well stop being a vampire and grow accustomed to some form of natural light, sun or moon or otherwise. It is incredible how many moths hang out by the door. I count at least sixteen of them before I go back inside. This may very well be the day in which I stop being so much of a depressing dipshit. Though of course, in the end, I've got a lot more to work on in order to, as everyone's wanted me to do, fully "heal."

DECEMBER

The day after Thanksgiving, I wake up to the sound of tapping on my bedroom door. Knowing full well that neither Devin or Kyle are polite enough to knock, I'm not as surprised as I thought I would be to see Rachel standing there, wordlessly offering me a plate of leftover pumpkin pie. It's a wonder that any of it still remains, given how good it was and how we're all young adults with insane appetites, so I very gratefully take the slice to my bed and begin eating what I've decided will be my breakfast. What I don't expect is Rachel to sit down next to me.

"Don't you have anything better to do?" I ask with a mouthful of pie filling.

She shrugs. "I'm living vicariously through you by watching you eat."

"Ah, like a kind of foodie voyeurism. Nice."

Rachel grins and rolls her eyes, but not in a condescending way. She then playfully punches me in the arm, which doesn't at all feel like the way she struck me on the hand with that flashlight about a month ago. It's a lighter, friendlier gesture, one that doesn't bruise my already overwhelmingly sensitive skin. Maybe — shock and horror! — she's warming up to me.

We begin to talk, and I mean really talk, for the first time since Rachel arrived at the property. For the first couple of days bleeding into December, our conversations are nothing special. They mostly consist of commentary on what we see or hear or taste or smell. For instance, one day, I walk out to the creek for once, and I see Rachel already there, ankle-deep in the greenish brown water and loving how cold it is. I don't dare wade in, but I perch myself on one of the rocks nearby, and we end up talking about, I shit you not, waterdogs. We only somewhat change the subject when Rachel mentions grabbing a garter snake from a stagnant pond when she was six years old, thinking it was a cool, colorful stick. I give her ten points for that story.

"What if the snake had bitten me?" she jokes. "Would I have gotten more points or less?"

"More," I answer, "especially if you didn't cry."

"Joke's on you. I'm not much of a crier."

Somehow, I find myself not believing her. She may look tough, but I get the feeling that Rachel can be kind of a softy. Not that she'd ever admit to that or anything.

A week later, we spend time together outside our rooms long into the night, even after Kyle and Devin have migrated to their own cabin. Instead of just sharing boring observations, we talk about our work and how our days generally went, since we don't do the same stuff in the same place all the time. Rachel likes to tell me how much I shouldn't worry about representing some rebellion against feminine expectations, because there's nothing inherently wrong with being feminine, and honestly, who around here cares? "Me," I point out, and I get her to laugh. It's nice to hear a laugh from her that's not derisively directed at me, and from what I can tell, she's not so put off by my attitude anymore. I don't know if it's higher tolerance or the fact that I'm less of a bummer. Or both!

Of course, now that Rachel and I are staying up too late in the living room, listening to Stevie Wonder records while I slowly succumb to drinking Riesling, we're not getting a whole lot of shut eye. Devin lets us off the hook in terms of sleeping in for the first few days, but he starts teasing us when we still show up at the table in the morning, yawning and cursing at Father Time under our breath. I don't mind Devin's haranguing, and I don't think Rachel does, either. We just sneak in, "Really?" smiles or practice our good old eyebrow dialect during breakfast, while Devin sings improvised and off-key songs, continually failing to make good omelets.

Kyle wonders aloud just what the hell's gotten into everyone. "Seriously," he chuckles, "when did we all start getting along? Is it drugs? Tell me it isn't drugs."

December is another slow month guest-wise, save for a group of guys staying over during New Year's, though I do not intend to be in Pensalado by then. I've promised my parents that I'd stay with them, starting about three days before Christmas Eve and ending my vacation on January fifth, meaning the others are on their own until then. Devin intends to be gone for Christmas Eve and Christmas Day, and that's it. Kyle has been invited to the Abrega household for the holidays because his homophobic family, in his words, "can go choke on a rainbow flag and enjoy the taste." But I'm not so sure about Rachel's plans, and when I ask, she blows it off like I've just asked her, "So, what do you think the weather's going to be like tomorrow?"

"I'll be fine," she says. "Don't worry about me."

Too late, I think. Then I wonder: When did I ever imagine I would worry about her?

It's not cold enough to snow in Pensalado, but it sure rains, and hard. I don't get much weeding done, and pretty soon, all we're doing is interior decorating and reorganization. No painting, no chopping, no outside labor. I think Devin's getting a little bit stir crazy because after becoming indecisive on what comforters we should put on the beds in the guest room, he begs for Kyle to drive him to Hearnsville so he can get some air, no matter how waterlogged said air is. The roaming side of his brain is starting to retaliate against him, and we're not even halfway through our nine-month stay yet.

The guys do end up taking off one night halfway into December, even though the road's extremely muddy and the rain isn't stopping, so that leaves Rachel and me in the main cabin, taking care of ourselves. I haven't cooked anything since the mashed potatoes, so I just heat up some popcorn in the microwave and call it a meal. Rachel tunes her guitar in the living room, her face bronzed by the fire that's just starting to whimper out.

"When do you think they'll be back?" she asks as I sit down on the couch, holding a full bowl and smelling like butter and too much salt.

I stuff a handful of kernels into my mouth and shrug. "Who knows. Could be in an hour. Could be tomorrow. Could be after Kyle hooks up with a hot stud at the bar, and Devin has to drive him home shit-faced."

"I wasn't even aware that Kyle was looking for someone."

I sneer, suddenly in a teasing mood. "Maybe he can give you tips."

"On what?" Rachel asks. "Picking up gay men?"

"Well, no. I mean, there've got to be some guys in Hearnsville who like boobs, right?"

Rachel gets tired of strumming her guitar. "Do I look like I need help finding a guy?"

"I plead the fifth on that question."

She punches me in the knee, and I almost spill my popcorn. Then she steals some kernels out of the bowl and munches on them as I pretend to complain.

"Mine!" I whine in my best obnoxious teenager voice.

"Tough, Jamie girl," she smirks, still chewing.

I sigh and lean back on the couch with oily fingers. "So, what are you doing for Christmas?"

"You already asked me that."

"And I'd like an answer this time."

"Meh," is her one-word response.

For the first time, I persist. "C'mon."

Rachel raises her eyebrows. "I told you, don't worry about it."

"You're being cryptic," I point out. "Like...I don't know...inexplicably cryptic."

"Inexplicably?" Rachel repeats. "You sure you didn't want to get an English degree instead of a history one?"

"Fuck off," I mutter. I can't help blushing about my word vomit. Sometimes, it just happens.

"Okay, how am I being 'inexplicably' cryptic?"

"Well, you know." I take a breath. "I figured you'd just say, 'Oh, just spending time with relatives,' or, 'Yeah, maybe crashing at a friend's place.' I mean, it's a pretty straightforward question."

"Actually, with Aaron gone, I can't exactly visit my old house," retorts Rachel. "As for friends, well, they're all scattered."

"What about Washington? You were visiting a friend there before you came to Pensalado, right?"

"Hmm." Rachel thinks about this. "Yeah, but I think she's gonna be in Bozeman. You know, that college town in Montana? Her grandpa has a ranch there."

I begin massaging my temples with my fingers, ignoring the fact that I'm essentially coating my forehead in leftover grease. "You're telling me that you don't have any Christmas plans? I mean, even if your dad's in Portugal, don't you have other family to see?"

Oh, geez, I've said something wrong. Rachel has gone painfully quiet. She's not mad; she's just quiet. She lifts her guitar off her lap and lays it flat on the carpet. The Randy Newman record that we've been playing has stopped and is waiting for us to flip it onto its other side.

"Sorry," I murmur.

She doesn't say anything.

"Sorry. Was it something I said?"

"No." She laughs. "Well, kind of. Devin didn't tell you, huh?"

"Tell me what?"

"That I'm not his biological cousin."

I give her a look. "You're not?"

"Nope," Rachel replies, wearing way too big of a grin. "I'm adopted."

Hold it. This new revelation pretty much sucker-punches me in the gut. I feel like I've been cast in a low budget soap opera without a script. "Wait, what?"

"Dude, I'm not kidding. I was in a really bad place for a long time." Rachel says this all as bluntly as she can, as if there's any other way to convey it. "And Aaron, well, he saved my life. You've met him before, right?"

"Yeah, at a reunion party a few years back." I pause. "Which, come to think of it, I didn't see you at."

"I was probably in Washington or something. Feels awkward for me to be at events like that, you know? I'm not really close to anyone else in Aaron's family except for Devin." She shrugs, as if she's just told me some inane story or run-of-the-mill anecdote. "I was kind of dumped on my ass in this shitty foster care center for, like, five years or something. My dad died when I was eight, and my mom decided that cocaine was her new best friend a few months after his funeral. And Aaron, being a big old bachelor with no kids, had decided that he wanted to be a foster parent. So he took me into his home when I was thirteen, and he adopted me about a year later."

Okay, that's a lot to take in. I'm having trouble following her every word. "Wait, slow down," I stutter. "You were in foster care?"

Rachel exhales and nods. "Yes. And like Harry Potter, I had my fair share of foster parents who acted like the Dursleys." This comment is meant to be funny and culturally relevant, but I'm not laughing. I seriously don't know what to say, so I just let her keep speaking. "But yeah, Aaron's not my real dad. Couldn't you tell?"

I do remember thinking about how different Devin and she were physically. Then again, I know people who look nothing like their siblings or cousins all the time, so I never questioned their family connection or wondered if this was anything out of the ordinary.

"It might have occurred to me when I first met you, but I never thought that you were adopted," I explain. "I just sort of assumed, I guess."

"Look, it's a big old sob story," Rachel sighs. "I get it. It's like something out of one of those stupid Lifetime movies. Look, let's talk about something else, okay? I don't want to drag you down with this shit."

Me? Drag *me* down? What is she even saying? *I'm* the one with the stupid sob story. She has some legitimate trauma to deal with. She makes me look like a sissy.

"Look, if it's any comfort to you," I say, "my issues are a hundred times dumber than, I don't know, having a dead father or a mother on drugs."

"Okay, fair enough."

"I'm serious. You make my break-up look super petty. No matter how long I was with her."

"I get it, Jamie," Rachel replies. "I'm agreeing with you."

I don't know whether to feel affirmed or insulted by that.

"Do you miss her?"

It takes me a moment to realize that Rachel's posed a question to me. "Hmm?"

"Do you miss Emily?"

Okay, it's a rhetorical question. "Of course I do."

"Even after she kind of bossed you around, told you what to do?"

"I never said she bossed me around," I object.

"Sorry," Rachel says, though I don't think she's really sorry. "It's just that, when you mentioned studying to be a teacher because of her...well, I figured she kind of told you what to do with your life."

"Eh." I try to handle the whole thing casually. "Not like I could succeed in any other field."

"You can't say that."

"Rachel, I'm not even allowed to carry an axe here. I don't have much to offer."

"You could be a stand-up comedian. You've got the self-degradation down to a tee."

I don't know if Rachel's trying to make me laugh or get me to shut up. Or both. "Yeah, and I'd have to start counting how many times I get food thrown at me," I counter.

"Extra points if it's something fancy. Like caviar. Or crab cakes. Or some other kind of seafood." Rachel suddenly frowns. "Why is seafood considered fancy, anyway?"

"Look." I try to wrap up the conversation in hopes of veering the topic off Emily because I'm kind of not in the mood. "You do things for love, right? I did a lot of things for Emily, and I loved her. She made me feel...not so useless. I mean, she really thought I could be a good teacher, so I just tried it out. Not her fault that I can't even master what I learned. I think I was just trying to be happy."

"Or trying to make her happy," remarks Rachel.

"Okay, I was trying to make both of us happy."

She gives me a look. "But mostly her."

I feel myself stiffen. "You don't know her."

Rachel concedes then because I've admittedly delivered one of those rebuttals that you just can't waste time arguing over. "You're right," she groans. "I don't know her. But maybe being away from her will allow you to understand yourself more. No sappiness intended."

"Heh, good luck to me, then," I say snidely. "There's not much left to go around."

Rachel gives me a look that's a cross between, "Stop being such a stupid sad puppy," and, "*Let me hug you, damn it!*" It's very confusing. I know I've been doing better with the whole socializing thing, but it doesn't change the fact that I still call myself a failure when it comes to...well, everything. I'm surprised that she's not so annoyed by my irritating self-criticism anymore. Again, it might just be that she's adjusting to my bullshit when she's around me.

Then Rachel seems to get the bright idea of going into the kitchen and fetching some wine. Relying on booze to feel better should lighten the mood, right? She's switched it up a bit, so now I'm being poured White Zinfandel and feeling kind of overtly girly drinking something that's a faint shade of pink. It does taste good, though, and I enjoy every sip. I guess I have to stop trying to act all butch at some point in order to validate my existence after my ex-girlfriend politely told me to fuck off.

"C'mon," my cabin mate declares. "Let's drink too much and play music too loudly and forget talking for a little bit. We'll just depress each other."

"Well," I say, "I'm glad that's not a one-sided thing anymore."

We clink glasses and sip. I won't deny it — the White Zinfandel is definitely doing wonders to my mood.

And that's when I hear the crash.

[...]

I thought I was a pretty shrill screamer, but Rachel, for all her physical and mental strength, sure beats me in the high-pitched shrieking game, even though I definitely put up a good fight. We both nearly spill our wine, and I kick the table and send the rest of our now cold popcorn flying onto the carpet. I swear that the floor rattles just a little bit under our feet as the sound we heard subsides. Then: Long, uncomfortable silence.

I don't hear anything for a moment except the rain falling outside. Then I get down on my knees and start picking up scattered popcorn as if I'm on autopilot. In the middle of my sporadic clean-up, I cast a look of panic at my friend.

"Earthquake?"

"No," Rachel gasps. "Car crash?"

"Shit, I hope not. Devin and Kyle better be — "

"Oh, *fuck!*" she suddenly shouts, and in the next moment, she's dashing out of the cabin.

"Hey, wait!"

I drop whatever kernels I've collected and follow her outside. I'm barefoot, but I'm not exactly paying attention to the sharp, stinging pains in my heels, as I hop across prickly leaves and weeds and rock clusters. The rain has lessened somewhat, but it's still there, nibbling at my face and making my sweatshirt feel like a heavy quilt against my back. The two of us run down the rocky path toward the gate, both anticipating a car wreckage, and I morbidly and graphically picture Kyle bent over the steering wheel, while Devin tries to stop blood from pouring from his forehead.

But it's not a car crash. It's still not a good thing, though. Not as bad as a car crash, but I'll explain.

We see Devin and Kyle, not a scratch on them, with Kyle's unscathed car idling on the road. They are surveying what appears to be a fallen tree — a rather large oak, in fact. And one of its most prominent branches just happens to be blocking the open gate that separates the property from the real world.

"Oh, no," Rachel breathes, as she sweeps wet hair out of her eyes and examines the scene.

Devin looks more than a little shaken, but he manages to nod. "We only just got in here before it fell," he says, a noticeable quiver in his voice. "One second later, and we would've had a crushed car on us."

"And possibly crushed people," adds Kyle, his buzz cut and beard gleaming from the mist that's still wafting through the air. "But we're okay."

"Dead tree?" I ask.

"Yeah. Fucker didn't have much time, I guess," says Devin. "I was going to get to it after we cleared everything around the cabins, but...hindsight is twenty-twenty, huh?"

"So, what, we can't get out of the property anymore?" I demand to know.

I don't need anyone to answer me because I'm already making my way toward the tree, and I can see how much it's obstructing our exit. The biggest branch hovers a little bit off the ground, meaning that we can slip under it or climb over it, if need be. But there is no way on God's green earth that we can drive a car through. The tree's too close to the gate, and the barbed wire fence around the property stops us from maneuvering out by automobile any other way except through the creek. We certainly can't get Rachel's truck through, and it's definitely not big enough or sturdy enough to roll over the tree trunk like one of those monster vehicles I've seen in the commercials. I turn to Kyle, ready to ask if we can move the tree ourselves. He shakes his head, once again seeming to read my mind.

"The thing's too heavy," he claims, and I notice that he's rubbing his left arm, where the sleeve of his flannel shirt has been pushed up. "I tried it already. May have pulled a muscle."

"Suck it up, big boy," snaps Devin, clearly not in the mood for any complaining, even though I'm sure he's ready to cuss everyone and everything out. "C'mon. Drive up to the cabin. I'll make some calls."

"What are we going to do?" I ask. "It's Christmas next week. I'm kind of expected to be home."

"And what about food and shit?" adds Rachel. "Last time I checked, we needed to do a grocery run. And I don't think any of us are going to walk all the way down to Hearnsville. Not on that crazy road."

"Fuck, we should've gone shopping," Kyle keeps repeating under his breath. "Fuck, we should've gone shopping. Fuck, we should've gone shopping. Fuck, we should've gone – "

"Knock it off!" Devin abruptly yells. "All of you! Kyle, we had a very nice burger outing, and I very much enjoyed my beers, and I am not going to let you all upset my stomach. Jamie, to answer your question, I'll call someone from Fort Lawrence to come down and clear this tree away. They should be here in two days tops."

I feel my eyes narrow into slits. "How can you be so sure?"

"Just trust me, okay? I'm the fucking caretaker – I know what I'm supposed to do!"

With that, Devin storms back to Kyle's car, gesturing for him to come with him and drive. I guess he's too pissed off to, you know, just walk the few yards back to the cabins, but I don't push it, and Rachel doesn't push it, and Kyle really doesn't push it. Rachel and I stay next to the sad fallen tree after the boys have started rolling up the path, the last remnants of the night's rain peppering our hair.

"If I didn't know any better," Rachel says, "I'd say my cousin is getting way too into this job."

"That," I reply, "or he's starting to hate it."

It's hard for either of us to say for sure. All we'll know is that by tomorrow, Devin will try to keep it business as usual, while I continually wait for some guy to show up with a chainsaw so we can restock on wine and fresh food, and I don't have to resort to crackers and popcorn like I'm preparing for the zombie-robot-alien-global-warming-Mayan apocalypse. It is getting close to December 21st, 2012, after all.

Or maybe I should stop being overdramatic and just expect the tree to be removed in two days.

[...]

Only the tree's not removed in two days. It's not even removed in three or four. Devin gets back on the phone after I harass him about it, and he gets the same apology and the same, "We'll be there," from the people at Fort Lawrence that he got a day earlier. The rain has lightened to a drizzle, so it shouldn't be too hard for the tree guys to make it down here. But as it stands, we're kind of running out of options.

Our supplies aren't lasting as long as we thought they would, either. We soon run out of milk for coffee, which makes Kyle unhappy. We run out of eggs, which makes Devin unhappy; I guess he really wanted to make some more weird omelets or something, I don't know. We run out of wine, which makes Rachel unhappy. Then we run out of beer, which makes *everyone* unhappy. I start becoming accustomed to only drinking water, and I'm not eating much, even though our refrigerator's still well stocked. Food's not exactly an issue, but we certainly don't have a wide variety of meals to choose from anymore. Mostly, it's been toast, leftover veggie plates, and random boxes of dessert snacks that we've been throwing together for main courses. And the dessert snacks in particular are murdering my intestines.

More than the food, as the days go by, it's the holidays that I'm worried about. I do want to be with my parents for Christmas. There's a kind of sentimentality to being home for the holidays, and this year, because I missed Thanksgiving with my family, I just feel like it's more important than ever. My parents especially want me to make it home, and I wouldn't mind being by an actual Christmas tree, drinking eggnog and enjoying a second helping of turkey and mashed potatoes.

And since we can't leave the property to buy stuff, it doesn't feel like the Yuletide season. There's no tree; there are no presents; there are no candy canes or other treats to enjoy. Kyle finds some old Christmas lights bundled up in the closet in Rachel's bedroom and hangs them across the eaves of the main cabin, but only half of them light up in scattered blues and reds, since all the green and orange ones seem to have burnt out. Needless to say, they don't help much. Not even playing Christmas records makes us feel better, and we only have two of them, anyway.

It's when a week passes after the Dreaded Tree Collapse, as I've decided to call it, that I start to feel desperate. Christmas Eve is in two days. I've already had to call my parents and apologize for not being home sooner. I told my dad about how the guys who are supposed to help us out still haven't come to clear away the tree yet, and he almost swore to come up to Pensalado and cut it up himself. But the emphasis lies on the word, "almost," because I know he'd never actually drive up here, and I can't force him to, either. So we keep waiting, and I don't like it.

The day before Christmas Eve rolls around, and for the first time, Devin calls up the company responsible for the tree removal and gets a voicemail wishing us a Happy Holidays. Instead of simply hanging up the phone, he mercilessly slams it into the receiver about six times until he's satisfied. Now everyone is getting tense. I'm not the only one who's had to call home and explain the shit that's been going on.

"Ham," is the first thing Devin utters when he walks into the living room where we're all glumly situated.

He sits down on the floor in front of the coffee table and starts fiddling with a couple of red, nearly transparent dice, which just lie around because we don't know which board game they belong to. I'm sitting across from him with a newspaper from two months ago that I've read about a dozen times already; I've even completed two crossword puzzles, which normally aren't my forte. Kyle, despite being cranky due to his lack of booze, is apparently curious about Devin's minimalist declaration.

"What about ham?" he asks quietly.

"Ham," Devin explains, "is one of the main things I was looking forward to at Christmas this year because it'd be the first time in four years that I've eaten it. Because for the past four Christmases, I've been in Ohio, Georgia, Illinois, and Maine, respectively."

"Thanks for the sharp geographical memory," I grumble. "But what about the fucking ham?"

"You don't get it, Jamie. You just don't." I can feel the hot air bursting from Devin's nostrils from where he sits. He's like an angry bull ready to charge a matador. "*Ham.* Hot, orange-glazed ham. Made by my mom. With baked potatoes and spinach casserole."

"Devin," moans Rachel, her face buried in a pillow as she lies face down on the couch. "I'm going to murder you if you mention any more food."

"Fine! Do it!" snarls Devin, and I sincerely hope that he's joking. "Because I can't have my ham, and I'm sure as fuck tired of hanging around here without so much as a piece of bacon to munch on! Wait, I take that back. Don't murder me until I castrate the assholes who were supposed to get rid of the fucking dead tree already!"

"At this rate, they won't help until after Christmas," adds Kyle, a little too sadly for my liking. He's nursing a tall glass of some generic lime-flavored soda, which I'm sure isn't soothing his palate much.

I can't believe I'm doing this, but I'm becoming the determined one out of the four of us. I won't call myself optimistic because that just feels weird.

"Look," I pipe up, "isn't there something we can do about this? Like, anything?"

"You want to be a hero and chop up the damn thing yourself?" Devin asks coolly. "Be my fucking guest. God knows, we can't rely on the people who do that for their fucking job. I'm going to douse my sorrows in...sweet Lord, water. Jesus Christ. *Water!*"

He excuses himself, and I maneuver to the nearest window and watch his silhouette plod along to his cabin. Kyle gives me a nod that can only be translated to, "Sorry, bud," and goes after Devin; maybe he's going to give him a pep talk, but I doubt that a chat with a burly, yet sassy, lumberjack would do much good. I mean, if that guy isn't going out with an axe to take, as Devin christened it, this "fucking dead tree" down, then I don't know who will.

And I've just taken my own thoughts as a personal challenge. Because before Rachel can lift her head up from her pillow, I practically fly into my room, pull on my boots, and trample out the door into the cold night.

It's dark as hell outside, and the rain's still drifting down in wet, icy spirals, but the main cabin's light guides me to the tool shed. I fling the door open and find a slew of axes and saws hanging from the walls. I snag one of each — the ones exposed to the least rust, specifically — and prop the axe over my shoulder like I'm trying to be a poor man's Paul Bunyan, the thin and springy saw dangling from my other clenched fist.

As soon as I march back onto the dead grass, I hear Rachel's voice emerging from the main cabin. "Jamie, what the hell are you doing?"

"Being a hero and chopping up that damn tree myself," I answer over my shoulder.

"C'mon, don't be stupid."

"Hey, I didn't say it. Devin did!" I call out, as I hurry my way down the path to the gate.

Leave it to Mother Nature to raise the stakes a little bit,

because as soon as I make it to the fallen tree, the rain starts acting more like rain. It starts descending on me like a violent shower spray, soaking me all the way through my jacket and my shirt. Still, that lonely corpse of an oak tree dares me to rip it apart and cart its bones over to the side of the path leading out of the property. Of course, the closer I get to the main offending branch, the larger and thicker it appears to be. It's at this point that I wish I had beaver teeth so I could just gnaw the thing into shreds.

I prop the saw at my feet and try the axe first. Swinging downward as hard as I can, I hit the thinnest part of the branch and shut my eyes as bark flies into my face and gets stuck in my admittedly way-too-long hair. The next few tries are lousy and poorly aimed. I'm all over the place in my strokes, the blade scratching the wood but never quite getting a deep enough cut. I can already feel my arms burning despite how chilled my skin is, and I don't even think I've been out here for more than five min-utes. Maybe I should just stick to weeding and laundry.

Then I mentally tell myself to shut up because I've made my decision. Time to carry this out, you punk. You dug your grave; now lie in it.

Eventually, I give up on the axe and pick up the saw instead, finding the deepest gash I've made and trying to hack through it. The almost papery blade keeps getting stuck in the groove, and every time I wrench it out, I'm worried that it's going to spring out of my hand and snap me in the nose. I quickly get tired of using the saw and go back to the axe. Luckily, my swings are much more coordinated now. The rain dripping into my eyes makes it harder to see, and I'm not even sure if I'm making any leeway. But I'm not stopping. Not until I get to see the Christmas tree that my mom and dad have set up, and Kyle and Devin get to have that delicious orange-glazed ham.

I'm ready to try out the saw again when I hear sloshing behind me. I turn around and, boom, there's Rachel, dressed in Kyle's denim jacket with that baseball cap pulled on tight over her hair, holding an axe of her own as she wades through various puddles to get to me. I wipe the water from my face, only to have it drenched again as I gape at her.

"Are you serious?"

"You think I was going to let you have all the fun without any help?" Rachel laughs, as she slips under the tree branch and emerges on the other side.

I realize that she means to chop away at one side of the limb while I chop away at the other, the open gate looming behind her as we get to work. We take turns swinging, bark and dead leaves spraying over our shoulders, our grunts audible over the downpour and the crazy wind. Rachel makes more of a dent in her first few attempts than I did, but I don't mind at all. At least I'm not the only insane person trying to clear a path out of this place. And apparently, we two aren't the last insane ones, either.

"*Woo-hoo! Make way for the lumbermen, ladies!*"

Yep, here come Devin and Kyle, both whooping and hollering, waving around axes and an enormous double-handled saw that I remember seeing in the gold rush documentaries that I was forced to watch in American History 201 back at my university. I don't know where they got that saw, but I suppose everyone has their tricks. Whether they saw us working or just figured that it was time to do something about our situation, I can't say. But seeing Devin's hair billow out behind him as he runs toward us and Kyle's

mouth hanging open in a loose smile like he's an excited mutt —
well, that makes me feel a hell of a lot better about possibly doing a
job that a hired hand should have done eight days ago.

Kyle and Devin take on another part of the branch, fairly close
to the section that Rachel and I have covered, yanking that double-handled saw between them like they're actually experienced
loggers. I've gone back to my personal saw because the gash I've
made with Rachel has gotten, surprisingly, pretty deep, and I can
cut through the limb without the blade's teeth getting jammed.
Rachel keeps chipping away at any remaining wood, and while the
two of us are eerily quiet, Devin and Kyle shout encouragement to
each other like they're fraternity bros, the purring of the saw and
the pounding rain accompanying their voices.

I start to get numb instead of cold in the winter night, my nose
feeling almost non-existent on my face. My arms squeal for mercy
as I saw away. I can hear my own harsh breathing as my lungs try
to cuss me out, but I don't stop. Not until I hear the sudden creaking and crackling of the branch beneath my hand.

"Rachel!" I cry, breaking my silence. "We got it! We got it, we
got it, we got it — "

"Shut up!"

But she's laughing as she screams that, and forgetting our
tools, we push down with our hands and feel that specific part of
the tree give until it sounds like bone is breaking. The branch splits
apart, and our side of the work plummets to the ground. Thank
God that Devin and Kyle, unbeknownst to me in my enthusiasm,
have successfully lopped off a fat chunk of the tree before they
were dragged down in the descent. The large, intruding limb lies
in two pieces at our feet; with hearty grunts, we lift them up from

the muddy leaves.

"Fuck!"

"C'mon, c'mon..."

"Jesus Christ!"

"Knees, not back, knees, not back."

"Easy now!"

"Knees, not back."

"C'mon, c'mon!"

"Yeeeeaaaaahhh!"

I practically howl it out, all in one breath, breaking the string of grunts and profanity. Rachel and I heave our part of the tree into the darkness, hearing it land with a dull thud beside the creek. Kyle and Devin lob their handiwork after ours, and then it's mayhem among the four of us. The gate is exposed once more, accessible by car, and we go absolutely mad.

"How about that?" I holler at Rachel. "How a-fucking-bout that?"

Rachel jumps up and down in the storm, pumping her fists to the sky, her face glistening with sweat and dirt and rainwater. Kyle swoops me into a hug from behind and lifts me up into the air, like he's Rafiki and I'm baby Simba being crowned king of Pride Rock. And Devin, completely overcome with adrenaline — and most likely the happy thought that he can have his Christmas ham after all — throws his head back and bellows to the clouds above, drawing out his voice for longer than I ever imagined him being capable of.

Before this, I was a scraggly, unkempt, melancholy shadow of a twenty-something who couldn't even leave her bedroom unless she wanted something besides fried rice for dinner. Now, while still being scraggly and unkempt, I'm standing here in sopping wet clothes, a dirty axe and saw at my feet, not feeling like a badass but more like I did something worth my time. Something worth more than pining for a girl who I'm slowly beginning to realize wasn't so amazing after all, or bemoaning my seeming lack of natural talents. I helped clear a tree away from the road so we could all get home for Christmas. Yes, I realize, I helped save Christmas.

Somehow, I wonder if what I just accomplished — being in the moment, improvising, doing something crazy and making a difference for people I cared about – could have impressed Emily. But then the wonder subsides, and I'm left with the unyielding euphoria of how my irrational plan to deal with the forces of nature actually paid off.

Devin and Kyle keep yipping and celebrating as they cavort around the grass, holding hands like giddy schoolboys. I, on the other hand, turn to face Rachel and see her propelling herself towards me, wrapping her arms around my torso as she gives me the biggest laugh-filled, we-just-kicked-ass hug she can muster.

[...]

"Fuck, I'm freezing."

I've stripped down to my bra and boxers after stumbling back inside, and I feel no shame in doing so. Rachel fake-grimaces at my lackluster physique before draping a blanket over my shoulders. Kyle is bundled up in a similar fashion, using cocoa packets to make us all hot chocolate, while Devin, far from the excited man who was launching praise after praise at us for being ballsy as he ran back into the main cabin, is curled up on the couch, covered in two thick comforters.

"This is why I need to eat more ham," he comments, making me chuckle despite my chattering teeth. "Because I have no blubber to keep me warm when we do something stupid like, well, what we did just now."

"How the hell did you put up with east coast weather?" asks Rachel, her hair sticking out because she just ran a blow dryer across her entire body. "Because this temperature can't be as bad."

"Hey, wearing gloves and a hat with ear flaps while hiking in the snow with some buddies is one thing," Devin explains. "But chopping up a tree in the rain in Pensalado was never on my bucket list."

"You can cross it off, anyway, Dev," I grin before thanking Kyle for my mug of hot chocolate. My hands are still numb, so I don't feel the heat of the drink against my fingers. It tastes amazing, though.

We sit by the fire, warming up and drinking our cocoa like it's nectar from the gods, and we don't say much. We don't feel the need to. I'm not waiting for a whole lot of kudos because I don't think I could have done what I did tonight without everyone else's help. Tomorrow, even though it'll be Christmas Eve and the traffic will probably be horrendous going home, Devin and Kyle will be good sports and drop me off at my house before driving away to have that wonderful Christmas dinner that Devin gave us such excessive detail on. Everything will be locked down in the cabins until Devin returns on December 27th, and for him, it'll be back to work.

After Devin and Kyle finish their hot chocolate, they say good night without too much fanfare and leave Rachel and me alone again. Rachel hasn't really touched her mug of cocoa, only sipping it a couple of times, and I don't question her on it. Instead, I decide to question her on something that's probably far more personal and regarding a much touchier subject.

"So, have you actually made plans for Christmas?"

I expect her to get annoyed, but she giggles and smiles at me.

"You know what, I have. If only so you could stop bothering me about it."

"Hey, be nice."

"It's not anywhere we talked about, though."

"So, not Washington?"

"Nope."

I silently wait for an explanation.

"I know this guy in Port Lionel," Rachel starts her story. "He owns a pub there. We know each other from way back. He's one of Aaron's friends, but he doesn't really have family, so he always likes it whenever I see him around the holidays. I took your advice and I called him, and he's taking me in for Christmas."

Well, that's sudden yet good news. I didn't exactly advise her to call some dude from a place I've never visited, but I did recommend touching base with someone, so I suppose that's a good thing.

"I'm going to sound ignorant," I say, "but I can't say I've ever heard of Port Lionel."

"You wouldn't be the first," replies Rachel. "But it's where I've always kind of felt, well, safe. They say that if you're dealing with a lot of bad stuff, or you have a lot of emotional scars from your past or your present, you should at least have a place to go to or some refuge where you can be calm and happy. Could be your room, could be your backyard, another town, an entirely different country. For me, it's Port Lionel."

"Oh." That's all I can say as I slowly forget about my half-drunk hot chocolate.

"Port Lionel's beautiful," Rachel goes on, and she closes her eyes as if trying to imagine it. "It's right next to the coastline. Kind of a drive away from here, but it makes me feel so comfortable. I try to go once a year, and if I can't go, I'll at least think about it, and I'll feel a little better about everything. I'll think about walking around the little town area and sitting by the church, or having a drink at the pub and seeing an old friend. I can't always have that happy feeling, but I try to."

"Well, that's good," I manage to respond. "You're lucky to have a place like that."

"What about you?" Rachel's eyeing me now, though she can't really undress me because all I'm wearing are my undergarments. "You could use a safe place, too, right?"

I could. I really could. But as much as I think it over, I can't imagine where it could possibly be. I've never felt truly at peace anywhere in particular, unless I'm lying to myself, or I've forgotten, or I just have shitty luck. I shake my head, stand up, and dump the rest of my hot chocolate into the sink, watching the brown mass disappear bit by bit into the drain. Sorry for wasting a good packet of powder, Kyle.

"I should get to bed," I announce.

"Yeah," agrees Rachel. "Me, too."

"That safe place idea, though," I remark, making sure she doesn't think I was ignoring her. "I wish I did have one of those.

I mean, Emily was kind of my safe place for so long, so I wasn't relying on an actual location to feel like I was going to be okay. I guess, I don't know, we should depend more on places than on people?"

"Who knows," Rachel replies dryly. "Maybe we're onto something here. Unless there's an earthquake or hurricane or something that completely destroys that safe haven."

"How delightfully cynical."

"Yeah, Merry Christmas to you, too."

"Good night, Rachel."

I leave her by the fireplace and walk to my room, my bed's seemingly endless folds of sheets waiting for my embrace. I feel blissfully warm now — comfortable, stable, confident. Those aren't familiar feelings. As I sink into sleep, thinking about Christmas instead of my failed love life, Rachel instead of Emily, I wonder when my cabin mate will decide it's time for her to fall asleep, too. And I hope we both end up having good dreams.

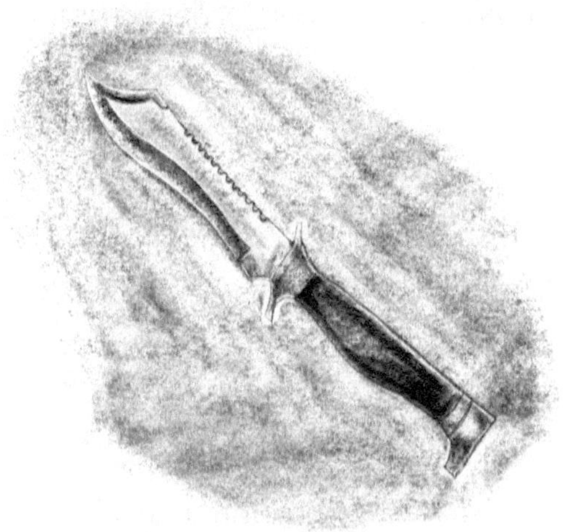

JANUARY

It's cold as hell, I'm back in Pensalado, and I'm ready to kick some more ass at my job.

I had a pretty good Christmas, even if it wasn't anything big. My parents were thrilled to have me come home after all, and of course, my mom called me crazy after I told them about the whole chopping up a dead tree incident. I'm not sure if maybe I was fooling myself, but I think my dad gave me one of those smiles that he used to flash at me back in high school and during my college years to let me know that he was proud of me in some way.

I got a handful of nice presents, even if most of them have to do with Pensalado and my caretaking gig. My parents bought me the usual new coat and socks and beanie cap with a sports team I don't pay attention to, but they also got me a compass, a walking stick, a brand new tool kit, and a big-ass knife. I'm not going to lie; I felt like a badass when I was holding that thing for the first time, knowing full well why they gave it to me. I joked to them that the first thing I'd do with my new weapon is slice up some pepper jack cheese for a sandwich.

But it's not Christmas that made me the happiest, which is a word I never thought I'd use for myself ever again. It's not the food or the tree or the presents, or the surprise visit from relatives whom I haven't seen in a long time — my Uncle Max somehow still doesn't have gray hair and still drinks way too much red wine. It's not New Year's, after three bottles of champagne and a trip to the Lair, where I ran into some of my nondescript high school friends and heard all their stories about community college and dead-end jobs. It's not even the fact that I looked forward to seeing Kyle's car pull up in my driveway, honking the horn at six AM, so we could race back up to the cabins and get back to work.

No, as I resettle into my room in the main cabin after another amazing dinner cooked by Kyle and two beers, I'm thinking about how for the entire time I was home, I never logged onto my computer and checked to see what my ex-girlfriend was up to. Not once.

I'm not joking. It just didn't cross my mind to even think about Emily. Not her smile, not her hair, not her tight tank tops or blue wedges. Not the selfies we constantly took, making goofy faces and kissing each other's cheeks and getting very, very drunk on Friday nights. Not her laugh, or the way she said my name when we cuddled on whoever's couch we decided to crash on that evening. Nothing. It's like I've finally pulled off the rose-tinted goggles, thrown them to the ground, and ruthlessly stomped on them.

As a result, I feel so liberated that it almost, ironically, hurts. Rachel certainly notices the shift in my mood when we start hanging out again. All I can do is talk about how good I feel, as we sit around the fireplace and Devin hands out presents that he bought for all of us.

"Well, if that doesn't make me feel all warm and fuzzy inside," I tease him, as I open up a poorly wrapped box of now outdated Christmas candies. I don't mind, though. Chocolate is chocolate.

"Devin knows me a little too well," is what Kyle grunts when he gets a T-shirt from Hearnsville, complete with a big fat rainbow sprayed across it with the words, "Kiss me, I'm queer," on it.

"Just don't wear it where you might get beat up," warns Devin, wagging a finger at his burly friend. "Otherwise, I'll feel super fucking guilty."

Kyle laughs. "I'd like to see them try."

"So where's my shirt?" I ask with a grin. "Or did they not have my size?"

"Sorry, hon," Devin sneers. "I'll be sure to get you the gayest clothes ever next time I head to town."

"That better include a neon bowtie."

Rachel gets a brand new capo for her guitar from Devin, and I kick myself for not getting her a gift of my own. I want to ask her all about Port Lionel, and when I do, she smiles and tells me that it was really nice, and the guy who took her in was a total sweetheart, and they had Christmas dinner together. I ask her how old he is and whether or not he's hot, and she punches me in the knee again.

"You just really like abusing my leg, don't you?" I ask, as she unscrews the cap of another bottle of Riesling.

"Correction: I like abusing you, period." Rachel fills a glass to the brim with wine and passes it to me. "Here. Drink up. It's good for you."

I do what she says and secretly savor the sweetness. Some habits of ours don't change after New Year's, and sure enough, we're staying up together and talking and listening to music every night, just like the month before.

It occurs to me that, while with Rachel, I feel a lot more relaxed and calmer and just overall, well, good. I mean, I feel really, really good. Being with Devin and Kyle and Rachel all at the same time is fun, too, especially during the weekend before I jump back into work. I even go on a hike with them, even though I still haven't visited Hearnsville. Kyle tries to scare Rachel about finding rattlesnakes, but not only does Rachel refuse to be perturbed, but she also calls him out for the fact that you don't exactly find a whole lot of mobile snakes in the winter.

More and more often, however, I find myself enjoying just being with her, whether it's during dinner or while we're playing a board game or whenever she decides to whip out the guitar and play us all a song. The night before I'm thrown back into my caretaker schedule, Devin tries to come up with his own lyrics, and Rachel plays along to them as best as she can before we all crack up. I absolutely love hearing her laugh. And we still like to communicate with each other using our eyebrows, though we now add smiles to the mix, too.

I'm not sure if I can believe it myself, but it seems like I really am healing. Emily is stuck way in the back of my mind, and when her face does pop up, I mentally shrug and carry on with my life without so much as a self-pitying sniffle. Devin helps. Kyle helps. Rachel definitely helps. They all remind me that I'm more than just an ex-girlfriend. And maybe, just maybe, I can actually move on with my life without so much as a relapse.

I'm ready, new year. Bring it the fuck on.

[...]

Since I've been away for the holidays, the whole property has been designated a dead tree zone. We're no longer taking any chances since that fateful night that one of those wooden suckers almost ruined Christmas, and as a result, Devin, Kyle, and Rachel have been slowly but steadily removing them in my absence. Kyle even brought up two chainsaws so we could be lumberjacks living in the twenty-first century for once. Basically, if we can't rely on experienced people from a neighboring town to cut this shit down, then we'll do it ourselves for free, no problem.

To my not-so-secret delight, I'm invited to partake in said tree clearing. Specifically, I get to take the blocks of wood that get sent my way after the three of them pulverize each trunk, and I split everything into neat bits of firewood. It's tough to use the axe, but I'm getting the hang of it, and I'm entertained every time Kyle roars, "Timber!" when a tree's ready to come down. I obviously get to do the housework when we're not cutting down trees, but thank God that I'm not the only one now. Devin's been kind enough to take up laundry once in a while, and Kyle's better at vacuuming than I am. I think they'd make better stay-at-home dads than I would make a stay-at-home mom, which amuses me because I don't think Devin would be caught dead living in a condo, sweeping floors, and dusting furniture for the rest of his life. And he never would be interested in having kids.

January is a month for business, and we have quite a few people stay for a handful of days at a time. We make the guest cabin presentable, and we get nothing but good reviews about the property and the hospitality. One middle-aged woman, in the presence of her husband, thanks me for being such a beautiful helper when I carry her suitcases into the quaint little bedroom. The look I get from her spouse is an odd one, like he thinks I'm trying to ruin their sacred union. I sincerely hope that he's not plotting to kill me while I'm sleeping; who knows how queer his wife truly is.

Personally, I'm doing my best to go outside and enjoy the open space more. With so much weeding done and so many dead trees being cleared away, the property looks really nice. It's way too cold to dip my feet into the creek, but I still walk alongside it until I can't see the cabins anymore. I find Rachel down by the edge of the property a couple of times, hanging out under the bridge where two big, black "No Trespassing" signs loom over our heads. I have no idea who owns the acreage next to us, but they sure mean business with their written warnings. Needless to say, it becomes another hang out place for us when the workload is a little lighter than usual.

Oh, yeah, did I mention that it's cold? Because it's super cold. I wake up every morning to see frost clawing at my window. Kyle's decided to put together a hot food menu and looks at me funny whenever I drink something chilled, unless it's a beer; he'll forgive me for that. He offers me things like spiked hot cider and toddies as a substitute, as they'll actually keep my innards toasty, but sometimes, I just like my good old suds.

Sometimes, it's so frigid out that we forego the hikes that we've decided to do nightly and just stay inside, putting on the same old vinyls and bunching up on the couch to play more of that outdated trivia game. I never thought that learning about horned lizards that can squirt blood out of their eyes could be so conducive to getting cozy on a January night.

"How do they do it, you think?" I inquire once we've packed up the board game. Kyle's won with three wedges ahead of all of us. He's kind of random, at least intelligence-wise.

"How do what do what?" asks Devin.

"The lizards. Squirting blood. I mean, what's the deal? Does it hurt?"

Devin takes some time to think about my questions, pursing his lips and making a somewhat dopey, "Hmm," sound. But the answer he gives sounds encyclopedic enough.

"Well, I could be wrong, but I think I heard somewhere that the little guys try to stop blood from leaving their heads, so it all backs up behind their eyes and breaks a shitload of eyelid vessels." He shrugs. "Last I checked, the blood can shoot out as far as five feet."

"Gross," Kyle grimaces, shaking his head.

"Let me guess," jokes Rachel. "You heard this from some nature guy in Arkansas or something?"

"Nah, Texas, if I remember correctly. Only they call them horny toads, not horned lizards."

"Leave it to you to learn shit like that in Texas," I sneer.

"Yeah, well, you travel to Goliad or Sugarland and come back with something better."

"No, thanks. I'm not a cowboy."

"I'll say," taunts Devin, shoving me and snickering as he gets up from the couch. "And now, to bed, my pretties. Another day, another dollar."

He struts out of the cabin with Kyle in tow, leaving Rachel and me behind yet again. We don't move from where we're sitting.

We're too warm to disturb our nest, and even though we're sitting on opposite ends of the couch, since Devin and Kyle took up the space between us, I can almost feel her body heat radiating against me. I know that in the guest cabin, a young couple is putting their six-year-old daughter and four-year-old son to bed. The husband is a fisherman, and I expect him to be up early tomorrow morning, searching for crawdads in the creek.

Rachel decides to endure the chill and gets up to grab her guitar. She tries to tune it as quickly as she can, though her fingers visibly shake as she adjusts the pegs. I'm not a musician, but I can tell that the low temperature's made all the strings completely out of tune, so it takes some effort on Rachel's part to correct the sound.

"I can't help it," she tells me. "I gotta play in this weather. I get so damn fidgety when it's cold."

"I just get numb."

She giggles as she finishes tuning her guitar. Unfortunately, once she double checks the first string she tweaked, she discovers, to her annoyance, that it's reverted back to its old, incorrect note. After some valiant attempts to fight off winter's influence on her instrument, she finally gives up and decides to just play a song, pitch be damned. It sounds pretty, anyway, and I can feel my whole body relax as she tries out a tune that I've never heard before. When I ask her what it is, Rachel smiles. She tilts her head back, and lets her voice carry itself across the floor.

"Rock me, mama, like a wagon wheel, oh, rock me, mama, any way you feel..."

"You sound good."

"Thanks," she murmurs. "And it's called, 'Wagon Wheel,' by Old

Crow Medicine Show."

"Cool."

"But the chorus was written by Bob Dylan. He just never used it, I guess."

I prop my head against a couch cushion and pop the bones in the back of my neck. "Why not?"

"Shit, I don't know. Maybe he just couldn't think of the right song for it?"

"I find that hard to believe."

"Why?"

"Well, he's Bob Dylan. Can't he write anything?"

"Apparently not."

"Well, nobody's perfect." And isn't that the truth.

Rachel plays, "Wagon Wheel," again and kind of exhales the lyrics, rather than the usual rough and raw tone she gets in her voice when she sings. She sounds sweet, especially when she's sleepy, and she keeps closing her eyes and letting her lashes flutter up and down. I hug my knees against my chest as I watch and listen from the couch, focusing on her lips as they part and move back together with each word she enunciates.

Wait. Why am I focusing on her lips?

"Fire's going out," Rachel suddenly observes as she sets down her guitar. She doesn't bother putting the thing back in its case. She just walks up to me, looking at me expectantly. I realize that I've wrapped one of the blankets around me like I'm making myself a cocoon, since the embers in the fireplace are whimpering out.

"You want me to share?"

Without saying anything, Rachel pulls the fabric away from

my torso and sits right next to me. And I do mean right next to me. We end up sharing the blanket, our shoulders pressed together, our feet bobbing above the floor. Then she touches my ankle with her toes, and the touch startles me. Her feet aren't cold; they're actually very warm. I like the way they feel against my legs.

I don't think that either of us one hundred percent realize what we're doing, but before I even say anything, we are legitimately cuddling. Under the blanket, I have one arm draped across Rachel's shoulders like a limp scarf, and she huddles against me with her face pressed against my collarbone and her arms squeezing my abdomen. She just holds me there, like she's afraid she'll let go, and I'll fall into the couch and completely disappear beneath the cushions. I can feel the hot breath from her nostrils grazing the sleeve of my sweatshirt, ruffling the cotton only slightly, as all I can hear is my own rattling heart like a wind chime on a typical stormy Pensalado night. I try to tell myself that she's only doing this to keep warm.

But maybe she's —

No. She's doing this to keep warm. I try to convince my nervous brain of that. And of course, it doesn't believe me.

Does this count as cheating? No, I remind myself, I'm single. I'm not cheating on Emily. It's not cheating if you're no longer together with someone. It's interesting how quickly I think about my ex when there's another girl in the picture now, making physical contact with me that I can't fully interpret. I don't know if this is platonic or not. I don't know if I should be made uncomfortable by this or not. I'm in a mental space that's ambiguous and murky and weird, so Emily emerges like the Loch Ness monster from the lake, as if reminding me of what I've lost in order to make me lose focus on what I've yet to gain.

But I manage to ward off those intruding thoughts, and I don't pull away. I just cling to Rachel, our bodies cozy against one another, watching the flames wisp away in the fireplace, our breathing loud but comforting.

I'm not sure what to think. I'm not sure what to say. Rachel doesn't say anything, so I don't, either.

And it feels really, really good.

[...]

I wake up on the couch the next morning with the blanket coiled around my ankles like a thick, woolly serpent. My head swims, and my neck aches, given the fact that I most likely fell asleep while sitting up. I examine the once person-filled spot beside me. No Rachel to be found.

As I lift myself up from the cushions, I can smell eggs and toast and salt and pepper from the kitchen. Then Kyle pokes out his big, bushy head from around the corner as if he's checking on me. He's still dressed in his pajamas — or more accurately, his oversized pink T-shirt and heart-covered boxers - but he is up and as peppy as ever.

"Morning, sleepyhead," he coos, a smile dancing on his bearded lips. "I'm making you an egg in the basket. Do you want your egg over easy or over hard?"

"Where's Rachel?"

"Still sleeping, I think," replies Kyle. "I figured I shouldn't bother you two. Devin woke up with the sniffles, so I think we're just going to have the day to ourselves."

"Oh." That's a relief. I feel sore all over. Guess I'm still not used to chopping wood.

The frying pan begins to sizzle in the kitchen, and I suddenly feel very hungry, like I haven't eaten in days. Everything edible starts to smell divine.

"Was Rachel in here when you came in?" I ask, as I push myself off the couch. I can feel my hair sticking up from my scalp, like static's caught in it. The blanket untangles itself from my feet, finding its freedom on the floor.

Kyle blinks at me, probably wondering why I keep asking about my cabin mate. "You mean in the kitchen?"

"No, I mean in the living room. On the couch. Was she with me?"

"Nope," says Kyle. "Just you. You were out like a light. Seriously, easy or hard, dude?"

"Um. Easy, I guess." I'm a sucker for runny yolk.

I make a rather large effort to move myself to the dining area, slowly positioning myself into my chair as Kyle brings out a plate of steaming egg and carbohydrates. I start tearing into my simplistic meal, which isn't quite the same as waffles, but I still enjoy it for what it is. After mopping up the salty yolk with the remainder of my crust, I accept a mug of coffee from my personal chef just as Rachel trudges into the room, all tousled hair and sleepy eyes and suddenly looking, as much as I don't want to acknowledge it, cute.

"Rach! Morning! Easy or hard?"

"Not in the mood for trivia, Ky," Rachel grumbles, sitting in a chair across from me. She looks equally as groggy as I do, if not groggier.

122

"I mean your egg in the basket."

Rachel gives Kyle an incredibly drowsy stare as if she's expecting him to be holding an actual basket full of eggs or something. It finally registers for her what he's asking, and she mutters for her egg to be done over easy. Which somehow makes me happy that we have similar tastes in eggs, even though it's not that big of a deal.

I try not to think about anything. I intend to blank everything out from last night and ignore the possible scenario that my brain's conjuring up in its limited studio space. Me and Rachel? No. That's ridiculous. It's way too much like an overused movie trope. Hell, it's even clichéd from the beginning: A meeting based on misunderstanding, an initial phase of hatred or apathy, a later mutual recognition of our flaws and past ghosts, and finally, a strong, beautiful friendship. And now I'm crushing on her? Come on. Why is my life trying to imitate art so much?

We eat our breakfast together in silence, and I don't dare instigate any conversation. I excuse myself to walk around the property, and Rachel doesn't invite herself along. I guess once Kyle tells her that Devin won't be working and we can take the day off, she's very likely decided to go back to bed.

All I want to do is calm myself down as I saunter along the dirt path. Rachel and I were cuddling last night. Big deal. Friends cuddle. Even guys group together when it's cold enough (no homo, of course — they'll be quick to remind you of that). That doesn't mean that we all have to start sucking each other's teeth off. I'm not in the mood for any remotely romantic ideas, and I'm sure that Rachel isn't in the mood, either.

I make my way towards the creek and listen to it whistle

across the rocks for a while, if only to soothe my anxiety. A few minutes later, I spot one of our guests — the husband of the family — hiking up a small slope next to me, carrying a bucket and a bunch of sticks with raw strips of bacon dangling from them. I was right on the money with him, though I wonder how many crawdads he was able to snag. And I'm not sure if he actually plans to cook them and eat them, either.

I never thought I'd say this, but I try to tell myself that I'm fine without anything happening between Rachel and me. Hell, it's like I don't even *want* anything happening between us. Not that it would be bad. Rachel is tough, probably with more toned muscles in her arms than I have in my whole body, but I like that about her. I remember a lot of my guy friends from school claiming that it wasn't good for a girl to be buffer than they were, but I never cared. I can't believe I'm confessing this, but my cabin mate is gorgeous. Yes, that's the right word: *Gorgeous.* From her dark hair, to her olive skin, to her eyes rimmed with both brown and green, to what cheesy romance novelists might call, "her rippling biceps." Rachel's a looker, wannabe macho boys' expectations and insecurities be damned.

Also, she might be tough on the outside, but she's genuine on the inside. And when I say genuine, I don't mean that as synonymous with, "soft." She's not super gentle or secretly sweet and mushy, like finding a gooey caramel center in a thick layer of chocolate. Honestly, maybe there's just chocolate. It's not like I want to crack Rachel open and expose a brand new side of her. She makes me laugh, she teases the shit out of me, and she's always had this thoughtful side to her that you'd expect from anyone with her kind of background. No need to analyze her like a Freudian subject, as much as I habitually scrutinize every interaction I have with everyone I know. She's just unapologetically her.

In short, there's nothing that says manipulator or trickster about her, unlike what I assume Emily always was deep down. Rachel's open, blunt, talented, and, most importantly, real. And the more I think about it - from her jaunty smile, to her sharp tongue, to the way she strums a guitar, to the way she swings an axe — I'm beginning to realize that I am unforgivably attracted to her.

This was not on my agenda when I took this job.

FEBRUARY

I'm beginning to wonder if Pensalado has any type of weather besides, "You don't get to have any feeling in your nose for the whole day." For the rest of January, we hardly get any rain, but the chill's incessant, and I find myself bundling up a lot more. February is no exception to the "Jesus Christ, it's freezing," rule. I'm amazed that I don't see icicles dangling from the roof when I go outside to do my chores.

The guests don't seem to mind, though. Nothing's staving them off now. I learn that when Devin and Kyle went back home for Christmas, they took some time to write up advertisements and post contact information for the property, so it probably got plastered all over the good old Interwebs and people's email lists and what not. I wouldn't be surprised if every time those two go to Hearnsville, Kyle brings along a stapler and a stack of flyers and goes around sticking the things to telephone poles and stop signs in the hopes of someone noticing.

In short, we are booked solid for February. Which, of course, means that I get very little free time, and now I get to be busboy for the bigger families who partake in the little nature wonderland that we have to offer. Everyone now has a daily list of jobs to tend to. Devin's gotten even less lenient about the house cleaning, so sometimes, I find myself in the guest cabin twice a day when our clients are out and about, cleaning tables and sweeping floors and scrubbing sinks and making beds. I am one step away from becoming a hotel maid, and I'm not alone. Even Rachel's started to complain about how many times Devin's asked her to mop the kitchen floor.

"I swear to God, it's like one bread crumb falls, and I've got my cousin on me like a fucking vulture," she gripes to me and Kyle, as she props the mop against the nearby rack of firewood after finishing yet another tedious soaking of the linoleum. Kyle and I are washing and drying dishes, and I'm already getting a sore arm from trying to scrape away sticky rice and starch from a pan we used the night before. "'It's just for business,' he says. 'Just do it and stop whining,' he says. Yeah, I'll stop whining after I take this broom and shove it right up your – "

"He's just trying to give the guests the best experience possi-ble," Kyle coaxes in his best little counselor voice, which sounds like a cross between an English doctor and a little old lady.

"The way you side with him all the time, Kyle, it sounds like you'd like to give him the best experience possible, if you know what I mean," Rachel sneers, finishing off her sentence with a goofy wink.

I can't help it; I have to cram my face into a towel that I'm using to dry dishes in order to muffle my laughter. She's not done yet.

"Seriously, do you want me to oil up this broom handle for you? I think there's some Vaseline in Jamie's and my bathroom. Cabinet, top shelf, to the right."

"Fuck you, Rachel, fuck you, Rachel, fuck you, Rachel, fuck you, Rachel," Kyle chants with each stroke of the scrubbing brush against a particularly stubborn pot covered in potato grime.

Despite the fact that, once the guests wrap up dinner and head to their cabin, all we want to do is collapse, we still find the time to play one card game and tell one story per night. Usually said story is another one of Devin's adventures in the Oregon wilderness or sailing against the Washington shore. He's talked so much about the Midwest and the East Coast that now we're getting the Western installment of his ventures now. Nothing but states lined up next to the Pacific Ocean these days. I'm expecting an ice-fishing epic from the Aleut Chain in Alaska by the end of the month.

Of course, the guests we get here now come with their own idiosyncrasies that I have to put up with. They're sure as hell no Sally and Cindy, I'll say that right now — and by that, I mean they have all of the quirks, but none of the charm. One redneck-looking family asks me if they can practice sharp shooting with beer cans on the property, but for the sake of everyone's safety and ears, Devin fetches a map and directs them to an appropriate shooting range. Two brothers stay for a few days and argue the entire time, routinely driving off in the middle of the night in each other's trucks and showing up for breakfast in the morning with half-empty bottles of wine still clutched in their drunken fists. It's a wonder that they're both still alive, and I desperately hope that they haven't killed anyone on the road yet. A mother comes up with her adult son and tells us all about his "sinful" sexual escapades and how she's praying for his soul. I rummage through the dresser drawers in the guest cabin for any leatherbound Gideon bibles once they've finished their stay. To both my surprise and my chagrin, I actually find one — small and humble-looking. No leather, though. I take my time reading it one night before tossing it into the corner of my room. No more of Isaiah's prophecies for me, thank you.

Overall, not exactly people I'd care to socialize with. I'll just stick with maintaining a professional relationship with them, thank you very much. So of course, that leaves me to mostly interact with, you guessed it, good old Rachel, and I really can't help the fact that I'm enjoying every chat we have. But why not, when she's totally contributing to my happiness, which I never thought I'd ever get back after a pretty horrid summer that I don't wish to repeat?

More often now, we're straying away from the living room and spending time in each other's bedrooms — and no, not in that way, you rascals, you. Whether it's me on her bed and her sitting on the floor, or her on my bed and my sitting on the floor (seriously, it always happens that way, and I'm not sure why), we find it a little more comfortable to be away from the big fireplace and the record player so we can just talk without musical accompaniment or any other excess noise. It's like our rooms are little hideouts for us, where we can slip away and talk without the world spying through the window, and the moon casts the covered glass in this pretty cool silver glow that just adds to the ambience of the whole set-up.

As we open up to each other more, Rachel and I begin to talk about our pasts. She mentions some dude she dated named

Garrett, who doesn't exactly pose a threat to me, even though I'm still trying to prove to myself that I don't have any minute feelings for this girl whatsoever (and failing at it, mind you). She tells me that they broke up for one simple reason: He tried to "fix" her. I guess he was really preachy and sort of undermined all of Rachel's struggles after all those shitty years she spent in foster care, and he always gave her these pep talks and tried to raise her up on some sort of pedestal, like she was some shining example of steadfast courage, or something. You know, the kind of person who goes, "You can do it, you can get over this, you're strong, I believe in you," but that's it. Just bloated words of stale confidence and empty platitudes. Not a real, well-conceived relationship, in which the guy should have just listened and nodded and hugged her and kissed her and told her in basic terms that it was okay and he was there for her, regardless of whether or not she was actually strong or courageous or whatever.

But if that's not bad enough, guess what? Rachel had to relive the whole excessive and dramatic routine with another partner. This time, her name is Sophie, all angelic and well-meaning and what-not. Funnily, or sadly, enough, the story with Sophie sounds nearly the same as the story with Garrett. All, "Let me help you," and, "I know you better," and all that bullshit woven into some stupid tapestry of the same old "soulmate saves other soulmate" narrative. At this point, I start to feel bad for Rachel. Not because I'm a sucker for sympathy, but because it all sounds so stupid and snotty from her so-called significant other's end.

"I'm not some broken toy that needs to be wound up again," she informs me as we sit in my bedroom. Of course, she's on the bed, and I'm on the floor. "I just sometimes want to talk about stuff.

Stuff that bothers me, stuff that gets to me. I shouldn't be force-fed motivational speeches every time I just want to spill my guts."

"You think Garrett and Sophie meant well, though?" I ask, attempting to play devil's advocate.

"I'm sure they did, but..." Rachel sighs loudly. "If I wanted a person to say shit like that to me all the time, I would've signed up for therapy."

Of course, this gives me the perfect opportunity to talk about the very person who embodied my entire existence for the past near half-decade: Emily. Rachel seems unexpectedly excited to be hearing about her again, like my ex-girlfriend has been some huge enigma ever since I made those comments about her both at Thanksgiving dinner and before Christmas. I've purposely tried not to talk about her that much since then, but in this moment, it just erupts from my throat like acid reflux, burning my tongue as I talk, and I just can't seem to get myself to stop.

"So *she* asked *you* to prom," Rachel mutters, leaning her back against the bed's headboard, her dark curls gathering in clumps around the nape of her neck.

"Yeah. She liked to tell me she admired me from afar. Though, thinking back on it, I'm not sure why."

"Maybe because you're such a rugged rebel."

"Don't be such a bitch."

"No, no, Jamie," she corrects me. "I'm being an asshole. Get it right. So, after prom night, the fairy tale began?"

I sigh. "Fairy tale" is a good way to put it if you like to omit the obligatory happily ever after tagline.

"It really was like everything was coming together so perfectly and so easily," I tell her. "No complaints from our families — they

132

were all accepting and open-minded. We both decided to go to the same college before we even started dating. I was pretty much undeclared major-wise until Emily just went on and on and on about my being a good teacher. I don't even think I'm that great of a talker. Again, all I did was bullshit."

"Hey, I, for one, think that bullshitting is a necessary tool to keeping an audience's attention," quips Rachel. "C'mon, how do you think writers do it?"

"True, but..." I linger on the word, "but," for a while, stuck in my own thoughts for a moment or two. "Like I said before, it's not like I'm actually good at teaching. I mean, sure, I did student teaching, and it was okay..."

"Did the students like you?"

"Don't even go there."

Rachel laughs. She drums her fingers on her thighs, waiting for me to continue my story.

"I can't believe I even did that well in school, actually," I say. "I mean, maybe I figured, hey, Emily's happy, I'm happy if she's happy, and it just helped me be super temporary-smart or something."

"I've heard that before from you."

"What, 'temporary-smart?' I just made it up. Aren't I clever?"

"No, I mean the whole, 'If she's happy, I'm happy,' spiel. I've heard you say that."

She has. I really do sound redundant.

"Look, Rach, I cave, okay?" I groan. "I didn't exactly look out for myself when I was with Emily. But it wasn't like I was aching to do anything else, or she just swooped in and ruined my one true dream. It's not like the movies, where someone thinks she's happy and then, I dunno, she finds out she's really good at playing the ukulele with her toes, and all of a sudden, it's epiphany time and time for breaking things off and frolicking into the sunset. Or something like that."

"See, maybe you'd make a good screenwriter," Rachel comments, her voice sharpening in the typical way it does when she's teasing me. "I can see that film making big bucks and snagging a few Oscars. Only make sure the ukulele player has no hands, so playing it with toes seems heroic."

"Yeah, well, you can write it. Just send me royalties for the concept, and I'll be happy."

"So, why did Emily break up with you? If you don't mind me asking."

I pause for pseudo-dramatic effect. "You're going to find this hilarious," I whisper. "It's because she felt like I was too programmed and predictable. Like a robot."

"Ha!"

"And she said she felt like I wasn't doing anything exciting or new anymore. Like she thought I was always supposed to be some great action hero or intellectual who didn't follow the satisfy-your-girlfriend-at-all-costs script. I don't know. She kind of gave me a laundry list."

"So, in short...she got bored with you."

"Yep," I grumble. "Even though I did every little thing she asked for or whatever came out of her little mental fantasy diary."

"Hmmm. 'Little Mental Fantasy Diary.' That can be the name of the screenplay you write!"

The whole conversation, which I swear only feels like ten minutes but really lasts for about three or four hours, keeps going on like this. I reveal something about Emily, from her constant reminder that I was the only one for her, to her insistence that I follow the path I'd already paved for myself educationally when I questioned it, to her brilliant timing of breaking up with me after college like she was finally being liberated from my presence. And in return, Rachel has a barb, a joke, something to lighten the mood. I don't think she's trying to be dismissive or downplay my feelings. In fact, I think she's legitimately trying to help me in terms of making this whole thing easier to stomach.

And you know what? It's working. I feel open and relaxed the whole time we're sitting in that bedroom together, trading off jabs and sarcasm like we're passing around a fat bottle of cheap booze. And more and more, as I cast an eye on the photo albums I brought up to the cabin, I notice that a very thin film of dust has started to crawl and settle over them. I realize that I'm even having a harder time picturing Emily at all. Her face is nearly a blur to me, her hair fuzzy around her jaw, like a Polaroid picture that just didn't come out right. And in her place, stark and vibrant in my imagination, is Rachel. Rachel, with her lazy grin and her arched eyebrows and that look she always gives me when I've done something she likes. That sharp, amused look that's to die for. Her hazel eyes lingering with me long after she's already said good night and gone to bed.

I bury myself under the covers as soon as I'm left alone. The cold doesn't get to me; I just feel like a ball of warmth and good-ness and, "Here I come, world," mantras. And I know that most of the reason why I feel that way is because of my cabin mate.

I really am a hopeless case.

On Valentine's Day, I expect to be mentally flooded with depression at the very thought of not being with Emily. Instead, Kyle and Rachel invite me to accompany them to Hearnsville. Devin is staying at the property to take care of some guests who are expected to arrive later that night, so he won't be tagging along. He hates Valentine's Day, anyway. Color me fifty shades of shocked.

Usually, I've said no to going to Hearnsville. Now, especially since it's Rachel who's asking me to come and not just Kyle, I'm much more inclined to take up their offer. I figure, at this point, that staying active and distracted is the best way to ensure that the progress I've made doesn't completely disappear. I'm not in the mood for getting caught up in lovey-dovey memories and ultimately feeling super sorry for myself. I'm over that.

So I say yes. Kyle literally howls with excitement, like he's a coyote. I guess he's pretty ecstatic that he's finally getting the reclusive loner Jamie to actually leave Pensalado. Rachel laughs as Kyle hugs me, and after he finishes his happy dance, I start thinking that maybe he has ulterior motives, given that Devin's not coming.

"He needs a designated driver, doesn't he?" I ask Rachel as I pull on my shoes; I keep my socks on in the cabin because it's so damn cold.

Rachel sneers. "Maybe."

"Great. So I'm his babysitter *and* his chauffeur. Why can't *you* drive?"

"'Cause I want to drink more than one pint of beer. Duh."

I roll my eyes. Rachel notices this and goes into salvage mode.

"Hey, having you be the DD isn't the only reason we asked you to come," she insists. "I mean, if we really didn't like you, then I'd just be the DD instead. Against my will, of course, but DD nonetheless."

"So, you and Kyle really do want me to come?"

"Mostly me."

"Aw," I warble in a high-pitched, lisping voice. "You're so sweet."

"Have I given you diabetes yet?"

"Nope. But give it a couple months. It'll happen."

We hop into Kyle's car around four o'clock in the afternoon and bounce along the narrow bumpy road to Hearnsville, blasting music the whole way. I'm not used to hearing songs out of an MP3 player these days — Rachel brought one up, and she's got quite a few tracks on it, mostly...symphonic metal? The songs don't have the same rough, yet comforting, sound as they would if they were on a scratched vinyl. I'm not trying to be a hipster here, but I currently prefer records over CDs or musical apps. I think I'll have to grab a record player from a pawn shop or a thrift store the next time I go home.

Okay, no, I'm definitely a hipster now. Oh, sweet Jesus, it's happening. Tell my parents I love them.

Kyle doesn't speak much because he's always been a cautious driver, but Rachel and I spend the ride talking. It's amazing that we can always find something to chat about, given where we currently live. The only updates about outside civilization I get are from the newspapers that Devin fetches from outside the Pensalado general store, or the occasional reports I hear from his portable radio when I work near him on the property. Most likely, when we're talking about politics, we're not exactly up to speed compared to the rest of the cultured, cyber-wrapped world, but we don't care. I never thought I'd say this, but I'm kind of over the Internet.

Oh, geez, this is just reiterating my newfound hipster status. I need a cold shower and a slap to the face, stat.

"Yeah, you say that now," says Rachel in response to my growing indifference about the worldwide web. "Then when this is all over, you'll go home and get sucked in again."

"Not like a whole lot of people miss me."

"I was never the social networking type, either," Rachel admits. "So that's never been a problem for me."

"You don't talk much with your friends?"

"I don't have a whole lot of them. Just my old roommate and my Washington buddy."

"Chris Lynch says that you really only need two friends, so maybe you're okay," I point out, remembering a book I read back in middle school for sixth grade English.

"Who the fuck is Chris Lynch?"

As we approach Hearnsville, I start noticing that there are a lot more rainbow flags flying outside stores and other establishments than I remember, which is an impressive feat. In fact, I notice something else that I'm not used to — mainly that there are a lot more men. Really big, brawny, bearded men. Some of them aren't wearing shirts, regardless of whether or not they've got abs or flab. One guy trots by our car wearing nothing but daisy dukes, exposing more of his inner thighs than I'd prefer to ever lay my eyes on.

"Um," I manage to utter after my eyes have been assaulted by a guy's impressive pair of moobs. "What's going on here?"

"Oh!" Kyle cries, the first time he's spoken in a while. "I forgot to tell you. It's Wolf Weekend."

"Wolf...Weekend?"

"Yeah! Like Bear Weekend, only they say wolf here. You know, 'cause they want to be different and stuff."

Okay. There is no way Kyle "forgot" to tell me. This has to be the main reason he wanted to go to Hearnsville in the first place. On Valentine's Day, no less.

"So, let me get this straight," I conclude, knowing full well the irony of that statement. "You invite me to come with you to Hearnsville, and I finally say yes, and when I do show up, it's filled with gay men?"

"Uh, yep. That's about right."

I make a frustrated fluttering noise with my lips. "You think I could have been updated or something?"

"Aw, what's wrong, Jamie girl?" taunts Kyle. "Can't handle some extra man in your life?"

"You know I'm almost too gay to function."

"Well, so am I. It's Valentine's Day, and I'm splurging. Deal with it, homie."

I can't argue with that. I won't deny just how happy Kyle looks as he pulls into a spare parking space next to the grocery store. Rachel gives me a look that begs, "Just have fun," as we get out of the car, and I suddenly feel very wiry and wimpy against some of the big and fabulous men walking around. All that mopping and cleaning and wood splitting, and I still don't have a whole lot of muscle to show off. Especially not compared to this male mob.

Hearnsville is a lot more colorful than I last remember it, with or without the "wolves," but maybe that's partially because I'm a little less disdainful about the world as of late. Once we start walking, I become accustomed to seeing exposed skin from some of the bears shuffling around town. One bearded mammoth sashays by with his nipples bursting from two purposely cut holes in his white T-shirt. When he catches me looking at him, he chirps, "Oh, don't worry, honey — I don't bite."

Nothing against these guys, okay? I just really, really like women. And *only* women. And Wolf Weekend is doing a really good job of reminding me of that.

It's getting darker, but that's not stopping anyone else. We follow a swarm of buff and burly men into the River Bar, which is practically spray-painted with gay pride, and settle down to have dinner and drinks. The place is packed with guys in flannel shirts and baseball caps, belching and laughing and sitting at little round tables, while someone plays guitar on a tiny stage in the corner. It's a cozy spot, but it's loud and rambunctious and, yeah, I'm kicking myself for not coming here sooner.

The pretty waitress among dozens of men takes our orders. I settle with the brie burger and a glass of lager, and I notice that some guys at a table across from us are giving Kyle coy looks and smiling.

"You've got some fans," I say to him.

"Course I do, silly!" exclaims Kyle. "I'm beautiful."

I decide to play along with the whole scene, like it's some sort of matchmaking game. "Let me know if I can help you out in some way," I tell my friend, taking a smaller sip of beer than usual because I'm DD and want to savor my only drink of the night. "I'm sure I can assist you with some of these guys."

Kyle smiles. "Thanks, but I've already got my eye on someone else."

He does. I notice a pretty good-looking young man sitting at the bar, watching the football game where one team is surely clobbering the other in the sportsiest of fashions. He's dressed all preppy in a collared shirt and slacks, so he's more cleaned up and conservative-looking than the other patrons. But he's built like a brick and has this magnificent goatee, and while my gaydar isn't stellar, he exudes a glorious level of homosexuality.

If I were straight, I'd be competing with Kyle for this guy, fuck our friendship. But since I'm not straight, and this handsome stranger's also not straight, I instead keep looking at Rachel. She refuses to take off her cap even when we're eating, sucking down her beer like it's water. It's kind of hot.

"Why don't you go say hi to him?" I ask Kyle, knowing full well what strategy my brain is devising and not even bothering to put a stop to it.

"Say hi to who?"

I jerk my thumb toward Kyle's object of affection. It doesn't seem like the dude's even with a friend. "Him."

"Oh." Kyle hangs his head like a nervous puppy. "I don't know. I've said hi to him before, and..."

"So you know him?"

"No!" protests Kyle — a bit too much, methinks. "I've just said hi to him once!"

"And what? He said hi back? At least he'll recognize you! Try speaking more words!"

"I just don't know if I'm his type..."

I get what he's hinting at. It's no secret that as much as these men are out to have a good time, most of them would not want to get with Kyle for one reason: His race. I'm sure he's had his fair share of comments like, "Sorry, I only date white guys. It's just a preference," or, "I only like black dudes if they've got it where it counts." It's bound to make him nervous about approaching any-one, let alone men of the Caucasian persuasion.

But I'm a stubborn, pseudo-woke white bitch, so once again, I fail to keep my mouth shut.

"Okay, dude," I snap. "Look at you. You are a smoking hot mountain man who chops down trees and hangs out in the wil-derness for a living. That guy is sitting all by his lonesome, having a beer with no company, watching some stupid sports game, and I'm sure he'd love to talk to you instead. Has he ever acted all shy when he sees you?"

"Yeah, but Jamie, I don't— "

I grab Kyle's enormous arm and look straight into his eyes.

"Buy him a drink."

Kyle's mouth falls open. "Dude."

"Buy him a drink, or I cut you," I threaten him. "Like a steak."

He doesn't argue with me. Gulping down his first helping of ale like it's liquid courage, Kyle stands up and starts walking toward the bar without waiting for his fish and chips to show up. I sigh and lean back in my chair, my stomach audibly growling as I think about my upcoming meal. Then I notice Rachel gazing at me.

"What?"

"Dude," she says. "You totally pumped Kyle up."

"Guess that's what friends are for."

Don't tell her you also just wanted to be alone with her, Jamie.

She does not need to know about your stupid secret plan.

"You know, when you're not being emo," Rachel opines, "you're actually pretty cool."

I snort. "Why, am I still emo?"

"No!" Rachel quickly replies. Then she can't help giggling. "Not as much, no. I mean, not as much as when I first met you. Sorry, am I being rude?"

I smile and shake my head. "Nah. I was a huge downer."

"Okay, but now look. You're in town with us, having a beer, and helping a buddy out. I'm impressed."

"Thanks." That's all I can really say to that. Otherwise, I'm just enjoying the onslaught of compliments.

Rachel bites her lower lip as she looks at me. "You're having a good time, right?"

"Yeah. Course I am."

"Okay. Just making sure."

I finally get my burger and eat about half of it in less than five minutes. I make loud noises as I do so, laughing when Rachel tells me to stop. I want to act like a bear, but she says I'm more like a pig. I snort at her, and she laughs again. We just keep acting goofy as we eat, all while we shoot glances at Kyle as he sits next to his crush and has a drink with him. So it's a win-win for all of us.

"So, have you thought about what you're going to do when this gig's over?" Rachel asks out of the blue as I gnaw on the rest of my burger.

I stop chewing for a second. "Isn't it a little early to be thinking about that?"

She shrugs. "Three more months until Aaron's supposed to come back, right?"

"Oh. Yeah."

"So...?"

I swallow a thick lump of ground beef. The grease sticks to the back of my throat and makes my voice come out all rough and clogged. "I haven't really thought about that, no."

"You can still teach, right?" she asks.

"Yeah."

"But you don't want to, do you?"

"Not really."

"What else do you want to do?"

I sigh. I drink more of my beer, but it's lukewarm and not as appetizing anymore.

"Rachel," I announce like I'm revealing a great truth, "I have no fucking iota of a fucking clue what I'm going to do once I get out of Pensalado. Honestly. I don't know where I'm going to live, where I'm gonna work, what I'm gonna do about friends or family. I mean, so much of my life was Emily. That was it. And you know what, it's coming back to haunt me now. I'm worried..." I correct myself. "No, I'm *terrified* about what I'm going to do next. I used to know. Now I don't."

I seem to do really well with unprompted speeches. The last quarter of hamburger left on my plate has lost the rest of its appeal, but that's because whenever I get passionate about something, my appetite just fades away into the great beyond. Rachel just nods at everything I say, not seeming disturbed by it at all. She just sips her beer and makes affirming noises as I vent.

"So," she summarizes for me, "you have no plan."

"Yeah. That's pretty stupid, huh?"

"Not really," she retorts. "You think I've got one?"

"Got what?"

"A plan."

"You don't have a plan?"

"Jamie, I've never really planned out anything ever," confesses Rachel, folding her arms against the table as the din around us seems to subside temporarily. "You think my dream was to work at a big box store for the rest of my life? Live in the same apartment? Stay with Garrett or Sophie or whoever else was on my radar before I decided to come out here? Hell, no. My whole existence used to be plotted out for me. When I was in that foster care facility, I'd be told when to eat, when to sleep, when to do anything. I'd be sent to a family I'd have no say about, and then I'd be taken out a month later, no matter what I thought or what I did. So now, when I finally don't have anyone giving me a schedule? I improvise. Because I like to."

Improvise. That's the word Emily threw around when she broke up with me. It subsequently makes me feel a bit defensive, so I decide to play devil's advocate again. "What if you can't improvise?"

"Dude, you can always improvise," Rachel argues. "It's not bad to have a plan, but it doesn't mean you *have* to have one."

"But look at Devin," I counter. "He used to improvise. Now he's a goddamn homebody. It's creepy."

"Yes and no," answers Rachel. "Sure, right now he's gonna stay in one spot and do what Aaron tells him to do, but look at him. He's not going to stick around here after his work's done. He wants to travel again and do crazy random shit with crazy random people. I think it's cool that he does that. I mean, I wouldn't personally sneak onto a bus and travel to Louisiana and eat gumbo every day, but I know what it's like to do things on a whim or take offers as they come along. Maybe not having a plan isn't so bad. Society's too scripted sometimes. We shouldn't need so much structure."

"And yet, we're told we need it to survive."

"E-fucking-xactly," she enunciates. "And you should know that more than anyone else."

This assertion throws me off guard. "What do you mean?"

Rachel gives me a look. It's a knowing look, not a pitying one. She expects a lot from me, which is better than expecting little or nothing.

"You were a history student," she states. "What's the core of all of human history? Society building. Constructing civilizations. Everything must have an order and system and story and reason. There have to be laws and government and people telling you what you can and can't do. And I get that. Anarchy isn't fun, either—you can't just do whatever you want. But sometimes, you get too tethered to this idea of having everything in your life make sense or have a point. Look at how you dealt with your break-up with Emily."

"Oh, you have to bring that up again," I whine, though only somewhat seriously. As I've already made clear, it doesn't bother me as much now.

Rachel ignores me and continues with her rant. "My point is, when you build up all this stuff you're expected to do, and it doesn't work, then you feel like you're left with nothing. All you've got is the past, and all the things that were and could've been, but you never stop to think that what happens next doesn't have to be based on anything you've done before. You can start fresh. Move away from history. Learn from it, of course, but don't feel tied down to it. Rules change. So can the way you live your life."

I can't help thinking this, but the way Rachel is talking, all informed and self-aware and even philosophical, energizes me in a good way. She shows off her intellect when I least expect it, and it reminds me that I'm not the only one who can act all deep and poetic when I feel like it. I grin and decide to add my own quip.

"Don't look backwards," I offer as an adage. "Move forward. Onwards."

"Yep." She smiles, and it's beautiful. "Onwards. Like right now, I'm moving onward to finish my beer, and then I want to dance. And you, my dear, are going to dance with me."

"Wait, what?"

"C'mon," she urges, grabbing me by the wrist and trying to pull me off my stool. "Let's go."

"I don't get a say in the matter, do I?"

I leave my unfinished food and drink behind, and I'm dragged toward the stage where the musician's still strumming away. He's playing some song that I'm sure I've heard before, but before I can try to remember its name, Rachel's chugged the rest of her beer and shoved her pint glass onto an already bottle-cluttered table. I notice that some of the guys are already crowded in the space we've just infringed on, which has been cleared off as if they had planned to dance. And dance they do.

"You'd think Kyle would be dancing with that cute guy already, instead of us awkwardly dancing," I observe, deciding to be snarky instead of begging for Rachel to let me go back to the table and not embarrass myself in public.

"He seems a little occupied," she replies, nodding her head toward the bar, where Kyle and his romantic interest seem to get cuddlier and cuddlier with each other. "Now focus on me, asshole, and not your big gay buddy."

There's nothing I can say to get out of this now. Rachel starts to groove to an upbeat song that the guitar guy's warbling onstage. I try to follow along with her, but I feel like all I can do is step and sway from side to side without looking like a complete asshat. Then, before I know it, Rachel twirls me like we're swing dancers, and I start to get dizzy. But it feels good. Being with her feels so good.

Pretty soon, it's all just drinks and dancing, even after the guitarist wraps up for the night and they turn on the stereo to make up for his absence. I buy Rachel several dark ales, and in return, she buys me a Cosmopolitan, which the bartender makes with gusto. Kyle offers to finish the pretty drink for me because he knows I'm going to need a level head to drive back to Pensalado. The guy he's been wooing, whose name is Warren (white collar name for a white collar looking fellow), becomes friendlier and friendlier to me the more alcohol he imbibes.

"Kyle's a good guy," he slurs to me after what appears to be his third shot of tequila. Yep, he and Kyle have moved on to shots. "So you must be a good person, too."

"Thanks for the vote of confidence," I chuckle. That's all I can get out before Kyle hops onto the bar counter and starts singing that good old standard Journey song.

Yeah, it's true. I'm having a good time. I'm even having—holy shit—a lot of fun. Rachel gets giggly when she drinks, and she slumps against me as we dance to slower songs, her face buried in the sleeve of my jacket. Kyle starts pretty much humping Warren next to us on the dance floor, and he winks at me in this adorable drunken way, which just makes me feel that much more special. I have to look a little off-putting to people here. Awkward sometimes, even. But pretty soon, I feel like I just love everyone. I love all the gay men and all their female BFFs and, shockingly, the one or two straight men at the bar.

Fine, I'll say it. This is a good way to spend Valentine's Day, even if I don't technically have a Valentine. I don't care. Life is beautiful right now, and I don't think anyone could screw that up.

[...]

I'm tired from all the dancing, but I feel like I'm floating above the seat when I drive a snoring Kyle and a sleepy Rachel back home. The whole time, she and I keep exchanging glances and giving each other these timid smiles. We don't want to say anything, not because we're exhausted, but because we just don't want to spoil the quiet. That, and we feel like we don't have to talk to each other every given moment, anyway. We don't make much of an effort to practice our eyebrow language via the rearview mirror, either. We just smile at each other.

Devin may have his adventures, but now I have my own story to tell. Me, an awkward college graduate who believed she had little to no purpose in the world only two or three months ago, now appreciating evenings filled with good music and good food and good conversation. I may not have a plan, but I don't feel so stranded anymore. As Rachel and I agreed upon, we're moving forward. We're moving onwards.

I try not to fall asleep behind the wheel of Kyle's car as I crawl up the slopes leading to Pensalado. All I can feel is calm creeping over me as I roll through the gate onto Aaron's property. The cabins are waiting, dim and still. At least, I think they are at first. That's before I see the intruding glow of another vehicle's head-lights.

I'm only temporarily disoriented, swerving just a little bit on the narrow road. As I inch between the guest cabin and the main cabin, I see Devin outside. It seems a bit late for our guests to arrive, no matter what he said previously about having to stay here and wait for them. But sure enough, he's standing patiently by the guest cabin, and I see the statuesque silhouette of a man stride to a blue Prius and fetch some bags.

I park Kyle's car and wake its owner up in the process. He gurgles a little bit as he attempts to get his seatbelt off, and Rachel has to help him while also being still tipsy. As I push myself out into the night air, I notice just how marvelously the man who's staying with us is dressed; specifically, he's wearing a navy blue sports coat with a bright red necktie. It's more than a bit stylish for being out in the wilderness, but I can tell he's confident as shit. He exchanges some words with Devin that I can't hear, and then I see blue wedges emerging from the partially opened door leading to the guest cabin.

"Jamie girl!" Devin crows as he sees me move toward him like a zombie. I'm not looking at him, but I hear him. "Have a good time in Hearnsville? Where's Rachel?"

"Right here," Rachel speaks up from behind me, and I can hear her shoes crunching against the frosted leaves.

But I don't look at her, either. I'm watching the young woman with long, bouncy, artificially red hair who's strolling towards us. I gawk at her as she smiles at Devin before snaking an arm around the well-dressed man's waist. I see her eyes and that smile that I never thought I'd have to see again in my life.

"What."

She turns to look at me, as the lone, yet direct, word tumbles out of my mouth. Shallow breathing tells me that Rachel's next to me now, staring in just as stunned a fashion as I am. It doesn't take a genius to figure out who our guests are, whether or not I've shown her the photos.

Devin gets it, obviously knowing who she is. The man definitely gets it, and he doesn't look happy about it. And the woman we're all ogling, most of all, gets it. She lets her mouth hang open like she's been struck in the back of the head. Her fingers overdramatically flutter toward her bottom lip.

"Jamie?" she asks.

"Jamie?" Rachel repeats.

"Emily," I manage to croak out, not able to take my eyes off her in my shock. "What the fuck."

MARCH

The conversation I have with Devin — which takes place about twenty minutes after that ugly dramatic reveal and dragging a whole bunch of suitcases into the guest cabin — goes a little something like this:

"So, were you going to tell me my ex was staying here, or…?"

"Jamie, I swear to God, I had no idea."

"Seriously? No idea at all?"

"Dude, the guy called me, not her. All I knew was his name and that he had a girlfriend named Emily. It's a common name. How was I supposed to know it was *your* Emily?"

"Wait. She's his girlfriend? Emily's with a dude?"

"Yeah, man. Did you know she was bi?"

"No!"

"Me, neither. So you can't get mad at me for this. Okay?"

"Okay. Fine. I get it."

"…Still don't be mad, please."

"What."

"They're also staying for a month, and that's a fuckton of money we're getting. So..."

"God damn it, Devin!"

"I said don't be mad!"

Emily and her new boyfriend — whose name is, out of all possible names, Leroy — are planning to stay up here for a month. A whole month. It's bad enough to see Emily again, but to have to see her for thirty days in a row? I'm ready to punch Devin in the goddamn mouth for advertising this place now.

I want to be over her. Actually, come to think of it, I *am* over her. And now she's here, like some tumor that I tried to cut out of my brain, but it grew right back. Not only that, but she's with a guy who happens to be a columnist for a super shiny, pretentious fashion magazine. Yes. He writes for a magazine called, "Star Face," in which he gives dating advice.

I ask Kyle if he's read Leroy's articles before. He has, and he admits, a bit sheepishly, that he likes them. I feel betrayed, but I think Kyle feels more betrayed by the fact that Leroy, who supposedly identified as a homosexual for years, is dating a girl. But not just any girl: My ex-girlfriend. Who is staying at the guest cabin in Pensalado. And is currently in a relationship with a guy who may very well have had sex with more men than Kyle ever has.

Not that I know how many men Kyle's had sex with. I've never asked. And obviously, I don't want to ask.

I don't know why they decided to come up here, or what the occasion is for them. Maybe Emily's being as cheesy as she was when I knew her, and they're celebrating their six monthiversary or something stupid like that. But she's here, and it bothers me.

I even toss my photo albums into my bedroom closet not just because I don't want her to see them, but also because I have to put up with glancing at her face now every morning and every night.

I wish I could avoid her, but I can't. Her very presence is annoying. The dismissive laugh and pseudo-cheery, "How are you? I've missed you!" comment that she gave me the night I first saw her were both agitating as all get out. The way she keeps giggling that giggle I was so used to hearing, and actually liked hearing, for four years, now just pisses me off. But she's here, and I have to put up with her and her boyfriend, who, by the way, is a total fucking snot. He even puts down Kyle's cooking one day, talking about how he's making bank and able to eat from the finest restaurants.

"I never go anywhere that has less than two stars in the Michelin ratings," he brags, as he pushes away a plate of some of the best quiche I've ever eaten. "I've even been to three-star restaurants in Japan. They're just to die for. Emmy, I just have to take you to Tokyo."

Oh, God. He calls her, "Emmy." Emily used to hate that nickname. Now she's okay with it?

"Oh, Leroy," she coos, "I like it here. It's so cozy. You have a beautiful property, Devin."

"Don't tell me that," Devin jokes. "Tell my uncle. He built this property from the ground up."

As he speaks in that painfully chipper voice, he keeps looking at me with this mixed expression of, "I am so sorry," and, "Don't blow the best gig we've ever gotten." I am less than amused.

"Oh," Emily breathes. "It's so admirable that your uncle made this all happen. Isn't it wonderful to know someone who's ambitious and works hard for their dreams?"

"Agreed," Leroy replies with a sneer. "You should've seen the scholarship I got for my journalism degree. Top honors, by the way. I had people calling me by the dozens before 'Star Face' snagged me as a columnist."

Oh, my God, I can't take much more of this. I excuse myself so I can escape from the table and get to work outside, and I decide to take out my unbridled rage on a poor piece of wood that's already reached metaphorical rigor mortis. With each strike of the axe, I imagine either Emily's beaming face or Leroy's simpering smirk rising from the splinters. I'm normally not this violent, but I can't even hide in my room now without hearing their voices trilling like lovesick songbirds through the main cabin. It's getting close to unbearable, and they've only been here for a couple of days.

As I hack more at the stump we use as a chopping block rather than the actual log I chose to destroy, I notice that Rachel is a few paces up the nearest hill, taking down loose tree branches with clippers. The way she acts as she works the shears, she must be just as frustrated as I am, too. However, I suddenly feel a shiver scurry down my back when I contemplate the fact that most likely, we actually share the same ire about the same thing.

"Rach!" I call out to her.

She doesn't look away from a limb she's attacking. I trek up the slope toward her, propping my axe on my shoulder.

"Rachel!"

"Hey," she mutters, still clipping.

"So." I lift my shoulders in a casual shrug. "How about this whole set-up, huh?"

"Yeah," she grunts. "How a-fucking-bout it."

A huge chunk of tree drops right on top of my right foot. Thank God it doesn't fall hard enough to hurt. I shake the branch off and sigh, stretching my toes out within the confines of my boot.

"Look," I say, "if you think you hate this situation, please remember that I hate it a whole lot more."

"Does she talk to you?" Rachel abruptly asks.

"Who, Emily?"

"Yeah."

"No." Okay, that's a lie. "Well, sometimes. But not much. She'd rather be with Leroy."

"Right. She's his little Emmy."

"She told me she hated that pet name," I scoff. "When did she change her mind?"

"When did she decide she liked men?"

"I don't know! Love's a great mystery, I guess!"

"So you don't want her here?"

"No! A thousand times no!" I snap. "I'm not interested in a rebound, and I'm sure as fuck not interested in getting back together with her."

"That's not the tune you were singing a couple of months ago."

Wait. Is Rachel accusing me of still being in love with Emily? Why would she think that, after all of the conversations we've had? How much faith does she have in me to move on?

But all I actually respond with is: "Things change."

Her retort is almost equally as terse. "We'll see about that."

I give up right about then and let Rachel work. I don't know why she's so uppity about this. Never once has she implied that she's interested in me, so why would she give a shit about what I thought about Emily? Maybe she doesn't want me to get hurt, but the vibe I'm getting from her is more territorial than concerned. I try not to think about it. It's just too weird.

As I slide back down the slope toward the main cabin, Emily waltzes out and loudly inhales the cool air, sighing dramatically as if she's trying to play the part of a nature woman. She sees me with my axe still resting against my body and decides that it's a good idea to open her big, fat mouth.

"Ooh!" she whistles as I try to pass her. "Looking good, mountain lady! When did you start chopping wood?"

"After you broke up with me," I reply candidly.

Emily makes that pouty face that I had once adored. "Oh, c'mon," she tries to coax, "don't be all unfriendly with me. I never said I didn't want to see you again."

"And I never said I wanted to see you again. Yet, here we are."

"Jamie..."

"Excuse me," I cut her off, shuffling toward the tool shed and doing my best not to angrily swing the axe down into the rotting floor next to the chainsaws.

Once I return to the main cabin, I blatantly shove my way past a doe-eyed Emily and look toward Rachel. She's watching me, all right. Those clippers keep on clipping, but she's observing my every move.

Just my luck. First, I have no women in my life. Now, I have to put up with the emotions and confusion of two of them. This is going to be a fun month.

[...]

So. Couple of things as we transition into March. First of all, I hate Leroy. Like, really hate him. And I don't use that word lightly. He's full of himself, he talks way too much, and he criticizes everything he sees, hears, touches, tastes, or smells. He gives every respectable magazine columnist and love guru a bad name, and he constantly puts down Kyle and Devin's efforts at hospitality. And I swear, if he decides to insult Rachel's singing or guitar playing, I'll choke him with one of his own ties. Which, by the way, he shouldn't be wearing in the middle of nowhere! Who is he trying to impress?

Oh, right. My ex-girlfriend. Fuck my life.

That's another thing: He really does show off being with Emily. It's like as soon as he found out I was here, he was ready to rub in my face just how much better he is and how much happier Emily must be with him compared to when she was with me. Whenever we're at the dinner table, he slings his arm around her shoulder while eating with his free hand, negatively reviewing the meal the whole time. I want to kill Leroy before Kyle gets to him first; I may not have much time, though, seeing how Kyle scrunches up his napkin and forces a smile every time the guy opens his mouth. I'm guessing he's not as big of a fan of his dating advice column anymore.

Okay, so Leroy sucks, but Emily, in all honesty, is more of a pain to deal with, in my humble opinion. I can tolerate her being here, provided that she stays away from me and lets me do my job without probing too much into what's been going on in my life since our relationship ended. But she won't leave me alone. One day, she's asking if I still want to be a teacher, so I tell her I will always be a classified bullshitter, regardless of whether or not I'm officially bullshitting in front of a classroom full of jaded pubescent wannabe rebels. Then she's playing vinyls in the living room of the main cabin, when I just want her to go away and not intrude on the one place where Rachel and I should be left alone after seven o'clock in the evening. Then another time, I'm vacuuming Devin and Kyle's cabin, and she stands at the door the entire time, reminiscing about all the years we spent together and trying to bring up every good memory she apparently has about our relationship.

"Hey, remember when — "

Yes, Emily. I do remember that random moment we spent at the Lair or in the university library. Now would you kindly turn yourself around and fuck off?

Why. Why does she think I want to be reminded of all the "good" memories? I'm done with all that. And no matter how much she tries to get me to smile about the last time we, oh, I don't know, shared a milkshake or had sex in my college dorm, all I have to remember is that every night, she's getting comfortable with good old fashionista Leroy, who's probably, I won't deny it, way better in bed than I'll ever be. Though I don't want to think about it too much. Call it stereotypical, but hetero sex makes me shudder like I got cold water dumped on me.

The worst part of it all, though, is that I'm feeling more and more distance between me and Rachel, which sucks because that's the last thing I want to see happen. This whole time, I want to talk with Rachel and drink wine with her and get away from the fact that my ex and her new man are here, disturbing my little bubble and bringing me back to bad thoughts about myself that I was working really hard to stifle. But whenever I try to talk to

Rachel or invite her to my room to listen to music or just chat, it's always a different excuse. She's tired. She's not feeling well. She's had a rough day. She's just not that talkative right now.

"Rachel, can you stop acting like a stereotypical girl, please, and just tell me what the hell is going on?" I demand one night, two weeks into Emily and Leroy's stay. Which, of course, feels like an entire year.

"Great. Now you think I'm stereotypical." Usually, Rachel would say something like that with a smile and an arched eyebrow. This time, she's not joking. She's looking at me like I'm a maggot-covered piece of meat.

"Well, I'm kind of acting like a guy right now, aren't I? As in a stereotypical guy who can't infer shit from how you're acting. So I just need you to tell me, straight up, what's wrong."

"I'm just feeling kind of lousy, okay?"

"Why?" I push. "Are you sick? Are you angry with me? Are you jealous?"

"Jealous!"

She laughs, but it's not sincere.

"Well?" I press. "Are you?"

"Jamie," she snaps, "the last thing I'd ever be when it comes to Emily is jealous. You think I give a shit about who she is or what she does?"

"I never even brought up Emily," I reply calmly.

Rachel stares at me like I've caught her in some kind of trap. All I can think about is what she told me at the River Bar on Valentine's Day: Onwards. This doesn't feel like we're moving onwards. This feels like we're cars spinning our wheels in the mud.

"Look, let's just chat, okay?" I ask, breaking the tense silence between us. "I need a buddy. I need someone to bitch with."

"Talk to Devin," she offers, as she pushes her shoulder against the doorframe, blocking me from entering her bedroom unless I fight her (and she'd definitely kick my ass). "I'm sure he'll tell you all about Alabama and how he made cheese grits for a family of seven."

"I've heard that story before," I gripe. "Just like all the others he's told."

"Good. He can tell you it again."

Then she slams the door right in my face.

I can't believe it. Rachel is the one person I want in my life right now. Not Emily. Not the girl who gives me all this unwanted attention like she's trying to be friends and make up for four years of head-over-heels romance and act like it's all rainbows and sunshine with me now. I want attention from the girl who currently doesn't want anything to do with me.

I literally have no one to talk to. No one I want to talk to, anyway. I can't talk to Rachel. Kyle's trying to keep busy just like I am, so we don't have to deal with our guests too directly, and we've never been exactly close enough to share our feelings. Plus, he keeps going to Hearnsville to see Warren, who I expect to see at the cabin any day now to have dinner with us, given how much Kyle gushes about his new romance no matter how much Leroy rolls his eyes. And of course, I've never been hugely open with Devin, even in high school, and nowadays, he's definitely more my boss than my friend.

Rachel refuses to socialize with me, not even after another week drags by, and I'm just about ready to bash my own brains out with a rusty shovel. I try to stick to my chores and ignore the

162

public displays of affection that Emily and Leroy partake in while returning from a hike or a walk around the creek. It's not just kissing, either. Leroy looks ready to fuck her right on the grass about half the time I see them making out. Either he's straighter than a line on graph paper, or he is seriously compensating for his repressed feelings for dudes.

I can barely focus on my tasks anymore, since I can't help dwelling on my current predicament. The vacuuming's half-assed. The weeding's inconsistent. The house cleaning's worse. I put whites in with darks while doing laundry and turn one of my favorite shirts from white to pink. Devin nearly screams at me about a table that I barely dusted in the main cabin. I refuse to go into the guest cabin, and he lets that slide, only to harass me about it every day and accuse me of being a baby. I'm kind of sick of Devin acting like a discontented landlord. He needs to stick with what he does best and fly out to Ireland so he can hang out with the drunks and the storytellers and the rugby players. At least he'd have something new to talk about instead of just repeating his old antics like one of the broken records we still keep in the living room.

But I put up with all of it. I'm not going back to the way I was before. I try to think about Rachel, even though I know that trying to talk with her is futile. I hope with all my heart that once Emily and Leroy leave, everything will be back to normal, and Rachel will be over this whole thing, and we can sit together on the couch and she can play guitar and we'll be okay again.

I really cannot tell if Rachel is doing this because she likes me. Normally, she flat out tells me what's on her mind — she doesn't imply it, or hint at it, or expect me to figure it out like I'm a poor man's version of Sherlock Holmes. And maybe that makes me the stupid one.

One more week, is what I tell myself, as I try to ignore another wave and giggle from Emily as I take out the trash. Just hold on for one more week, and then I'm free.

[...]

The final week of Leroy and Emily's stay, at long last, comes around, and sure enough, Kyle announces loudly and proudly that Warren is coming to visit Pensalado. He's like an excited preteen during the three days before his new boyfriend shows up, not to be disturbed by Leroy's callous remarks.

"I sincerely hope that this man is more tolerable than that slob I was with two years ago," he scoffs, winking at Emily as if to remind her that he still loves her. "Quite the looker, but God, he had no taste. His name was Gilbert. At least he had somewhat of a sophisticated name."

"My Warren is super sophisticated," Kyle says cheerfully; his mood will not be crushed. "No one pulls off a collared shirt better than he can."

"I hope so," snorts Leroy. "Gilbert didn't last very long. Last man I dated, actually. I suppose I'm on an Emmy binge now. I can't imagine ever going back."

"Oh, you," Emily titters, pinching his cheek and making me feel sick. I try to imagine this Gilbert guy in Emily's place as they kiss, in order to make myself laugh. I chuckle just loudly enough to receive Leroy's token scowl, so I go back to sweeping the floor, while Kyle sings a song that he just made up about Warren and him.

"Warren and me, oh, Warren and me. We're as happy as two gay men can be!"

"I think that's enough of Kyle the Musical, big boy," I hear Rachel quip, as she walks by us without even looking at me and disappears outside. I don't bother following her out or trying to interact with her. It's not worth the effort right now.

The day of Warren's visit takes way too long to come. Turns out that Kyle really wants to make this work, and I'm going to help him make it work. We clean up the main cabin, and we buy groceries and lots and lots of alcohol. Kyle starts making perhaps one of the most impressive meals he's ever prepared. It's definitely a runner-up to Thanksgiving: Roast beef, double baked potatoes, yams, spring mix salad with a homemade vinaigrette. All matched up with the right wines and the right utensils and the right every-thing. And of course, I'm enlisted to be his apprentice while he makes pecan pie.

"It's Warren's favorite," he explains. "I grilled him about what his favorite foods were, so this should be perfect. Please say it's going to be perfect?"

"It's going to be perfect, Ky," I encourage him, and I crack a smile as he snickers in eager anticipation.

I don't mind helping Kyle out because it gets me away from Emily and Leroy the clown, not to mention it means no more awkward eye contact with Rachel. Devin seems to be conversing with her just fine, and Rachel seems way too over-the-top when speaking with him. She really is trying to avoid me, and I have to focus extra hard on measuring out the pecans so I don't go down the old, "I'm a failure and nobody loves me," road.

Once the cooking and baking's finished, it's getting dark, and Emily and Leroy are nestled in the living room, listening to a jazz CD on the player that Rachel had brought up when she first got here. I really feel like they're infringing on my turf, and like every other time, it takes me so much effort not to say anything. Whenever I walk by with a dust rag, Leroy's eyes shift, and he puckers his lips like he's judging me. Like he's thinking, "How in the world did my Emmy girl stay with that sloppy dyke for so long?"

Finally, I hear a car hum its way into the driveway and then feel my ears ring, as Kyle starts yelping like an excited puppy. He rushes out of the cabin, his arms flailing, and I go to the side door to witness him tackle and smooch a very nicely dressed Warren. Warren, of course, is rosy and cheery, giving his boyfriend an aluminum foil-covered plate before they walk back inside, holding hands.

"You're so thoughtful!" Kyle is chirping to Warren, as I make sure the table's set to his liking. "You didn't have to bring anything!"

"I can't walk onto this gorgeous property without at least bringing my shortbread cookies," Warren replies with a deep chuckle, as he brushes a speck of lint from his waistcoat. "My mom's recipe."

Leroy, Emily, and Warren sit down at the table, and I start bringing over plates loaded with potatoes and yams and salad and juicy roast beef, thinly sliced and well peppered. Warren rubs his hands together in delight, while Rachel walks in and sits down in the chair next to him that's not reserved for Kyle. Devin sits down on her other side, leaving me to awkwardly plop into a chair diagonal from Emily, who watches me with those big brown eyes

166

and that once lovely, but now obnoxious, smile.

"Bon appetit!" Kyle cries, walking back into the dining space and inviting us all to dig in. And we do, but not without having to listen to Leroy's condescending running commentary.

"You know," he says with a mouthful of roast beef and a clear look of contempt on his face, "I once went to a beautiful little restaurant in Los Angeles, where they served beef thick as slabs. But they were tender and marvelously seasoned. Left my mouth watering for more. And the potatoes were so fluffy — just light as air. It was truly like coming home from a long day to my mother's cooking."

"Oh, you mean like the food we're having right now?" I hear myself interject. One warning look from Devin, and I shut up.

"Well, if I may be honest," Warren replies, patting his beard with his napkin, "I think Kyle's roast beef is just divine. Did you use garlic, honey?"

"Sure did," warbles Kyle. "Also some good old-fashioned salt and pepper. Little bit of rosemary, too. I don't like to get too excessive with my seasoning."

"Correct me if I'm wrong," Leroy points out, "but isn't rosemary better suited for chicken?"

No, Leroy. Rosemary goes on everything. Fuck you.

"So!" Emily cuts in, as if she's all too aware of the consequences of Leroy's nasty and tactless critiques of everything around him. "How did you two meet?"

She's referring to Warren and Kyle, obviously, only somehow, I wish she were asking about Rachel and me. Rachel concentrates on her food, but I can see the heat pulsing behind her eyes every time Leroy or Emily decide to speak.

"Well," Kyle tells Emily, "funny story. I was super shy about saying anything to Warren, and I saw him in Hearnsville all the time, always at the River Bar. All we'd do was exchange hellos, and then I'd scurry back to my end of the bar like a scared pup. And who should help me pluck up the courage to talk to him but good old Jamie."

Truthfully, I'm shocked that he brought that up. I swallow my spuds, laugh nervously, and wave at the group of people who are now staring at me for an explanation. "Hi."

"Jamie?" Leroy repeats. "What on Earth did she do?"

"So glad you asked, Leroy, my boy!" Kyle guffaws at his own rhyme. Rachel laughs, too, a bit too forcefully. No one else reacts. "See, it was Valentine's Day, appropriately enough, and Jamie, Rachel, and I went out to Hearnsville to celebrate Wolf Weekend. We got food, and Jamie saw me ogling Warren over here, and she told me to get over my fears and just have a drink with him. And you know what? I never thanked her for it. So I'm thanking her now. Thank you, Jamie, for helping me land this delicious hunk of man who's now sitting next to me."

I can feel my face flush as Kyle, glowing, raises his glass of wine to me. Warren raises his glass, too, and I know he's mentally thanking me without saying it out loud. Emily seems to think that this is all very cute, like a rehearsed display, so she also lifts her glass and cries out, "To Jamie!"

"To Jamie," everyone else echoes, some less enthusiastically than others. I grin awkwardly and drink my wine with a slight grimace.

"See, if it were me, I would have taken the slow, debonair approach," suggests Leroy, even though no one's asked for his opinion. "You ever read, 'Star Face,' Warren? My column's in there every week."

"Oh, I don't read magazines very often," Warren responds with a thin smile. "Especially when it's about romantic advice or something cheesy like that."

"Pity," Leroy scoffs. "I write an advice column for men looking for other men. See, the Debonair Approach is simple. It's all about the body language, keeping a polite but seductive aura to you as you say hello. But your choice of wardrobe helps, too. You seem to have the successful businessman aesthetic down pat, Warren."

Warren grunts, though I can tell that he's been rendered silent by Leroy's unsolicited feedback. He instead attacks his potatoes and salad rather than choosing to stab the man in the eyes with his fork, which I admittedly am tempted to do. However, Leroy is not finished yet. He now turns his attention on Kyle, who averts his eyes to the tablecloth.

"You could learn from your boyfriend, you know," he lectures, his voice turning into a low, patronizing hiss. "The Debonair Approach could work for you, too, if you want to keep your options open. So for future reference, Kyle, shirts and jeans that don't have holes in them and actually fit your figure tend to attract more eyes when you present yourself in public. Especially if you want to avoid the racial stereotypes."

I am just about ready to throw my wine in Leroy's face because of his outright disrespect for the way Kyle is. Leroy has always been bold, but this is the most daring — and certainly the most prejudiced — he's been so far, trying to knock down my friend when the boyfriend he was able to snag is sitting right there. I can see the look of horror seeping onto Warren's face, and he casts a sharp glance at Kyle, whose expression is like rock behind his silverware. No one talks. No one, that is, except for good old Emily, who honestly never knew when to stay quiet.

"Oh, Leroy," she chirrups. "Always looking out for everyone. You know, he's been able to work exclusively with the best dating gurus and fashion designers for men. They take him very seriously."

"I've got people on TV begging for me to come on their shows and give advice," Leroy adds, and I'm waiting for him to puff out his chest like a dominant bird, given how arrogant he is. "I believe that mainstream media ought to address same-sex dating more frequently. Representation is key, you know."

"Maybe they ought to invite people who aren't judgmental, racist fucks!" I hear almost out of nowhere.

Of course, it's got to be Rachel. She's put down her fork, and her food lies abandoned on her plate as she glares at Leroy. Leroy appears startled at first, then angry, then suddenly stern like he's speaking to a child.

"Media, as of now, only enforces stereotypes and cardboard cut-outs of what beautiful men should do to find other beautiful men," he says coolly. "With my writing, I plan on providing more diversity. Not less."

"Bullshit," Rachel spits. "You just completely put down Kyle for being more rugged instead of polished. Hell, you just put him down for his *skin color*. If there's anyone putting gay men into tiny boxes, it's you. With your debonair crap and your stupid wardrobe. It's Pensalado. You don't dress like a fucking car salesman in Pensalado."

"Hey, knock it off," Emily interrupts before Rachel can continue her sudden tirade. "Leroy wasn't asking to argue with you."

"Yeah, well, actions speak louder than words, sweetie," hisses Rachel. "And your boyfriend's actions, as of now, earn him the label of total pompous asshole."

"Can we please stop?" I try to ask, but my voice comes out all thin and quiet.

"You don't have to stand up for me, Emmy," Leroy cuts in. "I know jealousy when I see it."

"Jealousy!" There's that word again. Rachel presses her hands against the table as if she's ready to stand up and challenge Leroy to a duel. "You think for one second that I'd ever be jealous of you? You, a garishly dressed fop who works for an overrated rag?"

"Hey, hey, now! People are eating here! Settle down!" Devin hollers. He's clearly becoming panicked, but his words go unheard.

"My dear," Leroy says in his usual superior tone, "I'm sorry if what I'm trying to do to make a difference in this country doesn't satisfy you, but then again, I guess that's what happens when you're stuck here with no real access to the modern world."

"Would you just shut the fuck up?"

There. I manage to get my voice out loud enough for everyone to shut their traps. All eyes, once again, are on me. Warren keeps eating his meal as he looks at me, his spare hand straying over to Kyle's tense fist and squeezing it as if to calm him down.

"Excuse me?" Leroy finally exclaims, his pupils reduced to dark, angry dots.

I gulp down a wad of mucus-clotted nervousness. "You heard me, Leroy," I rasp. "Shut up, and stop criticizing everyone at this table. You're the guest. We're the hosts. And...and you need to respect us."

I should have expected laughter, because oh, boy, does Leroy laugh. He wraps his arm around Emily's waist as if to directly spite me, his lips dangerously close to her ear. Emily's demeanor, I notice, has entirely changed, and she looks at me with an expression of contempt that is far different than the extraneously cheery glances she's sent my way for the past four or so years. It's like talking back to her beautiful boyfriend, unlike anything else I've done, is the last straw.

"Emmy," Leroy croons with amusement, "tell me again what you saw in this girl."

"Oh, you know," Emily murmurs with a slight sneer, and I realize that she's no longer interested in being nice to me. "She was sweet and all, but nothing like you. She didn't really have... ambition."

I'm ready with my comeback, but my eyes widen as Rachel beats me to the punch. "Jamie sacrificed everything for you!"

"Oh? And how do you know that?"

"She was going to be a teacher for you," Rachel growls, her face tinged with red rage. I want so badly for her to stop talking, but she won't quit. "She gave you four years of her life. She had to deal with bigotry and hate to be with you. She was going to do everything you ever asked her. Because she loved you that much."

"Aw, honey," snickers Emily, "you don't have to defend her! I loved her, honest, but then I realized that it just wasn't right. I need someone with more spirit, more independence. You know, someone who actually has balls."

"Em..." I try to choke out. Whether or not she means the balls thing figuratively or literally or both, it hurts like hell. I can feel the ache starting, twisting its way into my stomach like a metal corkscrew. The anxiety attack is imminent. "You…"

"It's okay, Jamie," she whispers to me, and suddenly, all I can feel is hate for her. "I still like you. But I can't help it if you didn't offer enough for me."

With those words, she verbally slaps me across the face. I can feel the wind rushing out of my body, my tongue trying to form words but failing to do so. Devin has gone totally white, and Leroy is just grinning from ear to ear, like he's proud of Emily for trying to undermine me like I'm a whimpering, pathetic little girl. But that look doesn't last long, because in the next moment, Rachel flies in a shrieking blur towards Emily, her fist aimed straight for her beautifully rouged cheek.

Leroy is quick and blocks the blow with his forearm, and before any of us can say, "Holy shit!" the two of them are fighting. And I really mean fighting, like brawling, only Rachel happens to be a lot tougher than Leroy is. He slaps and claws at her face, sure, but she grabs his wrists and pins him to the table, shaking the surface and sending the salad bowl plummeting to the floor. Then she starts hitting him — really hitting him. Her knuckles leave red, angry welts on Leroy's chin and cheeks, and to both my shock and my hidden delight, he starts bawling like a child who's being bullied for his lunch money.

Emily screeches incoherently and tries to pull the thrashing Rachel off her beautiful, emasculated boyfriend, but I finally get myself to move and wrench my ex-girlfriend away, wincing as she strikes at my face and arms. All that housework and all those lumberjack shenanigans I've partaken in have paid off, after all — she cannot break free from my grip.

"Let me go!" Emily screams into my ear. "You stupid coward,

let me go!"

"Fuck you," I snarl in reply. And damn, it feels good to say that to her.

The next thing I know, Kyle is lifting Rachel, roaring and swinging, off Leroy's flopping frame. Emily finally yanks herself away from me and runs to assist her boyfriend, who's bruised and puffing and sniffling and checking to see that his fabulous green necktie hasn't been ripped. Devin has not moved from his seat the entire time; neither has Warren, though his expression of worry has turned into utmost admiration for his strong and brave Kyle. Also, I wonder if he's appreciating the free soap opera.

"Okay." Leroy is practically chugging down air, his chest rapidly rising and falling against his tailored shirt. "Okay. I'm fine. Okay."

"What the hell is wrong with you?" Emily squeals at Rachel. "You could have killed him!"

"Don't make me laugh," Rachel bites back, trying to break free from Kyle, who's pinned her arms to her sides. "Your precious celebrity boyfriend could be beaten up by a five-year-old. I hardly touched him."

The marks on Leroy's face say otherwise, but I don't dare argue with her. Not in this moment.

"I could get you arrested for this," threatens Emily, or she at least tries to. "I could sue you!"

"Yeah, for what money? Go ahead, take it. I've got nothing. Let me *go*, Kyle!"

"Not a chance, Rach," her restrainer rumbles.

I stare at Emily. The sadness she injected into me has curdled into outright fury and bitterness. Every drop of love I had left for

174

her is gone, like I bled or sweated or cried it all out. She hardly pays any attention to me, though, instead veering on Devin.

"You know," she says, her voice cracking like she and Leroy are the ones who have been wronged, not me or anyone else in the room. "We decided to come here because I considered you a friend, and I wanted to support you. But if this is the way you run this place, then I'm not giving you a penny for our stay."

Devin gapes at her, as if she's just spoken to him in an unknown, foreign language. "You paid upfront," he reminds her.

"You think I'm stupid, Devin?" hisses Emily. "I'm asking for a refund. In full."

"You're joking."

"Or I could just file assault charges on your cousin. You wanna deal with that?"

I can see all the color drain from Devin's face like juice being squeezed out of a browning orange. He doesn't say a word — no retort, no questions, nothing. Instead, he practically flies out of the cabin, and in record time, he returns with what looks like a signed check. We all watch, silently, as he proffers it to Emily, who snatches it out of his hands. The check is promptly ripped into confetti, the shreds settling onto the floor as the remains of her signature become illegible ink blots.

"Leroy, pack our bags," she orders her blue-lipped boyfriend. "We're leaving now."

"Em," Leroy rasps, still trying to get his breath back.

"*Right now!*" Emily bellows, and she storms out of the cabin, slamming the sliding glass door behind her and nearly shattering it.

We don't know what else to do, so we just look on as Leroy

struggles to catch up with Emily, wiping his eyes and trying to shrug off his moment of weakness. None of us return to our food, as our appetites have magically disappeared — except for Warren, who finishes off his roast beef with a flourish as if he's enjoyed both his dinner and his show.

I look at Devin, and his hands are shaking against the table as he tries to keep himself together. I look at Kyle, and his jaw is set like stone. I look at Rachel, and suddenly, I'm just as mad at her as I was at Emily. She just stands there now, still being held captive by Kyle, her mouth drawn into a furious line.

"Devin," I finally say, glowering at Rachel but speaking to him. "I didn't want this to happen."

"It's not your fault, Jamie," Devin replies in a low, harsh voice. It's the kind of tone he takes on when he's trying to stop himself from erupting like a volcano. "But I think my cousin here needs to say something."

Now we're all looking at Rachel. Kyle gingerly releases his hold on her. She brushes herself off and looks like she's trying to stay self-assured and strong against us, but her voice quivers as she talks.

"I was just trying to protect Jamie," she stammers. "I was trying to stand up for her."

"You didn't have to protect me," I mutter through clenched teeth.

"Rach," Devin insists, his voice still buzzing with exasperation. "You're lucky that they didn't call the cops. You could've been thrown in jail. What the fuck were you thinking?"

"Devin, I — "

"And not only that," my friend continues, as if he didn't hear his cousin at all, "we just lost a fifteen hundred dollar gig. Fifteen hundred dollars, Rachel. What the fuck do you propose I tell Uncle Aaron?"

As he demands an answer, we finally hear a car's angry whirr, and the rattling of wheels lurching down the path signifies that Emily and Leroy have left the Pensalado property once and for all. I look outside and peruse the dust cloud that the Prius's tires have left behind in its wake. It hovers there for longer than I anticipated, like an omen. Then, finally, the cloud disintegrates, and the outside settles, even though here in the cabin, everything is still close to a boiling point.

We know we can't fight to get that money back. The best that can happen is that they say no, but the worst that can happen is that they demand more money from us for harassing them and not the other way around. And at this point, it's better to drop it than to have a lawsuit on our hands. Scanning the room, I know that none of my friends want to even try persuading Emily and Leroy to make amends with us. So instead, I decide to be altruistic.

"Devin, I'll go to Hearnsville tomorrow and get you the money," I suggest. "It'll be like two months out of my paycheck."

"Jamie, no," Devin protests. "You didn't..."

"She's my ex-girlfriend, so when you think about it, I'm the cause of all this bullshit, all right?" I snap. "Take the money, or I'll shove it down your fucking throat."

Devin doesn't fight my offer. He just sits down, deflated, at the table. I can only imagine how he feels right now. He's most likely bummed and thinking that he's failed his uncle at a job that I'm not so sure he's as thrilled about having as he used to be. Or he's embarrassed that Warren had to witness all this shit. Or maybe he's disappointed that his own cousin pulled off such a stupid stunt. Or all of the above. Well, I'm not just disappointed with Rachel. Because while Kyle and Warren wordlessly retire to the kitchen to get more wine and a slice of pecan pie, I march out of the cabin and head toward the creek without even asking for a single crumb of dessert.

The rush of the water isn't relaxing anymore. It's loud and torrential, and it shakes me up. I try to skip a pebble across its surface, but the stone just falls into the current and doesn't go very far from there. The sky's getting darker above me, the only real light coming from the cabin windows behind me.

I want to calm down before I go back inside, but I can't seem to tamp down my temper. My anxiety, combined with my anger, is like a Molotov cocktail. If I make one wrong move, I'll blow up. I don't want any of the boys to deal with that; I don't even want Rachel to deal with that. It's tempting to chew her out, to rip into her, to verbally tear her limb from limb. But if I can avoid it, I will. Yet deep down — deep in my roiling gut — I get the sinking feeling that my efforts at keeping a level head will end in futility.

I sit by the creek for a long time before I hear footsteps rustling in the grass behind me. I turn my head, assuming that it's Kyle, asking me to come back to the cabin and be social with his boy-friend. I can feel my jaws lock up when it turns out that it's Rachel.

This isn't going to turn out well.

"Oh," I say. That's it for now. Just, "Oh."

"Oh," she echoes, quietly.

I don't give my feelings away at first. My voice is as frosty as the evening air. "Now you feel like talking to me."

Rachel averts her eyes. "I was just trying to — "

178

So much for staying cool. I immediately lose it. I break like a corroded pipe and just let the deluge happen.

"Just trying to what?" I bark. "Defend my honor? Be my knight in shining armor? Weeks go by, and you don't bother even talking to me. Then you decide I'm not strong enough to take care of my own baggage?"

"I don't think you're — "

"I'm not done!" I interrupt. "I thought that we were really good friends, that maybe you figured I could solve my own problems and you'd be there to support me. Well, guess what? I'm perfectly okay with going back to the way things were between us in October, because you did not act like a friend tonight."

"What the fuck, Jamie?" cries Rachel, her face paling in the dim light. "I was trying to help you! You were letting that bitch run her mouth on you, and I couldn't just sit there and listen!"

"I could have handled it!"

"Jamie!"

"I don't need anyone coming to my rescue!" I shout, rising to my feet and getting only inches away from Rachel's nose. "Okay? I'm not a pussy. I'm not a stupid coward. And I'm not going to let anyone push me around anymore, especially you. I don't want anyone acting like they want to protect me or take care of me or pretend I can't take care of myself because I'm tired of it. I'm done. Got it?"

Well, I've certainly torn her down a bit. Her mouth keeps opening and closing, but nothing comes out. She looks beautiful, even with her now pained expression. I ignore her saddened visage; I can't help it. I laugh as I step away from her, and I feel so heartless. But I'm also completely riled up, and the adrenaline's just surging through me, like a drug or a shot of whisky. I don't stop talking, just like Rachel couldn't stop back at dinner. I just dig myself deeper into the hole I've created for myself.

"You know what?" I throw at her. "This better not have been your way of showing you're in love with me. Because I'm not interested in having a girlfriend who can't deal with her issues like a normal human being."

Wow. Even I'm aware of how harsh those words were. How critical and cruel and reckless my comments really are. But in the heat of the moment, I don't care. I'm not even thinking about Rachel's trauma, or her reasoning for her actions, or her current state of mind. I've done what I've wanted to do, said what I think I've wanted to say. I've shut her up, and I'm now going to go to my room, and I'll sit down and breathe in and out, and she can do whatever she wants. I don't give a shit anymore.

Only the scenario I've cooked up in my head doesn't happen. Not at all. Because as soon as I finish my aggressive spiel, the look that appears on Rachel's face is foreign to me. Like she's suddenly lost something she dearly loved, and it's all crashing down on her.

Wait, no. It's not foreign. I know that look. The way she's trying to keep herself steady. The way she makes little sounds like she's suppressing the urge to cry, even though I can see the water leaking from behind her eyes. It's exactly the look I must have worn on my face as soon as Emily told me that she didn't want to be with me anymore, blurting it out right after graduation when we were supposed to be celebrating. It's the look of heartbreak. I'm all too familiar with that.

"Shit," I breathe. "You're actually in love with me, aren't you, Rachel?"

She doesn't answer. She just makes this horrible noise like she's muffling sorrow and wrath and fear all behind her tongue, and she tears away from me and hurtles toward the main cabin. Billows of dry dirt and dust kick up behind her, and before I can say anything, the front door slams, and she's disappeared from my view.

Once I can finally get my body to react, I try to catch up with her, but she's too fast, racing down the hallway and into her room as I lumber across the hardwood floor. As I scamper to the closed door, I see that Devin, Kyle, and Warren are already right behind me, Kyle still holding a plate of half-eaten pie.

"Rachel." I try the doorknob. It's locked. I bang on the door. "Rachel!"

"What's going on?" Devin demands. "Is she okay?"

"I fucked up, man," I moan. "I really fucked up. Rachel, please, open the door!"

"Leave her," Kyle pleads with me. "Jamie, just leave her alone."

They don't ask what happened. They don't push for details. I keep pounding on the door and calling out Rachel's name, and the guys all go back into the kitchen to finish their dessert and wait for whatever happens next. Time passes, but I refuse to let up, not until the door suddenly swings away from my hyper fist. Rachel, a stuffed bag slung over her shoulder, storms past me and toward the sliding glass door.

"Hey, Rachel, what—" I hear from the other room.

"Fuck off, Devin!" I hear her yell as I bolt after her.

I make it outside just in time to see her walking to her truck. I stumble across the path as I try to stop her. Silently, she throws her bag into the truck's bed and fetches her keys from the pocket of her jeans. I grope for her arm, and she pulls away without looking at me. But I can see the side of her face, and I know that it's wet with tears.

"Rachel, I'm sorry!" I splutter as she pushes herself into the driver's seat. "I'm sorry!"

Then I have to get out of the way. Rachel, her truck rumbling in the night, swerves around me and barrels down the road and into the shadows. No amount of running I do can help, as I try and fail to stop her. I slow to a halt by the gate, out of breath, watching as Rachel disappears down a curve and not moving until I can no longer hear the engine's roar.

For the first time, perhaps, in all the months I've been staying here, I cast my eyes upward and gaze at the brilliant, starry sky. It's more gorgeous than I could have ever possibly imagined. There's no skyglow here. No light pollution. Just vivid constellations and pockets of cosmic dust and an occasional shooting star sailing past the treetops.

What wish can I make now, I wonder? Does it even matter?

Then the sky becomes blurry, and I let my own tears fall.

APRIL

Rachel hasn't returned to Pensalado. I've lost track of how long it's been. I think, so far, it's been about three weeks, but it feels like it's been months. I'm starting to lose focus. I'm starting to emotionally fall apart.

Devin tells me that Rachel's done stuff like this before, mostly when she was younger. He says that when she first got adopted, she fled as far as the next city on foot, and Uncle Aaron found her at a café, eating a sandwich that some sympathetic sap had bought for her. He was able to calm her down and get her to come back home, and apparently, she stopped running away from him after that. It's easy to understand, given her background; she probably gets pretty emotional at times, and the only way she can cope is by escaping rather than fighting. But Devin also acknowledges that Rachel's never been away for this long, ever. Maybe she's taken off for a day, two days, three days tops — never over a week. So that means that the words I said to her and the things I did must sting a lot more than I could have ever possibly imagined.

To make things worse, there's no way to contact her. We try calling her cellphone from our landline, just in case she turned it back on, and get nothing. Devin stops by the Pensalado general store, and nobody knows anything in terms of her whereabouts. Kyle even proposes putting up missing signs in Hearnsville, but Devin says no, that Rachel's an adult and that she has to take care of herself. That doesn't change the fact that she could be hurt, or worse, dead. She could be dead because of me.

And that obviously makes me feel like shit. In fact, I feel like less than shit. I feel like if shit and I were running for President of the United States, then shit would win both the popular vote and the electoral vote by a landslide. All I can think of is that I made Rachel run away. I made things more difficult to deal with at the property. Me. Jamie. The bitchy emo strikes again.

It really doesn't help that she loves me. Of course she loves me. How did I not figure that out earlier? Am I really just like all those other schmucks who can't seem to understand romantic cues? Rachel was clearly unhappy with Emily and wasn't talking to me because she was scared of losing me. I was too stupid to realize that, and now I know that she was doing everything to show me her feelings except outright telling me.

So, yeah. That whole, "I suck," mentality I have now? Totally making me fall into a depression again. I've started to shirk off my chores, so that doesn't make Devin happy. Kyle, on the other hand, is a lot warmer and more open with me these days. I think after I helped him out with Warren, he's starting to finally like me more as a friend rather than just an acquaintance. He notices that I'm regressing back to the nasty habit of staying in my bedroom as soon as I choke down dinner, so almost every night, he comes to see me with a beer and lets me vent to him. He's no Rachel, but he's good company.

"I mean, it's like I fuck up every single time," I complain one night, and I'm getting major déjà vu because I'm fairly certain I've said this before. "I start growing a spine, and it makes me a jerk. I don't have a spine, and it makes me a push-over. I can't seem to find the happy medium. I mean, what's even the point?"

"See, this is why I'm glad I'm gay," Kyle sneers, as he drinks from a glass that he's brought in with the beer. "I don't have to deal with girls like you and Devin do."

I blink. "Honestly, my money's on Devin being ace."

"Can't bet against you. 'Cause I agree."

"So, what?" I say, redirecting the topic away from Devin and back to his missing cousin. "You think Rachel's being stupid?"

"Well, yes and no." Kyle shrugs. "She's stupid in that she thinks running away will solve her problems or make anything better with you. But she's kind of smart in that she thinks running away will keep her distant from you in general. I mean, let's face it. She probably thinks you hate her."

"But I don't."

"But you're mad at her, aren't you?"

"Not really." I let out a big, dramatic sigh. "Not anymore. It's hard to explain, man. I just blew up that night. I mean, Emily did try to verbally castrate me. She even said she needed someone with balls."

Kyle blinks. "But you don't have..."

"I know, I know. Metaphorically speaking," I snap before he can finish his thought. "And then Rachel got into it and tried to stand up for me, and it just pissed me off."

"So." I can tell Kyle is trying to figure all this out, and I can understand why he's feeling a little mixed up. "You're mad that Rachel did that, but you're not actually mad at her in general."

"No. I'm...I'm more mad at myself, honestly."

"Jamie," Kyle probes. "Do you love Rachel?"

I don't have to answer that: He already knows. I set my bottle aside and flop on my back on the bed. Kyle takes that as his cue to leave, and I'm back to staring at the ceiling. I'm not so thirsty anymore. I just feel dead.

[...]

I guess I've become so inert, and the workload's gotten so big, that Kyle's recruited Warren to help out, at least until Rachel hypothetically comes back to Pensalado. I wonder how Warren has the time to come up here because he's got to have a career of some kind to tend to, but once he starts staying in Rachel's room, I learn from Kyle that he quit his job a few weeks earlier and just jumped on the opportunity to be closer to us. He's pretty talkative with me, too, probably just as grateful to me as his boyfriend is.

"I had a pretty shitty data entry job at a credit card company, and it was sapping away my soul. So I thought, why not improvise?" Warren informs me as I watch him wash dishes. God, the word *improvise* strikes again. It will never leave me alone. "You guys seem to be good at this whole outdoorsy thing, and I figured I could be an outdoorsy person, too."

"I'm sure Kyle loves having you here," I comment.

Warren giggles. "Well, Devin's cool with it, as long as we're not sharing a room." He then winks. "Yet."

He is good to have around the property, especially when we're clearing away weeds and dead trees that grow more and more perilous by the day. He knows how to use a chainsaw. He knows how to pull invasive plants out by the roots so they don't grow back. He knows how to properly mop a linoleum floor without leaving greasy streaks all over the place. In short, Warren is practically perfect in every way, and Kyle is one lucky son of a bitch to have him. Yay, successful romantic relationships! Kill me now.

As for me, I've obviously gotten distracted, so one day, when I try splitting the firewood, I miss, and the axe gets really close to separating my toes from the rest of my right foot. As a result, Devin bans me from doing that kind of work, even though he claims it's only temporary. And because of that unilateral decision, I lose my temper and get close to throwing a tantrum.

"I just don't want you to hurt yourself, Jamie!" Devin tries to reason with me after I've defiantly slammed my fist onto the table. I don't feel any pain from it, but then again, nothing seems painful when you're either drunk or angry as hell.

"I'm already hurting, Devin. You don't have to rub it in that I'm useless around here!"

"You weren't useless last month, were you?" he argues. "Or the month before that, or the month before that. But now you're going into major funk mode again, and I don't know what to do about it!"

"You really want to know what to do about it?" I snap. "You really, really want to know what to do about my never-ending depression?"

"Yes! Enlighten me!" Devin snarls.

I stare at him without so much as a shred of fear. Even with his long hair and his returning goatee and his flashing eyes, he doesn't make me nervous with his glare. I've known him too long for that.

"If you want me to stop feeling like I'm a worthless speck of dust," I announce, "you will find a way to get Rachel back here so I can apologize to her."

"Oh." Devin breathes in sharply. He is far from amused by my declaration. "What a novel idea. How are we going to do that, exactly?"

I pause. My fingers twitch as I unfurl them from my palm. "I don't know."

"Of course you don't know! You don't know, I don't know. I can't just track down Rachel. I can't communicate with her through cousin telepathy or some shit like that. I mean, fuck, I hardly saw her in person before she agreed to work with us. What do you want me to do, Jamie? I'm better with a walking stick and a knap-sack than this bullshit! What the fuck do you want me to do?"

The way the anger melts from Devin's face and turns into a look of sheer, stark panic is more than alarming. I've seen my friend upset. I've seen him anxious. I've seen him angry. But I've never, ever seen him desperate. It's like the demeanor of a big, bossy leader that he's put on for so many months now is falling off him like an old, heavy coat, and he's going back to acting like the person he's always been: An impish, ragtag guy who's never been keen on following any sense of structure or order. He doesn't like going by established rules, or to-do lists, or planned out expecta-tions or duties or activities or schedules. But that's his whole life now, and I can tell he's ready to get away from it because to him, this particular adventure should already be over. It should have been over by the end of September, based on his track record.

And the fact that Rachel's now run away and added an extra reason for him to freak out? That definitely doesn't make things any better. But I can't help him. I'm not mad anymore. I don't even feel depressed. I just feel really, really hollow, and I don't know how to handle it.

So I walk up to Devin and shamelessly hug him. My head barely meets his shoulder, but I squeeze him against me like he's a really big, sad teddy bear. He doesn't cry. More than anything else, he's confused as hell.

"Um," he mutters, "as much as I appreciate the random sentiment, this is way awkward, dude."

"Yeah," I mumble back. "It totally is."

I release him from my weird embrace, and we sit down at the dining room table together, just staring at our hands and not saying anything. Warren and Kyle come back inside, arm in arm, their hair tousled from the wind and their clothes speckled with dirt and bark from a long day of work. When they see Devin and me sitting silently across from each other, they don't shy away or ask questions. They just sit down with us, like we're exuding a message of, "Hey, we kind of, sort of need to talk about something. Not sure what we'll say. Just come on over."

So all four of us sit there. And sit there. And sit there. The cabin is still chilly this time of year. April isn't much warmer than the winter months were. There's not as much rain, though — just cloudy skies and rough winds and this sense of impending doom. Whoever said that April is the cruelest month was spot on.

"So." Kyle tries to diffuse the silence and lighten everyone's mood. "Are we going to call this meeting to order or not? 'Cause

Warren and I really want to cuddle before we start making dinner."

"'Cuddle?' Is that your codeword?"

Warren snorts at Devin's sassy question. I, however, get down to brass tacks. "We're trying to figure out how to get Rachel back to Pensalado."

"Hmm." Kyle purses his lips. "Okay. How?"

"That's exactly what I asked her," groans Devin. "But she hasn't given me any ideas."

"I'm working on it, okay?" I retort. "I'm just trying to figure out where she could even be."

"Yeah, sort of throws a wrench into finding her, doesn't it?" Warren asks. "Not knowing where she is?"

"She'd have to be in a place where she feels comfortable," I brainstorm out loud. "With someone she trusts. Some place where no one else can bother her or put her down. I just need to figure out where — "

Oh. My God.

I cut myself off with the sound of my own palm cartoonishly slapping my forehead. How. How could I have not thought of it sooner? Rachel had talked about her refuge before. She had been there for Christmas. She had talked about it after New Year's. And I didn't remember it until now.

"Jamie?" Devin prompts me, arching his eyebrow. "Are you going to share what you're thinking with the class, or are you going to keep freaking me out?"

"Port Lionel!" I cry out. "Rachel is at Port Lionel. She has to be. Where else could she possibly go?"

"Port Lionel?" repeats Warren. "But that's — "

"Three hours from here," I interrupt him. "Little town, with a church, and a pub, and it's pretty, and it's exactly where she would be. It's her safe place. It's a place where she can go and be happy."

"How the hell could she possibly live in Port Lionel?" Kyle demands to know.

"She knows someone there. He's a friend of the family, some-one who'd be willing to let her stay with him. I don't know his name, but he owns the — "

"I know who he is!" Now it's Devin's turn to cut me off, and he bounces up and down in his chair as he talks. "I know who he is. His name's Reggie. I've only met him a couple of times, and that was when I was a kid. But I know Rachel really liked it whenever she and Uncle Aaron visited Port Lionel."

"This Reggie guy's a friend of yours?" Warren is trying to put it all together, desperately attempting to follow along.

"Yeah, a family friend!" Devin answers. "Reg owns the pub that Jamie was talking about, and it has rooms upstairs so he can live right where he works. Rachel could totally be there."

"So you know where he is?"

"Yes! I just said that!" Devin stands up with a loud grunt. "How the fuck did you think of that before I did, Jamie? I swear, it's like you know Rachel better than I do now!"

I crack my knuckles in order to stop myself from saying some-thing close to, "Oh, you have no idea, do you, Devin boy?" Devin gets it and quiets down, right as Kyle reaches toward me and pats me on the shoulder.

"What do you propose we do, Jamie?" he asks. "Go to Port Lionel and find Rachel ourselves?"

"I don't know," I reply. "It might be worth a shot."

"We can head out tomorrow," Kyle decides, suddenly very receptive to the idea that I've just tossed at his feet. "If we can't find her, then at least we can enjoy the trip. Is that cool?"

"Yeah," breathes Devin. "Sure. I gotta go somewhere new, anyway. I'm going insane here."

"Wait, are you guys serious?" I splutter. "I was waiting for you to tell me to shut up."

"Why?"

"Well, I...I just figured you'd think it'd be stupid to try to find her at this point."

"Jamie," Kyle sighs. "You're not the only one who wants Rachel to come back. She's my friend, and c'mon, she's Devin's cousin. I don't mind going on a little journey to find her, and from what you've told me, the chances of her still being in Port Lionel? Probably more likely than we think. So yeah. Let's do a road trip."

"Whatever we're calling it," Devin says curtly, "we're doing it. 'Cause we're awesome. And so is Rachel."

I'm stunned, honestly, so I keep challenging them to see if they're just messing with me. "But what about the property? What about our guests?"

"No guests until next week," replies Devin. "Besides, you don't worry about that. That's Papa Devin's job."

"I can stay here and take care of the cabins while you guys are gone," Warren volunteers. "I figure she's more your friend, anyway, so I don't mind."

"Oh, honey." I can tell that Kyle wants Warren to come, but Warren gives him a quick peck on the lips as if to remind him that he's going to be okay. It's sickeningly sweet, but I know they don't mean to make me feel worse about my botched potential relationship with Rachel.

I excuse myself so I can head back to my room and recollect my thoughts, which are scattered all over the place, and I just can't think straight anymore (not that I could ever think straight, anyway. Har, har, what a totally not lame and overused knee slapper!). I don't know if we really will find Rachel in Port Lionel, and if we do, who's to say that she'll want to come back with us? And how can I assume that she still loves me, or if she ever actually loved me in the first place? No, she did love me, but again, she might not love me anymore. Oh, my God, my brain won't shut up!

There is one thing I can assume, and that's about myself. I can tell because I've covered my photo albums in the closet with an old blanket, and I've never bothered to look at them again. I can tell because I've repeated the same music that Rachel and I used to listen to together on the record player, which I've once again stashed in my room night after night. I can tell because sometimes, I go into Rachel's old bedroom when Warren's out and about, and I look at her guitar in its case propped up against the wall, serving as a small hope that she could come back to the cabins of her own volition. I can tell because I distinctly remember Rachel's face, her hair, her smile, the way she moves and talks and laughs and cries.

She's so clear in my head. She's driving me crazy with both guilt and...well, something else. Not just infatuation. Not just lust. Something more. Something stronger. Something I'm now willing to admit has once again invaded my brain and grown roots there, unwilling to leave.

I am in love with Rachel. And I am absolutely hellbent on finding her and bringing her back to Pensalado.

I take some time trying to wrap my head around Devin and Kyle's willingness to go to Port Lionel with me, even though they gave me more than adequate reasons for it. We get into Kyle's car and wave goodbye to Warren, who waves back while scrubbing a skillet at the same time because he has to remind us of how wonderful he is. The sky is overcast, so the trees along the road block out most of the light, even though it's still early afternoon. Kyle flicks on his headlights and proceeds to drive like a nervous grandmother. My stomach churns like it needs more fuel, despite the waffles that I've managed to keep down, and Devin is already falling asleep in the front seat as we head toward the coast.

On a day like this, there's bound to be fog. It's not horrible, but it swirls around the windows, so I can't even see the ocean beyond the rocky edge of the winding road. Kyle puts on a jazz music station that's bloated with static, but every other radio station is playing Christian rock, and we obviously don't want to put up with that. I wonder if trying to fall asleep will make this drive seem any shorter, but whenever I try to nod off, something wakes me up, or I just can't get my mind to quit racing.

I think about Rachel, and I'm not catching a break. I already start hypothesizing about where she might be if she's not in Port Lionel. I can feel my heartbeat fluctuate every time I go from optimistic to pessimistic back to optimistic, like a tortured light switch. I'm seriously questioning whether or not I'll lose my sanity in the three hours we're going to be on the road.

Speaking of three hours, how long have we been on the road already? An hour has to have passed, right? I look at the clock on the dashboard. Twenty minutes? Fuck you, time!

So, yeah. The whole trip kind of goes on like this. The constant checking of the clock. The attempts at dozing off. The annoyance at the scratchy sound of the radio station we're trying to listen to. Nothing to look at, nothing to really care about beyond the car window. That is, until the fog lifts somewhat, and we see hills rising on our sides, white shops, and houses lined up in rows.

"We're here," Kyle exhales. "We made it."

"Oh, thank God," Devin moans, stirring from his power nap.

Port Lionel is this tiny town on the northwestern coast. Aside from the occasional rainbow flags and pinwheels around the shops, along with the random views of green hills accompanied by the sound of the sea nearby, there's not much else to say about it from a first glance. It's picturesque. It's cute. It feels...safe. Yeah, that's a good word for it.

Now I understand why Rachel likes it so much here. It's so close to nature, but it's also perfectly disconnected from civilization at large. I feel like I could spend an entire summer in Port Lionel, taking walks along the shore or eating at the local restaurants, or even running a little bakery on the street corner, and not realize how much time I've spent there until the leaves start changing color. Why run a bakery? I don't know. I like to think about random, "What if," scenarios.

We park by an abandoned church, which must be the one Rachel told me about. But as far as I can tell, as I step out of the car, there's no Rachel to be found. I don't even see her truck. I can tell that Devin's hungry after his nap because all he does is cuss and complain as he hobbles out of the passenger's seat. Obviously, we have no choice but to take him out for a burger.

"The pub," I remind them. "Let's go there."

"Do you even know the name of it?" asks Kyle.

"I do," Devin wheezes. "Flannery's. C'mon, my stomach's threatening to eat itself."

"Devin, you ate waffles before we left."

"Don't fucking argue with me, Ky!"

"Yeah, don't argue with a hungry Devin, Kyle."

We walk down the road even though there's no sidewalk, and trucks and vans breeze past us with surfboards precariously perched on their roofs. No matter what the season, everyone's eager to surf or boogie board or try out whatever other methods of putting their lives in danger they can think of while floating aimlessly on waves of the Pacific. I'm almost tempted to go down to the shore myself, just to see if Rachel is walking beside the water. But with Devin behaving like this, I'll never be able to get away with a suggestion like that without cramming food down his gullet first.

Again, as I walk through the town, I recognize that Port Lionel is really pretty. The stores are nice, and the little cafés we pass are quaint enough, and the whole area just seems tranquil and friendly. Kind of like an old friend welcoming you back to your hometown and then paying for your meal at your favorite restaurant, no questions asked.

We find Flannery's on the very end of what I can only guess is considered the downtown area, and it's open for sure. It's a split-level building, but the pub's what we get to step into first thing. Downstairs are the bathrooms, so say the signs, and upstairs must be where Reggie lives. Of course, I don't know what Reggie looks like, but I can imagine we'll see him sooner rather than later.

Devin, Kyle, and I all look around at the tables and stools, but still, we don't see Rachel. We head toward the bar, and there's a bartender in all his gray-haired, stubbly, middle-aged glory, mixing a drink in a dented cocktail shaker. I figure out pretty quickly that this is the guy who has most likely housed Rachel over the past couple of weeks.

"Hey, Reg," Devin greets him as he plops down on a stool. "Porter and a cheeseburger, please. Medium rare. How've you been?"

Reggie stops making the drink and takes a long, hard, watery look at the young man sitting in front of him. He blinks twice, slowly, before a huge smile seeps across his scruffy face. Then he vigorously seizes Devin's hand and starts shaking it, and I eagerly wish that my friend's body would flop around like a shaggy rag doll. It doesn't happen, but one can only hope for that kind of free entertainment.

"Devin, my boy!" crows Reggie, his voice rising in an almost stereotypical lilt. For a guy who runs a place called Flannery's, he's sure turned the Irish pep and demeanor into an art form. "Why, I haven't seen you in years! How are you? How's Aaron?"

"Uh-uh-uh." Devin wags a finger at him. "I asked how you were first."

"Oh, I'm old and tired, Devin. As usual. But really, how've you been?"

"Busy," my friend confesses. "Busy with all kinds of stuff. Traveling, but now Uncle Aaron's trying to turn me into a homebody. Pensalado property's good. I'm guessing you've heard all about it."

"Oh, good for you. Glad that you're taking care of it. I sure hope the guests still come."

"Oh, they do. Sporadically."

I clear my throat anxiously and claw at Devin's arm like I'm an hyperactive cat.

"Oh." Devin sighs and rolls his eyes at me. "Right. We're also looking for somebody kind of important right now."

"Well," chuckles Reggie, "I've seen a whole lot of kind of important somebodies in my life. Who's the somebody?"

"Rachel," I cut in before either of the boys can answer. "Devin's cousin. She was at your place for Christmas."

There's a silence around the bar as Reggie peruses me. And I mean that he seriously looks me up and down with these penetrating blue eyes, like he's analyzing every last detail of my clothes and hair and face, as if I have something to hide or some secret hidden motive. I try to look away, but there aren't a whole lot of other people to spy at, and anyway, they're just chewing away at their food and minding their own business.

"I'm certainly very close to Rachel, and indeed, she was here with me for the good old Yuletide," the man reminisces as soon as he's done inspecting me. "Like the daughter I never had. And you, little missy, must be Jamie."

I freeze. "How much has she told you?"

"A lot."

"Everything?"

"Just a lot."

"Where is she?" I demand, simultaneously excited and panicked.

But Reggie shakes his head. "Gone."

The word hits me like a fist colliding with my gut. I feel winded and bewildered. "What do you mean, 'gone?'"

Reggie looks at me like he's trying to comfort a child who's lost a toy. "I mean just that: Gone. She's not here anymore. Well, she was here, but she's taken off."

Well, that just kills me. I crash onto a stool right next to Devin, who I can tell is getting pretty impatient for that cheeseburger.

"When did she leave?" I ask.

"Well, that's just the thing." Reggie suddenly appears more curious than judgmental. "Because you have some rather odd timing."

I feel my eyes widen. "What do you mean?"

"Well, I mean, she only just left an hour or so ago. After she stayed with me for a few weeks."

"Are you fucking — *what?*" Kyle suddenly booms, which gets the attention of every other patron.

"Watch your language, my boy!" urges Reggie, waving his hand urgently in front of his face. "And look, I can't claim responsibility for her actions. What with the fog and how much wine she's got in her system, I kept telling her to stick around, wait for another night until it got clearer out. But she wouldn't hear of it."

"Well, where did she go?"

Reggie looks at the three of us apologetically. Devin is pale, but most likely because his insatiable appetite is slowly murdering him. "Trust me, if I had known this sooner, I would've told you to stay where you were and not bother coming down here. She said she had to get back to Pensalado, after all the things she vented to me about."

Devin takes this opportunity to start repeatedly slamming his head into the counter in front of him. Kyle yanks on his sleeve to get him to stop. While some of the customers are trying to ignore us, others are watching our exchange with a look of confusion or bemusement. Or both. Both is good.

"So, you did house her," I conclude.

"The whole time, and gladly," Reggie seems to boast. "Poor girl needed it. Mighty torn up about you, my dear. Can't say I can divulge much of what she told me — privacy is privacy. I let her stay upstairs, so long as she helped out in the kitchen once in a while. I kept waiting for her to set herself straight and go back to where she belonged."

"She stayed with you this whole time," Devin protests, "this whole fu — sorry, *freaking* time, and you didn't bother to call me and let me know where she was?"

"Oh, come on now, Devin," Reggie objects, "how was I supposed to call you? I don't have your number, and Rachel sure wasn't planning on giving it to me, knowing her."

I want to question him further on that, but more and more, I begin to trust him. He has to be telling the truth, given his candor. Reggie finally finishes putting together that drink from earlier and passes it to a very patient older patron sitting warily beside us.

"So," he says as he now pours the Porter for Devin, "I suppose you came down here to see if you could find her. Guess you care a lot more about her than she thinks you do, kiddo. Because she sure cares a hell of a lot about you."

Okay, now I feel my anxiety revving up like a car engine. After chugging down the Porter like a greedy bastard, Devin still wants that cheeseburger, but I tug on his shirt and scream at him that we have to go, we have to go *now*, even though at the same time, I'm wishing that Reggie could tell me more about Rachel and what she said, even though he won't reveal much at all. My brain's about to explode, and I promise to buy Devin all the cheeseburgers he wants in Hearnsville just so I can drag him away from the bar. Reggie waves us off, snickering, most likely about the fact that the three of us wound up here on an epic search for our friend only to head out about a half hour later.

"Well," Kyle grumbles as we sidle back into the car. "That was fucking productive."

"Yeah," Devin whines. "Like we could have known that Rachel would be going back to Pensalado today, right now."

"I know. That's what I mean. It's like the universe is fucking with us right now."

"How do you think I feel? We drive three hours here to find Rachel, only to talk to an old family friend of mine for, like, two minutes, learn that we basically came here for nothing, and now I can't even have my delicious cheeseburger..."

I don't listen to either of them. It's getting darker by the minute, and the fog is getting thick. Way too thick. Which means most likely on the way back up to Pensalado, the road will be covered in white. Rachel is, at this moment, driving a big truck in that fog, most likely at least somewhat intoxicated, because Reggie didn't stop her. Because I had to be a stupid douchebag and—

"Jamie." Leave it to Devin to snap me out of my own mental rambling. "Stop it. We can literally hear you thinking back there."

"No, you can't."

"Yes, we can."

I sigh. I have no patience for Devin's snark. "Literally, as opposed to figuratively, means..."

"You're supposed to be a history teacher, not an English teacher! Shut up!"

Not the first time I've been called out for being pedantic. Last time, it was Rachel, and recently, too. Funny how that worked out.

We start driving back the way we came, the crests of the cliffs that lead to the shore appearing closer to us in the mist. It's a good thing that on the way home, we can press up against a slope or a hill or some sort of solid landmass, so we don't have to worry about falling into the ocean. No, all we have to worry about now is knocking someone else's car into the cold, watery abyss below. We don't play music because Kyle's concentrating on the road, and I swear, we go ten miles an hour at some points, the three hours typically needed for this drive turning into a far, far longer trip than it ever should have been.

The whole time, I'm thinking about Rachel. Was Reggie right about her leaving only an hour ago? Does that mean she's still driving, and we just can't catch up? Will she even make it back to the property? Will she pull over if it gets too dark or too foggy? Can she even access the gate? Devin locked the gate, right? What about getting into the cabins? Does she still have the key that I distinctly remember her having back in October, when I tried to stab her with a poker? Why can't my brain shut up with all these theories? Shut up, brain. Shut up. Shut up!

I am this close to suggesting that I be institutionalized, as we disappear back into the woodier areas surrounding Pensalado. My right foot keeps jerking around as I cross and uncross my legs, much to the irritation of Devin, who's sitting directly in front of me and has to deal with my shoe occasionally burying itself into the spot where his back meets his seat. I curl and uncurl my fingers just to hear the joints pop repeatedly into place and out of place and back into place. I even have to fight the urge to start biting my nails because it would at least give me something else to pay attention to. The fog is so dense that it's soaking the windows of the car like rain. I don't know how much farther we can go without pulling over and waiting for things to clear up.

"We'll be fine," Kyle keeps reciting, mostly to himself, as he fidgets around with his high beams. "We'll be fine. We'll be fine, we'll be fine, we'll be fine, we'll be fine."

"*Stop!*" Devin suddenly shouts.

Kyle shrieks and brakes, hard. We skid along the narrow road, the trees looming above us, the base of their trunks being the only things we can see on both our left and our right sides. Luckily, Kyle doesn't lose control of the car, and we manage to settle on the edge of the road, the fog dampening everything as we try to collect our breath.

Kyle's fingers are rigid against the steering wheel. His knuckles are gray, but red is creeping into his dark face. "What the fuck, Devin? You could've killed us! I thought that— "

I shush him, managing to reach his shoulder and squeezing it in an effort to calm him down. Devin is frozen in his seat. He doesn't say anything at first. All he does is point.

"Look," he manages to squeak out.

I recognize what he sees immediately. It's hard to view anything past two feet ahead of us, but it's there, and it's obvious. The bulk. The color. The dents in the back bumper. Its lights are still on. Its emergency blinkers are flashing. On and off, over and over.

We've found Rachel's truck.

I rip my seatbelt off and wrench myself out of Kyle's car, staggering toward the vehicle. One look into the driver's side sends my heart plummeting into my diaphragm. No one's in there; the thing's been abandoned. I look at the ignition, and there are the keys, dangling from their tiny designated slot. The engine's off, but the keys are still there. I could drive this truck away if I wanted to, but I don't. I want to find her first.

Bounding across the asphalt, I ignore Devin and Kyle's yells for me to come back, as they also get out of the car. Hovering on the jagged edge leading to the hills below, I cup my hands over my mouth and call out Rachel's name, as loudly and for as long of a time as I can, my voice turning into a muffled echo within the fog once I run out of breath. The sound subsides, and I hear nothing in return except for the reverberation of another car in the distance, driving away from us. I cough loudly, steady myself, and holler again.

"*Rachel!*"

"Jamie, for God's sake!" Kyle calls to me, but I don't see him giving me any other, let alone better, ideas. He just stands away from me, his arms outstretched, but he doesn't try to pull me back.

I cough again, forcing air back into my lungs. Silence. I crane my neck, trying to see through the mist. Silence. I put a hand to my ear theatrically. Still silence. Then, a moan.

"Help...help me..."

Kyle yelps in surprise as I leap off the road and slide to the soggy ground below. It's not a very steep slope, and the jump's not dangerous, but my legs still shake and wobble as I make my landing on matted sheets of leaves. I struggle to keep upright and not slip, refusing to tumble into what must be the creek below. The trees rise up to meet me as I maneuver sideways down the hill, solid wooden checkpoints for me to brace my back or shoulder against in case I need to readjust my balance. I near a particular dip in the earth and stop in my tracks.

There's Rachel, all right, still weakly calling for someone to help her. She's curled up in the fetal position against a stump. She's covered in dirt, and leaves are caught in her hair. She clutches her right ankle with a whitening hand. But she's alive.

I hear thumping from behind me, and I turn to see Kyle charging down the slope like a furious black bull. We both kneel beside Rachel, but she doesn't say anything. She just looks up wide-eyed at us, like we're ghosts coming back to haunt her because she had the sheer audacity to run away. I don't speak; I don't want to. I just take one arm while Kyle takes the other, and we pull Rachel to her feet, drape her against our shoulders, and make the long, arduous uphill trek back to the car.

"It's okay, sweetie," Kyle says, filling the void when I can't do it myself. He seems to be directing his words to all of us, not just Rachel. "It's okay. We got you. We've got you. It's okay."

Rachel nods, but her limp gets worse and worse the higher we hike up the incline. She presses her body into mine to maintain her balance, and just receiving that physical contact sends oxygen back into my chest. I can breathe again. I can *think* again.

Above, Devin waits for us, his knees bent as he stands on the edge of the road, his serious expression visible even in the fog. First, he hoists me back up onto the pavement, since it'd be a bitch for me to climb on my own, given the noticeable gap between the earth's ridge and the manmade street. Then, he and I very carefully lift up Rachel, trying not to disturb her obviously injured leg. Kyle is last, and he doesn't need much help; he just grabs my open hand and uses it like the rung of a ladder, propelling himself up to meet us. I let Rachel fall against me again, still limping, as we head toward her truck. I feebly nod to Devin and Kyle.

"Dude." They both look more than concerned. "Can you drive that thing?"

"I'll be careful," I promise. "You two stay right behind us, just in case."

And they do, all the way back up to Pensalado. We're like tortoises bumbling up the road, but we don't care. It's awkward to drive the truck, and I feel like I'm suspended hundreds of feet above the ground. It doesn't help that I can barely see anything beyond the windshield. But I keep my foot steady on the rubbery pedal and my hands taut against the gigantic steering wheel, and I focus on what's ahead of me and not on the shivering, mumbling Rachel in the passenger's seat. I don't try to comprehend her words, instead listening for the ragged drone of a car engine behind me, making sure that our friends have our backs in case this little romp through the crazy weather goes directly to Hell.

I don't know if Rachel is sick, or hungry, or dehydrated, or maybe even delirious. I don't know how long she was lying on that hill, or how she even wound up there instead of in her truck. I don't know if she's still drunk, or if her ankle is really screwed up. I don't know what else I can do for her besides just keeping on driving. So that's what I do. I keep on driving.

All I know is that the fog finally begins to dissolve, as I climb higher and higher up the hill, until it all evens out, and that familiar gray gate waits for me to open it. Its metal grin leads me back to Aaron's property and into the safety of an empty cabin.

[...]

Kyle carries Rachel into her old bedroom, and he asks both Devin and me to stay in the hallway. When we're told to come in, Rachel is already in her bed, and our buddy, with a look that only reads, "Well, I wasn't going to let either of you strip her down, Mister Cousin and Miss Lesbian," carries her muddy clothes into the laundry room.

Devin doesn't stick around for much longer, instead only pausing to stroke the back of his cousin's hand before sauntering into the kitchen. Most likely, he's finally getting himself something to eat, and he's probably cursing the fact that we don't have anything in the cabin to make a proper cheeseburger with.

I don't know what time it is. I don't bother to check. I only go out of the bedroom once to grab a chair, which I drag over to Rachel's side so I can sit down where I can see her. She's already starting to drift off, and so am I. The drama of the day is weighing on me, and all I can think of doing now, besides worrying about the girl who means so much more to me than I ever thought possible, is falling into a deep, deep sleep.

There's a bad crick in my neck and a pain in the middle of my back when I wake up the next morning, still propped against that chair. My right shoulder feels slightly dislocated, though stretching it out makes it feel better, and my left foot's gone numb against the rug. I try to rub the tiredness out of my eyes, only to discover that Rachel's awake, and she's looking at me. I nearly swallow my own tongue, that's how I startled I am. She seems to notice, allowing a small smile to just barely crack open her lips. After all the shit we've exchanged with each other, she still seems to be amused by something about me.

I can't help it, but I move my eyebrows as if to say, "Thank

God you're awake." She doesn't respond in kind, her smile never wavering. I think she's too exhausted for our usual communication game. I get it, and I don't push her.

"You're okay," she whispers instead.

"Yeah," I get myself to croak out. "Are you?"

"I don't know." She winces as she tries to re-position herself under the blankets. "My ankle hurts like a bitch. What time is it?"

"I haven't checked. Sorry."

"No." Her head falls back down against the pillow. Her hair is pretty tangled after sleeping, and Kyle's attempts to get all the leaves out of the snags hasn't helped it much, either. "Don't be. *I'm sorry.*"

"For what?"

"For driving drunk. For putting myself in danger." She doesn't look at me now as she talks. She stares at the wall instead. "For running away."

I listen for Devin or Kyle, but they must still be in their cabin. Warren was kind enough to sleep on the couch after losing his bedroom to Rachel, so I'm sure he's either in the kitchen or still in the living room. I have no idea how early or late it is, and frankly, I don't really care. All I know is that after weeks of being away, Rachel is here, concentrating on the divots in the ceiling, not looking at me. I do my best not to get upset or angry, even though, once again, it's difficult to keep my cool.

"Well." I try to be sardonic instead. "I figured what I said was pretty stupid, but did it really piss you off so much that you had to bail like that?"

"Please don't."

"Rachel," I plead. "I was a shithead. I didn't mean what I said, and I didn't say what I meant. It's just that…so much crazy what-the-fuckery happened, and I felt like no one was on my side. I was trying to be a girl who, well, has balls."

"Oh, God, no, thanks. You don't want those."

"You know what I mean," I groan. "I wanted to be independent, you know? Someone who doesn't need to rely on anyone to stand up for her or…"

"You know that's not why I left."

"You're right," I admit. "I do know that."

We sit in silence for a while. I first take the tension as a bad sign. Obviously, we're both pretty shaken. I've been dealing with worrying about Rachel, and Rachel, well, she spent some time on the ground with a fucked-up ankle, probably wondering if she was going to die. But as Rachel noisily moves her tongue around in her mouth as if to moisten it so she can talk properly, I realize that my heart is pounding. I really did worry that I had lost her, but now she's back. And maybe, just maybe, I can stop being a brat and say the things I've wanted to say for a very long time now.

"Rachel, I—"

"I'm sorry," she cuts in, ending my dramatic speech before I've even started it. "I'm so sorry. I didn't want to stay away for so long. I hurt you and Devin and Kyle by running away. And it doesn't help that I fucked up the gig with that asshole and that bitch."

"Best word to use for my ex, though," I point out. "I'll give you credit for that."

I guess this is not the right time to be snarky. I've missed the humor from our conversations, but I know that until Rachel's told me her story, the friendly jabbing is going to have to wait.

"When I took off that night, all I could think about was how messed up I felt," she begins. "Just how ridiculous I was to ever... well, do the things I did or think the things I thought. I needed to clear my head. I needed my safe place. So I kept driving."

"You went to Port Lionel."

Rachel snorts, startled. "You remember," she says.

I decide not to tell her how long it took me to recall that information, instead replying with, "Of course I did."

"Reggie was closing up shop by the time I pulled up," she explains. "He was pretty disoriented by my arrival, too. I don't think he was expecting a grown woman to fall into his arms, bawling like a baby. But he took me in and let me stay for as long as I needed. So I stayed. I stayed for a really long time."

"Well, if you needed it..."

"I didn't, Jamie. I was just being stubborn." Rachel's hand strays from the covers to rub the back of her neck. "I was so focused on staying away from you. I mean, I was so angry and scared and just...well, to use a big grown-up word that Reggie likes to throw around, I guess you could say I was being pretty fucking juvenile."

"That is a good word."

"Isn't it? Yeah, but I thought if I went back, you'd never want to talk to me again. I didn't think you even liked me anymore." She pauses and presses her lips together. "Actually, no. I thought you hated me."

"What?" I'm shocked. "*Hate* you? I could never hate you! I thought *you* hated *my* guts!"

"What are you talking about?"

"I mean when Emily was here! And Leroy!" I exclaim. "You didn't want anything to do with me! Hell, I thought you'd never want to talk to me again!"

"Yeah, well, I was jealous!"

"But you said you weren't jealous!" I know she was jealous. I'm just prodding at her now.

"C'mon, man, I was lying! Couldn't you tell? I was jealous, and I thought that maybe, just maybe, you still had feelings for Emily. There. I'll say it."

It's a defensive confession, but it's still a confession. And yet, I don't let up.

"But there was nothing between us anymore!" I can't help snapping. "I didn't even want to look at her! You saw that! I mean, you had to have noticed that! I even told you I didn't like her, point blank!"

"Yeah, well, jealousy isn't exactly rational, is it?"

Damn it. She keeps putting me in my place. Rachel's back, all right, with a vengeance. And it doesn't set me on edge anymore. It calms me down, helps me breathe a little better. Looking at her now, I know that, no matter how dramatic her story is or how emotional she sounds or looks, I am just so happy to have her here, talking to me. Opening up to me. Appreciating me. Maybe more than appreciating me, or at least, I hope that's still the case.

"Anyway." Rachel lets out an airy laugh. "Finally, I decided to stop being such a bitch after drinking a few glasses of wine, and I told Reg that I was leaving. I went upstairs, and I got my bag, and I just headed out the door. Reggie tried to stop me. Obviously, I had had too much to drink, and I really could have hurt someone on the road. I was so stupid. But all I wanted to do was go back and see Devin and Kyle and you again."

"Mostly me?"

"Shut up, I'm not done," she grumbles, and I can't help chuckling. "It was foggy as all get out, and I was driving my huge-ass truck back up the road to Pensalado, when lo and behold, I got scared. So I got out and I went around to get...fuck, I don't remember what. I was really tipsy, so who knows what I was looking for. A flashlight or water or rations or a shotgun or something like that."

"You have a shotgun?"

"No." Rachel presses two fingers to her forehead in exasperation. "Don't get distracted. I'm stumbling around, trying to find the bed on my own truck, and sure enough, I lose my balance, and I slip off the fucking road. I can't believe it, but I just drop. I roll down that slope like a goddamn bowling ball. And I crash into this tree, and my ankle's all messed up, and I cannot, for the life of me, get myself back on my feet. It was like I was paralyzed. I really thought no one was going to find me."

My throat is tightening as I listen to this. I'm no visual artist or cinematic genius, but I can picture the very scene she's reciting to me. Her screaming as she loses her footing on the edge of the road. The crackle of the leaves and branches as her body topples down the hill. A horrid moan issuing from her mouth as she lies limply against the thing that may have saved her from falling further down. I try to snap myself out of it, but I clench my jaw, bite the inside of my lip, and try not to let the anxiety take over. I'm certainly not emotional enough to cry right now, like I'm normally quick to do, but I'm disoriented and just wishing I could throw my arms around Rachel already and pull her to my chest.

"And, yeah." She's wrapping up now, struggling to find the right words. "I don't know how long I was down there. An hour. Two hours. Felt like decades. And I kept calling for help. So when

I heard your voice...God, when I heard you calling me...it didn't matter how drunk I was or how much pain I was in. I had to call back to you. And..."

"And then I found you."

"Yeah." Rachel lifts her head and gives me another cute smile. "You had to be all heroic and come to my rescue."

She's right; I did come to her rescue. I was the most stubborn-headed out of the three of us — me, Devin, Kyle — when it came to actually going out and finding her. I was the one who got out of the car and called for her. Doesn't change the fact that I'm one whiny, over-the-top twenty-something, but it's certainly a change from the usual roles I've played earlier in my life.

Talk about moving forward and flipping the bird to the past, huh?

"Rachel," I whisper. "If I had known...if I hadn't been so clueless..."

"The most clueless," she corrects me.

"Yeah, whatever. If I had been smart enough to just think about how you felt, I wouldn't have said those stupid things. You believe me, right?"

"I do," Rachel murmurs, "Mostly because you are so easy to read when it comes to how you feel about people. I swear to God, you're like an open book."

I grin. "I'm that obvious, aren't I?"

"Jamie, I've been waiting for you to make a move on me for months. I mean, *months*."

"Hey, after four years of bullshit, you can't have expected me to just go running to someone else. I wasn't asking for a rebound."

"Yeah, but I'm not Emily, am I?"

"No. Thank God you're not. You're so much better."

"Thanks," Rachel remarks with a smirk. "Well, if it makes you feel any less guilty, I was willing to wait for you as long as you needed."

"Really? You, of all people, were being patient?"

"Yeah." Her eyes suddenly appear wet. "You're worth the wait."

We stare at each other quietly after that. It's like all the confusion, and all the guilt, and all the anger, and all the insanity have finally melted away. I imagine that a record is playing. In my mind, Rachel's playing her guitar. She's singing. She's screaming in the rain after we've chopped up a dead tree. She's hugging me. We're laughing. We're dancing at the River Bar. We're drinking Riesling. We're having a good conversation. We're loving each other. We've loved each other for so much longer than I first thought.

In the next moment, I lean forward and kiss her. It comes naturally, like walking or talking or breathing. Her cold lips feel so good against my hot ones, and I pull away from her, staring at her in a daze, watching as her eyes glaze over and she gazes right back at me with her mouth trembling as she props herself up on the bed.

I smile. She laughs. Then she turns back into the Rachel I know and adore so much, sneering and wagging a finger at me. Her eyes are lit with hazel fire.

"Next time we do that," she teases, "you better not be so subdued. I want tongue eventually, okay?"

I raise an eyebrow. "How about now?"

Rachel grins mischievously, wordlessly inviting me to go in for a second kiss, and this time, I don't hold anything back. Neither does she. We kiss until we need to come back up for air. We kiss until my throat goes dry and my jaw gets sore. We kiss until we feel like we've gotten everything we need from each other — at least, everything we need for now. And I give her all the tongue that she could ever ask for.

Then, after we finally pull away, we collapse into giggles, and I squeeze her hand. She reaches over and caresses my shoulder. We don't have to say anything else right now. It'd just kill the mood.

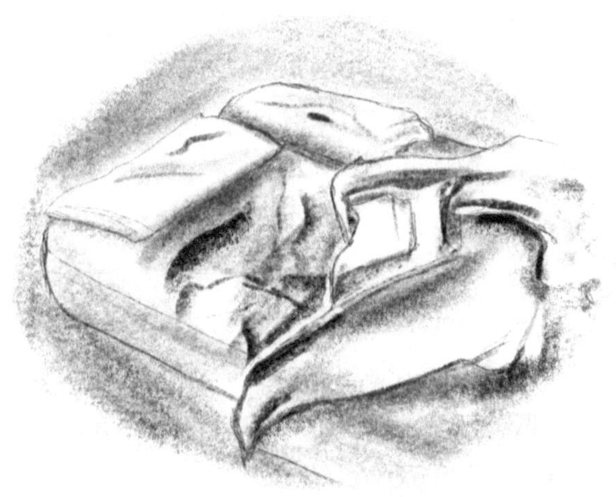

MAY

I'm in love. I'm in love, I'm in love, I'm in love, I'm in love. And I love being in love.

And no, this isn't Emily love. This isn't high school love. This isn't flashy college romance mixed with artificial commitment love. This isn't love that relies on a promise to do whatever the other person says you ought to do. No, this is healthy love. Nutritious and delicious love. Part of a balanced breakfast love. And there's nothing quite like falling in real love after four years of trial and error.

We don't tell Devin and Kyle about us for a while. We decide that we don't really need to. They're smart guys; they'll figure it out. And right now, they're doubling down on the workload with Warren, since Rachel's still got a sprained ankle and can't exactly do stuff like logging or weeding. By the way, yes, Warren and Kyle are now sharing a room. Devin sleeps on that hideous black and white couch in the main cabin whenever he's scared that they're going to have loud sex.

"We better not be too noisy, huh, babe?" Rachel whispers into my ear, as Devin comes into the kitchen for breakfast after another night spent in the living room.

"Shut up," I hiss, laughing as I try making an egg in the basket just as perfectly as Kyle does it.

The good news is, when we do it, we're not too loud. I do get excited, though. It's been a while, okay?

When May finally comes around, the weather's still delightfully cool, and I help Rachel explore the property again by being her support as she limps around. We display small gestures of affection, like holding hands or hugging or rubbing each other's backs occasionally, even when we're sitting at the table having dinner with everybody else. Rachel even kisses me on the cheek a couple of times while Devin's looking, and soon, the band of merry men makes a point to us that they know we're together. They just don't get to see us making out in my room, or snuggling up in Rachel's bed, or getting all cozy in more ways than one under the sheets.

It's not a big scene, either. When Emily and I were together, it was all about the presentation. As far as I could tell, we were the token lesbian couple who wanted to flaunt our relationship to everyone who had to deal with us on a daily basis. What I have with Rachel is not exaggerated. It's not show-offish. After so much craziness between the two of us already, we're happy to be, well, a normal couple.

And we continue to do the things we've always loved to do together, regardless of our status. We still stay up late talking into the night. We still listen to records together, or Rachel plays a song for me on her guitar while I try and fail to sing along without slipping out of key — of course, the songs we choose to perform together are a bit more romantic these days. We still go on walks by the creek and hang out near the bridge, where the same "No Trespassing" signs have started to fade around the edges. We still play our little eyebrow game. It feels good to have a dynamic that isn't forced or hackneyed or rehearsed. It feels natural. It feels real.

About two weeks after Rachel's return to Pensalado, she's walking on her own and doing a lot better. I guess the sprain wasn't as horrid as it could have been, and she's happy not to have to rely on someone else to be, you know, a high-functioning bipedal organism. She starts getting back into her old habits, and she resumes working on the cabins with us as she did before. Mostly, we're completing small tasks, like screwing in a loose door hinge or reorienting a roof shingle as needed. I can tell that Rachel enjoys every chore she takes on, even when she has to clean. I think she's just loving life right now, and I'm loving it right along with her.

With guests showing up for short stays and our work finally getting done, everything starts returning to normal around the property, with the addition of Warren. He gets involved in our trivia games and wins every time because he's apparently some kind of obscure fact wizard. I later find out that he used to be a frequent trivia night dude at the River Bar, and Kyle's thinking of restarting the tradition with him. I almost wonder if Kyle will ever want to leave Pensalado. Devin did mention that the guy wasn't cool with his family, so who knows where he and Warren will end up once this caretaker gig is finished.

Oh. Shit, right. It's been nine months. And good old Uncle

Aaron is coming back soon to check on us.

We get the call mid-May. Aaron phones us from the airport and says that he'll be visiting in three days. In response, Devin promptly has a panic attack. He goes through the books over and over again, though Rachel and I did manage to repay him for the Emily-Leroy fiasco, so we do have some revenue to offer for the boss. Because Devin is so focused on the numbers and profits, Kyle and I have to pick up the slack for our latest guests just as they head out the door. We end up literally scrubbing the bathrooms with toothbrushes as Devin parades around like a drill sergeant, barking his head off, while Rachel and Warren stick to dusting and vacuuming and don't talk back.

"Don't tell him it's overkill," I caution Warren in the kitchen while he's making dinner. Kyle has strained a muscle in his wrist after handling a particularly hair-clogged sink. "Whatever you do, do *not*—"

"Don't worry, Jamie," smiles Warren. "I'm not looking for an argument. The poor guy just wants to make the place present-able."

Forget presentable: he wants it fucking sterilized. He even wants our bedrooms to be spotless. I'm perfectly capable of making my own bed, but the morning before Aaron shows up, Devin marches into my room, rips the sheets off the mattress, and orders me to do it again, like I'm some army grunt or prison inmate. It's when Rachel and I both approach him with our hands balled into fists that he actually backpedals and lets us take care of our own rooms without his ever-watchful gaze.

Not like Rachel's bed's been mussed up lately, anyway. She and I have been sleeping in my bed recently. I know, scandalous, but

we like cuddling — cuddling, of course, being that good old codeword. And in the end, no matter what Aaron thinks, I'm proud of
what I've done and what I've ended up with during this entire stay.

[...]

The man of the hour pulls up in a modest sedan and emerges
from the driver's seat with an already massive smile plastered on
his creased face. He first examines the clearing where the piles of
firewood, which had once been mighty but also very dead trees,
are stacked up. He then navigates the exteriors of the re-painted
cabins and tool shed. He runs a finger against one of the main
cabin's walls, just like any eccentric property owner would do. And
when he sees us, he just laughs and nods.

The five of us are all standing by the sliding glass door — obviously not formally dressed for the occasion, but still managing to
get cleaned up and not looking so wild and, well, like we've been
camping out in the woods. Warren, of course, looks the preppiest,
but that's just the way he is, standing next to a partially groomed
Kyle. Rachel wears Kyle's denim jacket again, and she's always
looked amazing in it. I know. I'm just that gay.

We don't say anything as our superior strolls toward us,
the hems of his slacks brushing the tips of his sneakers and,
thankfully, not dragging in the dirt. While he's no Leroy, he's well-
dressed for the occasion, and he is ready to give his appraisal.

"Devin," Aaron first greets his nephew.

"Hi, Uncle Aaron," Devin says meekly.

His uncle responds to this with an enormous bear hug, and
I expect Devin to squeak like a dog toy once he's drawn into that

tight embrace. The man's not exactly ancient; he's strictly middle-aged, and he doesn't have too much gray in his thinning black hair yet. I kind of imagined him to get a little huskier and hairier since I last saw him, but he's just as shaven and dark-browed and bright-eyed as I remember him to be. I've always known him as a kind of sprightly individual, even though I only met the man once before. He's obviously not disappointing my first and only impression.

"You look good," Aaron informs Devin, brushing off his jacket. "Not so emaciated anymore. I knew settling down here for a bit would put some meat on your bones."

"I guess it did," Devin chuckles, though I can tell he's still uncharacteristically nervous about his uncle's presence and his scrutinizing, yet receptive, eye.

"And Rachel, my dear."

I can't help beaming as Rachel throws her arms around her adoptive father. It's true that they look nothing alike, but when they hug, they definitely seem like family. With one glance, I can see years of trial and conflict, but also of compassion and perseverance. Aaron never gave up on Rachel, and neither will I.

"I'm so happy that you decided to do this," Aaron tells Rachel. "Good for you to spend time with your cousin and get away from the chaos of your other jobs."

"It definitely beats working a cash register," replies Rachel with a grin. "But I did enough shirt folding to make up for it."

"To be fair, I did more laundry than you," I mutter to her.

She squeezes my hand as if to say, "Don't push it."

Aaron is especially enthusiastic to meet Kyle, who shakes his hand feverishly, flashing his teeth. Warren is definitely shy around

Aaron, but I think I win this round against him because as soon as the guy turns his attention towards me, I feel like I'm standing on a stage and he's my only audience. I smile and wave shakily, not exactly sure of what to do or say. Basically, I lose all notion of how to act like a normal human being responding to another normal human being.

"I remember you," Aaron says. "You're Jamie. Devin's old high school pal."

"That's me," I squeak out, like I'm spewing a catchphrase.

"After what you told me about your plans for the future, I wasn't aware you'd want to take on something like this." Aaron winks in Devin's direction. "My nephew has always been skilled in the art of persuasion."

Okay, now I'm finally feeling a little more comfortable, and he's absolutely right when it comes to his nephew. "Yeah," I laugh. "He's definitely steered me away from being a teacher, if that's what you mean."

"Well, we may as well not stand around the door," declares Aaron. "Let's go inside. Rachel, I hope you have some wine to pour for me."

"Riesling," says Rachel. "Your favorite."

Oh, so that's where she gets it. Or maybe she just got him hooked like she got me hooked. I still like reds, though.

We gather around the table, and Kyle, lo and behold, brings out a full meal. We've basically set the whole cabin up like a big welcome back party for Aaron, complete with snacks and drinks. But Kyle has never been one to skimp on treating a guest of honor. We have all the great "American" delicacies, since Aaron has been in Portugal for so long: Rib-eye steak, mixed green salad, mushrooms sautéed in killer garlic, roasted potato wedges. I personally would have gone for serving stuff like burgers, maybe even with American cheese, but the food is so good that I can't object to the selection. Aaron is obviously very thrilled and flattered about the set-up, and he can't stop thanking Devin and Kyle and everyone else.

He tells us all about Portugal, of course — from visiting the castles, to lounging on the beach, to having good meals and even better drinks near the ports. He talks about how Sintra is like a fairy tale and Obidos is like something out of a medieval saga. I've never heard of those cities, but the whole experience just sounds like a dream. I chew on a clump of fatty beef and shoot a look at Rachel, and from the glint in her eyes, I'm guessing that travel is something she might be raring to do some time in the future.

I'm totally cool with that, too. If I could afford it, I'd take her to Lisbon right now.

After dinner, we all pour ourselves wine of some variety, and Devin carries out the books and notes that he's compiled all neatly and obsessively throughout the months. I watch Aaron flip through the pages, and the tidiness of it all makes me wonder if some alien lives in Pensalado and decided last year to take over Devin's body. I have never seen him complete this much paper-work, and I went to high school with the guy.

"Looks good, my boy," concludes Aaron after a good half hour of perusing the papers, ending the small talk that we had started in order to pass the time. "Very, very good. Some dry spells, but that's what happens during your first year of hosting guests. If you wouldn't mind showing me the guest cabin?"

We don't mind at all. Once we show him inside, he scours the place like he's a health inspector, clicking his tongue at a chair while humming and nodding about a bed. He keeps making comments about what to add or what to remove or what to just change in general, and he's not being critical of us; he's just being a property owner. However, I notice that Devin doesn't seem to be thinking too hard about any of the suggestions or observations that his uncle makes, unless they're overwhelmingly positive or equal to, "You're awesome, my boy." He just seems happy to get this all done and out of the way, while Kyle, in contrast, is the best listener, asking questions and requesting insight.

"If you did rearrange the beds to be closer to the windows, what sort of earthquake precautions should we be taking?" he asks, as we step out of the guest cabin back into the fading sunlight. I'm not kidding; Kyle is actually discussing safety protocol for the place.

Chortling, Aaron turns to face the guy and slaps him on the shoulder. Kyle's a big dude, but even he shudders a bit from the blow, though his smile never fades away.

"Kyle, my good man," rumbles Aaron. "All this time, I was thinking that I was going to offer the keys to this property to my nephew. He's certainly proven to me that he can handle the place with your help."

"No, thanks, Uncle Aaron!" Devin cries.

I look at Devin. "Let me guess. You want to run around the country again, don't you?"

"Hey," says my friend, "I'll have you know that there are still a lot of places for me to check out. In fact, I've always thought about visiting all the small towns I can. For example, did you know that Great Barrington's tried to create its own currency so everything can be local?"

"Where the hell is Great Barrington?" I ask.

"Massachusetts," Devin clarifies, folding his arms across his chest as if he's revealed to me the truth about the universe. "One of the cool states. I'm just saying, a different currency? I'd totally be on that shit."

"Oh, you would. You really would," Rachel teases, punching her cousin in the arm. "Hipster."

I am not one to talk here. I'm a fan of vinyls now.

"Besides," continues Devin, rubbing his bicep while scowling at Rachel, "Aaron's trip to Portugal's really inspired me and made me think about what I want to do. Now, this whole thing? It was fun, but I think I'd jump into the creek if I had to stay here for another nine months. I've got lots of places to think about going to. Maybe I'll even sneak my way into Canada."

"Don't get attacked by wild moose," I warn.

"Or geese," adds Rachel.

"If it's any comfort to you, Devin," Aaron interjects, "I wasn't expecting you to say yes. Which leads me to ask the burning question here."

Kyle puffs out his chest and smiles. No matter how much administrative work Devin may have done, I have to ponder just how much of the load his buddy's actually taken on for the past nine months. I even wonder if there have been all-night brainstorming sessions in their cabin that I just haven't known about. And for that matter, I contemplate how many times Devin might have thrown a pillow at Kyle when the latter potentially recommended various ideas for the property. I think I'm onto something here with my theories.

Also, and perhaps for the first time, I realize just how at home Kyle seems to be up here. He was so excited about being close to Hearnsville in the first place, and ever since we began our crazy stint in Pensalado, I've hardly heard any complaints from him, not even about Devin's poor leadership skills. He's always been someone who's usually kept his cool, always someone who's known how to lighten the mood and bring people together and create a space that's safe and fun. He's done amazing work renovating the cabins and cleaning up the landscape, and my God, can the man cook. He's found his niche in a small, gay community, while also proving to us how responsible and level-headed he really is.

Devin wasn't really the interim manager of Aaron's property after all: Kyle was. He is, in a nutshell, the perfect landlord for this place, and I don't think he wants to leave. And from the way Warren fastens himself to his arm and looks at him all d'aw-inducingly, I'm guessing that Kyle's not the only one keen on the idea of staying.

"Kyle," Aaron suggests, "I would like to open two cabins for guests, rather than just one, to bring in more income. But I can't do it alone. I've still got my life away from here, taking care of the usual boring business. I need a good caretaker to handle the place — a custodian, a warden, whatever you want to call it. You could even have a whole family here if you wanted, since the main cabin would be all yours. Just imagine running your own bed and breakfast, but bigger and much more impressive."

"Just offer me the job already so I can say yes and start choosing new curtains for the dining area," Kyle pleads, his eyes wide and shining in the spring sunset.

We're all simultaneously amused and excited, and Aaron and

Kyle officially shake hands on it. It's settled: Kyle will be living here, and I'm one hundred percent certain that Warren will be staying with him. I can already imagine the things they'll be doing on the property: they'll pretty up the cabins some more with their ideas of rustic décor and vintage aesthetic, so I expect at least one pair of deer antlers. They'll provide complimentary meals to the guests, and if anyone complains about the food, they'll receive a fate worse than Leroy's. They'll raise their own family, and I think they'd be the best dads ever. Maybe they'll even add wi-fi to the place because, honestly, it'd probably add to the property value. And yet, I've gotten so used to not having the Internet that I swear, my laptop will look foreign to me when I get home.

Home. That's starting to sink in now, as we head back to the main cabin for some toffee bars lovingly crafted by Kyle's strong and manly hands, some music, and lots of good old-fashioned conversation. Aaron plans to send out the last monthly paycheck by the end of June, which means that Devin, Rachel, and I can't stay here after that. Devin obviously has his bases covered; he'll probably be bolting before the month is over. But Rachel and me? It's not clear. No matter how happy I am, or how confident I feel, I don't really know what we're going to do next. And I'd rather not go home to my parents if I have to.

This has been all I've known for nine months. Being a care-taker. Being a lumberjack. Being a lover. I wish I could say that was enough. Maybe for staying here, but everywhere else, not so much.

Aaron says goodbye, and Rachel and I head to my room. We lie on my bed for a while, Rachel's head pushed against my chest and my lips and nose nestled in her hair. She doesn't talk much, and at first, I think it's because she's sleepy and she figures I'm sleepy, too. But one look into her eyes, and I know that she and I are thinking about the same thing. No matter what, it's safe to assume that all we both want is a way to stick together, even if right now, we have absolutely no idea for how that's going to work.

JUNE

It's nine o'clock on a lukewarm rural night. Beside a bed in a dimly lit room is an opened suitcase with nothing in it. Next to the blatant display of reluctance and hesitation is a stack of photo albums that are nearly gray from dust, not having been cleaned off. And next to that, a half-empty bottle of beer, becoming flat and tasteless on the nightstand.

I don't want to leave Pensalado. Not yet, anyway. The last couple of weeks have felt predictably weird. Kyle and Warren have been making themselves at home, and as a result, Rachel and I aren't expected to do much around the property. They've already done quite a bit of shopping, even resorting to using Rachel's truck (with her permission, of course) to bring up new furniture that they've wrangled from discount stores and flea markets all around the region. None of the old couches are here anymore, not even that black and white one that was finally not looking so much like an eyesore to me. That smell I got from the place before

— mildew, bay leaves, and fresh dirt — is fading away quickly.

Not that it's a bad thing; I love what the boys are doing with the place. It's charming, and yes, it's definitely got that countryside flair I was expecting. There are no deer antlers, much to my disappointment, but there are chairs that appear to be built out of freshly cut tree branches. And a new floor lamp with a nature scene shade on it. And a four-foot-tall carved statue of a bear perched in the dining room because, hey, the place belongs to Kyle and Warren, after all. And of course, they just had to fly the rainbow flag, in all its glory, beside the front door. Their guests will know exactly what kind of show they're in for as soon as they agree to stay here.

Devin, as of two days ago, is long gone. He pretty much said he was done with Pensalado and took off, and Kyle let him leave. As far as I'm concerned, he could be in Puerto Rico or Ontario or all the way out in Indonesia, smoking a cigar or squatting in a million-dollar villa in Bali or something. Doing what Devin does best.

I have to give him credit. If it weren't for him, I never would have come here. I never would have tried something new. I never would have met Rachel. I owe him a lot. Maybe I'll train a falcon to recognize his face from a picture so it can fly cross-country and drop off a thank you card.

"Dear Devin: Thanks for changing my life. Don't get eaten by a Komodo dragon. Love, your archnemesis, little gayby Jamie."

The fact of the matter is, even though Rachel and I are waiting until our last paycheck comes in, we both think that we've overstayed our welcome. We're still living in the main cabin, and we both agree that we shouldn't be hogging it from its actual residents. Despite Kyle and Warren's assurances that we can be here for as long as we need to and they're comfortable in the blue cabin, we've promised to pack up by tonight or tomorrow. So far, I'm not doing a great job, and I'm not sure if Rachel is doing any better than I am.

I don't know what either of us will do once we leave. For me, it's easy to move back into my parents' place and start over, though what I'll do is up in the air. I could do all sorts of retail jobs; hell, I could probably land a career in hospitality, given my experience up here. I also could still become a teacher at my hometown's public high school, though last I checked, they were striking and demanding more than just a measly one percent pay increase. Plus, going into education feels daunting to me; I've become so used to being away from an academic environment that stepping back in feels unwarranted, like I don't belong there.

With Rachel, it's even more uncertain. She has no apartment, no job, and no real place to crash at. I doubt my parents would be willing to take her in, even if it's only temporary until we could figure something out. She could go to Port Lionel, but I really don't know how willing even Reggie would be to keep her around for too long. I mean, he seems like a generous guy and all, but after a while, it's hard to be patient with anyone trying to regain footing in the world.

So instead of packing, I sit. I try to play a record, but the music doesn't help my mood, so I sit. I try reading a book that I've skimmed multiple times before, but I get bored of it, so I sit. I try finishing my beer, but it's almost flavorless at this point, so I sit. And I sit. And I sit. Until it feels like an hour has passed, even though it's most likely only been fifteen minutes.

Then I hear someone knock on my door. What glorious timing!

"Come in."

It's Rachel, of course. She sees me cross-legged on the floor, my knee propped against my open suitcase. Her gaze wanders to the drawers jutting perilously out of my dresser like bad under-bites, my clothes still folded and tucked inside them. She steps toward me, sits down beside me, and snakes her arm around my waist.

"You okay?"

"Please tell me that's a rhetorical question, honey."

"Okay, fine. It's a rhetorical question." She gives me a token knock-it-off look. "Anything else you want me to say, darling?"

"Ugh. 'Darling.' That sounds so...stuffy."

"You never let me have fun."

"It sounds like..." I wince. "...Leroy."

"Okay. Never saying it again, then."

"I just wish we didn't have to — "

"Yeah, yeah." She drops her head against my shoulder. "I know. Are you really that nervous?"

I sneer. "Did Pope Benedict look like Emperor Palpatine?"

"Touché." Then Rachel's eyes light up. She has a plan. "You know what we can do, though? We can do some sort of symbolic send-off."

"Symbolic...what?"

My girlfriend raps my ribs with her knuckles. "I mean, do stuff to wipe the slate clean. Clear our heads a bit. Get us to be a little braver." She looks me up and down. "C'mon, don't you think there are still a few things you need to take care of before you force yourself out of this place?"

"Like what?"

She doesn't even have to glance behind her. With one jab of her thumb, she signals to the stack of photo albums next to my suitcase. I exhale. I know what she wants me to do. It's over the top and dramatic and cliché, but I know what she's implying. I'm just not sure how much it'll help, and this whole, "wiping the slate clean," spiel seems a bit stilted. But I happen to be crazy about her, so I can at least entertain her.

I stand up and trudge over to my collection, lifting the photo albums up, one by one, and feeling the grime stick to my hands. Tossing the things carelessly onto the bed, I lift my shoulders in a clumsy shrug at her.

"So..."

"So, what's in them?" she asks. "Pictures of Emily, I bet."

"Yeah. Lots of them."

"Do you still love her?"

"Do not even go there, Rach," I warn.

"Look, just hear me out," insists Rachel. "Do you even love her the tiniest little bit?"

"No. I love *you*."

"Okay." She stands up and takes my hand. "So, what do you think we should do with all those pictures of that girl you don't love anymore?"

It takes me a minute, but I finally understand what Rachel's trying to do here. I've never been one to burn bridges, literally or figuratively, but seeing as Pensalado was a way for me to escape reality, maybe it's better for me to eradicate the very thing that still makes me hesitant about going back. As much as I'm technically over my ex-girlfriend, there's still that nagging, irritating voice in the back of my head that people who suffer from anxiety always

deal with. It tries to tell me that I'm still pathetic and stupid and
not worthy of love because Emily didn't want it from me. Even
after all the bullshit she put me through — especially in March,
when I had to deal with both her and "Star Face" McGee — I still
have moments in which I validate my existence based on the time
I spent with Emily. Sometimes, I wonder if I was a victim of emotional abuse, of pressure to be someone I didn't want to be, only to
be rejected in a really shitty way. Somehow, of course, I don't think
that analyzing all of this will make me feel any better, in the long
run.

Instead, I pick up an album and I open it, and just the sight
of my younger self holding Emily, all smiles under a thick thatch
of badly cut hair, just feels outlandish to me, almost intrusive. It
bothers me, like I have the feeling of something crawling on my
arm, even though I can't brush anything off my skin. I almost don't
even recognize myself in these pictures. It's like the past I lived
was some bad fever dream that I finally managed to wake up from
and never want to remember ever again.

Acting on impulse alone, I tuck the photo album under my arm
and march out of the bedroom. My main objective: Burn it all. It's
the only way to be sure.

"Whoa, hey, cowgirl!" Rachel calls after me. "What are you
going to do?"

She follows me into the living room, where I fling open the
grating around the fireplace and scrape a box of matches off
the mantel. Rachel doesn't try to stop me. She doesn't even look
surprised, not even when I yank the first photo I can grab out of
the album and toss it into the forgotten pile of half-burnt logs and
newspaper clippings.

"Kyle better not come in here," is all Rachel says initially. "He'll kill you for stinking this place up."

"Isn't he in Hearnsville for Trivia Night right now?"

"Yeah, but you never know…"

I strike a match, and it grows eerily hot in my hand. I focus on my mission — my strangely dramatic and kind of creepy mission, but my mission, nonetheless. I let the flame slightly catch on the edge of the glossy photograph, and as it burns, the material crimps and twists, and the odor is just awful. I wrinkle my nose, but I watch the fire sear everything, from the high school scenery, to the foolish grins, to Emily's blue heels and purple tank top and red hair and luminous eyes. All turning black in front of me.

Devin took this picture around five to six years ago. It was during a football game, a home game, one that our team was losing badly. A parent chaperone had just threatened to kick us out of the stadium if we didn't stop acting like idiots, doing pelvic thrusts and throwing kisses to the visiting players and their cheerleaders. While on the bleachers, I turned my head to see who was watching us and caught Emily's eye. She laughed and winked. I smiled and gave the thumbs up, and she thumbs upped me right back. It was as if we could communicate through gestures — sort of like what Rachel and I do now with our eyebrows, only cheesier and way more obnoxious.

After halftime, Emily wound up sitting next to Devin and me in the lower part of the bleachers, and we introduced ourselves and cracked bad jokes for the rest of the game. She laughed at every single pun I made; now, I'm not so sure if she ever found them funny. Finally, Devin got one of his many disposable cameras out of his coat pocket, and Emily patiently snapped shot after shot of him and me, as we made faces, flipped off the lens, and practiced lewd gestures like that somehow made us rebellious. We were kids pretending to be recalcitrant douchebags because, for lack of a better excuse, it was fun.

I don't have the pictures of Devin and me from that night. I highly doubt that Devin has them, either. Why I didn't keep them, I don't know, but I have just burned the one I did save: The first picture ever taken of Emily and me. It was shot at a weird angle, of course, because Devin never liked doing things the "conventional" way. There I was, wearing my high school sweatshirt and a gray beanie, and there she was, with those bright wedges and those tank tops that she always had multiples of, no matter how long we were dating. We both had smiles so big that our faces could have splintered and broken into pieces — genuine smiles, despite how our relationship ended. And watching that all literally melt away in a fire is disorienting, yet liberating, yet confusing, yet inspiring, yet completely throwing me off mentally.

It's not until Rachel starts hugging me from behind, her hands caressing my torso and her lips moving up and down my neck, that I realize I'm crying. I'm not embarrassed, and I'm not sobbing. It's just a quiet cry, a necessary one. The kind of cry that makes me feel better once it's over and done with. I'm hyperventilating, and when I turn to say I'm sorry to the love of my life, she shuts me up by putting her mouth on mine and kissing me while she drags me over to one of the new couches.

We collapse onto the fresh cushions and keep kissing for a long time, even while the tears are still streaming down my face, and we don't make any comments about it. And it's nice. And then it's more than nice. And then it's just awesome, and I calm down and wrap my arms around Rachel, absorbing her warmth and enjoying the contact.

"Okay," she murmurs, disrupting the silence. "It's okay. We don't have to burn any more pictures."

"Yeah." I get myself to chuckle. "I'd probably run out of matches. And like you said, we don't want an angry Kyle on our hands."

I decide to put the photo albums in a cardboard box that we once used for recycling instead. I'm not going to throw them away, but I am going to keep them separate from the rest of my stuff, and I'm definitely not going to put them on some sort of literal or metaphorical pedestal whenever I settle into whichever place I end up in. So many of those photos are from Emily, anyway, taken on her camera, and she figured I would like the copies. So honestly, I just see myself putting the things away and starting fresh with my own photos. Though who knows how much I'll get back into social networking at this point in my life.

Once we've put the albums away, Rachel and I head to the kitchen and, big shocker, drink some very sweet wine. Rachel pours us glasses, and then she excuses herself to get something. My joke that I'm not ready to be proposed to yet makes her laugh, as well as earns me yet another punch in the arm. I don't think she'll ever stop doing that whenever I tease her; I know I deserve it. Besides, she never hits hard enough to hurt.

When she comes back, she's clenching something in her hand. She passes it to me as I swirl the crisp, cold Riesling around my tongue like mouthwash.

"Careful," she tells me. "You might get splinters."

I open my hand, and at first, I think I'm just looking at a piece of wood. And I am looking at a piece of wood: a gray, mangled, bumpy piece of wood. It takes me a while to figure out that this is tree shrapnel, and I hazard a guess that it's from the very tree that she and I helped chop up back in December when the monster was blocking our way out of the property right before Christmas. I look at my new treasure, then up at Rachel, then back at my new treasure, and I just don't know what to say.

"Taunt me all you want," smirks Rachel. "I don't know why I kept it for so long. I mean, I did want to remember that crazy night, especially when you were so sexy with that axe."

"Stop it."

"Never! But yeah, I figured that maybe we'd forget why we kept it in the first place after, I don't know, five or so years. So I did something with it."

I make a face. "What did you do?"

"Nothing bad."

"What did you do, Rachel?"

"Flip it over."

On the piece of wood, carved out by what must have been a pocket knife or something, is a little heart with both of our initials in it. Certainly a creative spin on the whole scratching your love into a poor, innocent tree, and yes, it's sappy, and I wonder how long ago she did this. But I can't help it. I grin a big, shit-eating grin, lean over, and kiss Rachel on the cheek.

"You missed, you fucking tease," she says, locking lips with me before I can protest.

"It's beautiful. I'll cherish it forever."

"Please don't put it under your pillow at night."

"But it loves me!"

Some things never change, and I don't think Rachel and I will ever stop poking fun at each other. As the wine bottle gets emptier and emptier, and we get more and more light-headed, I expect my anxieties to dissipate. They don't, of course, and soon, I can feel my brain practically squirm around in my skull, as I reach across the table and squeeze Rachel's fingers. They're cold from her wine glass, and I think they're shaking slightly.

"Hey." She squeezes my palm. "I can hear you worrying."

"What are we going to do, Rachel? I don't want to lose you."

"You're not going to lose me. Relax."

"You're my safe place," I continue, sounding sillier by the minute. "You know that, right? I tried to find an actual place instead of a person for that job, but then you came along and fucked it up. You've got Port Lionel, and I've got you."

"I thought you were supposed to be all independent and shit now? What happened to not relying on someone else to be happy?"

"That's not — " I take a deep breath, understanding the point that my girlfriend is trying to make but still being the hopeless romantic. "I get it. Maybe we won't last forever. I know I need to make sure I can imagine a life without you. But can we at least pretend this is all going to work out, you and me? Because I really, really, really like you."

"Hmm," Rachel sneers. "Little bit more pressure placed on me, but I'm still not going anywhere."

"Well, then what are we going to do?"

"Jamie, you know I like to improvise."

"I know," I sigh. "And I'm used to making plans."

"Well," replies Rachel, "if it's any comfort to you, I do have some ideas bouncing around in my head. Not sure if they'll work, but…"

"But what are they?"

"Fuck, they're vague, man. They really are. Maybe I made them vague on purpose. But they all involve you, Jamie. There's no way I'm moving on with my life without you beside me."

"Wow," I utter. "That's powerful."

"Well," giggles Rachel, "it's the best I can do for my girlfriend, who snaked her way into my heart after trying to kill me with a poker."

"Oh, c'mon. Don't bring that up again!"

"Look." She lightly touches my face with two fingers and her thumb. "You've got a college degree and a teaching credential. I've got years of shitty retail experience that could make great stories for parties. We've both worked nine months taking care of some-one else's real estate. So you know what, we've kind of got stuff going for us, résumé-wise. And if worst comes to worst, I'm sure Reggie wouldn't mind having us around his place, serving drinks or whatever, until we figure shit out."

Yep, Reggie's in the cards; I totally called it. I scoot over to Rachel and raise my glass to her glass. She sips my wine instead of participating in my toast. Her lips are cool against my skin. A curl of her black hair brushes against my forehead. She's wearing that baseball cap again. She'll always look good in it.

"We're rogues, you and I," she whispers into my ear, obviously being a little melodramatic. "Just rotten, rascally millennials who are up to nothing but trouble. You, a girl who's taken a break from the system, who's tired of being history instead of making it. Me, a girl who likes to act like she's rebelling when really, she's just aimless." She drops the histrionic tone then and becomes more casual. "And you know what, I'm okay with that. I'm okay with you. I'm more than okay with you. We don't have to impress anyone, and we can try whatever the hell we want to try, even if we fall flat on our faces. Even if maybe we crash and burn, and we never want to speak to each other again, we'll have some damn good memories, right?"

A girl who's tired of being history instead of making it. Now, that's a poetic way of simplifying my situation.

"'Try' whatever we want?" I tease. "Not 'do' whatever we want?"

"Very nice, Yoda."

"You, I thank."

"No, not 'do' whatever we want, 'cause we can't. Obviously. If so, I'd have found the secret to immortality by now." I can't help it. I will always laugh at her silly jokes. "But we can celebrate now. We can enjoy this night. And then tomorrow, we can get in my truck and just drive until we find another town."

"And we'll stick it out."

"Yeah." Rachel smiles. "E-fucking-xactly."

"This is our cheesy ride off into the sunset ending. A perfect Hollywood conclusion."

She knows I'm being sarcastic, and I think she loves it. "Deal with it, Jamie girl."

I want to deal with it. God, I want to. No more looking back. Only forward.

Onwards.

* 9 7 8 0 5 7 8 5 6 0 8 0 9 *